The Gardens of Nibiru

The Ember War Saga

Book 5

Richard Fox

For Kristy,

CHAPTER 1

The *Breitenfeld* shuddered beneath Lieutenant Hale's feet. His body and the gauss weapon clenched in his fist felt lighter as the shudder died away.

"Losing gravity. Activate your grips," Hale said. He pressed his heels against the deck and felt his armored boots hum to life as the magnetic linings latched him to the floor.

The team of Marines around him gave him a thumbs-up. He felt the individual thumps of their linings activate through the deck; there was no sound in the airless ship while it was under combat conditions.

A torn food wrapper floated into the passageway. Standish snatched the detritus and held it up to his visor.

"OK, who had the…white-chocolate-covered pretzels and failed to secure their trash, eh? Someone overlooks something little like this and the next thing you know we've got a pallet full of rockets bouncing around the armory like a loose cannon," Standish said, wagging the wrapper in the airless passageway like a disapproving finger.

"Weren't you eating pretzels right before the jump?" Corpsman Yarrow asked.

Standish froze, then stuffed the wrapper into a pouch on his belt.

"I thought they fixed the grav plates." Orozco thumbed the activation switch on his Gustav heavy cannon, spinning the three barrels so fast they blurred.

"They've been twitchy ever since Steuben's cyborg buddy used them to get us out of that gravity well on Takeni," said Bailey, one of the team's two snipers. She had a gauss carbine cradled in her arms

4

since her preferred weapon was locked away in the ship's vaults. The close quarters of the *Breitenfeld's* passageways were no place for a long-barreled rail rifle.

"His name is Lafayette." Steuben, the tall Karigole warrior, raised a hand and braced himself against the ceiling. He stomped a boot against the deck and slid it back and forth. "Why do these infernal things never work right?"

"Did you press your heel down long enough to activate the lining?" Hale asked.

"Your cursed boots aren't meant for my feet," Steuben snarled as his boot finally clamped onto the deck. Steuben had switched from his Karigole battle plate to Marine battle armor after they'd encountered the Toth on Anthalas. Adopting human uniforms meant he wouldn't make an obvious target on the battlefield.

Hale looked over at the two new additions to his squad, Marine Staff Sergeant Egan and Corporal Rohen. His team was down a communications specialist since Torni's death at the hands of Xaros troops; Egan filled the vacancy, but not the hole left in the squad's heart.

Rohen…Captain Valdar said the lithe Marine was a "mission specialist," another sniper for the mission to Nibiru. Both Marines were professionally competent and had integrated well during training, but both were standoffish. Rohen hardly ever said a word beyond what was needed, and Hale swore he'd never seen the man sleep. Every time Hale checked on his Marines in their berthing, Rohen had been wide awake, reading from his Ubi data slate or cleaning his sniper rifle.

"Are we there yet?" Standish asked. "These jumps are supposed to be instantaneous. If there was a fleet of Toth coming to eat our faces, you'd think the good captain would have told us to stick our heads between our legs and kiss—"

"Now hear this! Now hear this!" came through the ship's infrared system.

Standish widened his stance.

"Stand down from combat condition red. The ship will maintain amber until further notice.

Prepare for re-pressurization and cross-checks."

"Wait, things are going as planned?" Standish asked. "No boarders? No crazy pocket universe?"

"Don't jinx it or we're throwing you to the lizards first," Bailey said.

A vent opened in the ceiling and a cloud of compressed air rushed into the passageway. Hale watched as the pressure readings changed on his visor screen from red to green.

"Yarrow," Gunney Cortaro pointed a knife hand at the corpsman, "you get to crack."

"Sure thing." Yarrow attached his rifle to his back and hooked his thumbs under the front of his helmet. "Wait, isn't Corporal Rohen the new guy now?"

Yarrow pulled the front of his helmet away and took a quick breath before snapping the helmet back into place. "Clear. Good air."

The Marines and Steuben removed their helmets.

"*Corporal* Rohen outranks you, Yarrow."

Standish ran his fingers through his sweaty scalp. "You're the new guy until we get another lance corporal or below. Deal with it."

Yarrow shook his head and muttered under his breath.

"The next time your trash goes loose cannon, you will be demoted to a mosquito-winged private—again—Standish," Cortaro said. "Then you can take over all Yarrow's new-guy duties."

Standish held up a hand in surrender.

A sudden crush of gravity enveloped Hale like a giant hand had wrapped around his entire body. His armor locked against his body and the pseudo-muscle layer beneath the plates pressed against his body, fighting to keep his blood from pooling against the bottom of his feet. An icon flashed on his visor; the force of gravity against his body was nearly twice the Earth standard. As the press against him faded away, the gravity reading on his visor fluctuated a few percentage points above and below what the ship's gravity field should have put out.

"Bloody hell, when're they going to fix that?" Bailey pulled her boots off the deck one at a time with a loud snap. "The plating cut out the last time I took a shower. You know how hard it is to keep your shit together when you're floating wet, naked and covered in soap?"

Blast panels on the hull slid away from the windows. A sunset-hued nebula filled the void as reed-red gas filaments spread through a honey-colored cloud. A white dwarf star blazed at the center of the nebula, the remnants of a long-ago supernova.

"Definitely ain't Kansas," Egan said.

A text message popped up on Hale's visor.

"Gunney," Hale said. Cortaro stared out the windows, transfixed by the alien sky. Hale tapped his knuckles against Cortaro's shoulder.

"Sir? Yes, sorry." Cortaro turned away from the window.

"Captain Valdar wants me and Steuben on the bridge. We should have a couple hours before anything major happens. What do we need to train?" Hale asked.

"I'll run them through cloak drills, sir. Orozco and Yarrow are still tripping all over themselves. Then we'll hit the range," Cortaro said. He was his team's leader, responsible for everything they did or failed to do. The team's senior enlisted Marine since before the Xaros invasion, Cortaro took responsibility for the training the other Marines needed in order to accomplish whatever mission Hale had for the team. Cortaro knew each Marine's training record by heart, and given a few hours without any interference, he could make decent progress in fine-tuning the squad. Hale gave him a nod and turned away to catch up with Steuben, who was halfway down the passageway.

"Steuben," Hale said as he caught up to the Karigole, "you ever heard about this planet we're going to? Nibiru?"

"We lost all contact with the Toth after their betrayal. Before that, the Toth were confined to their home world several light-years from Nibiru." Steuben didn't look at Hale as he spoke, his clawed hands opening and closing into fists as they walked together. "I suspect Mentiq colonized the world to put some distance between himself and the Xaros maniple that should reach the Toth home system in the next decade. This is to our advantage. He is an easier target without hundreds of billions of Toth between him and me."

"You mean us."

Steuben grunted.

"Steuben, I know things are very…personal for you on this mission after what happened to Kosciusko and Rochambeau." Hale paused, trying to gauge Steuben's reaction, but the Karigole was a stoic as ever when Hale mentioned his dead comrades. "This isn't a suicide mission, you understand?"

Steuben stopped and slowly turned his head to Hale.

"The Toth massacred my people on Mentiq's order. When I and Lafayette die, the Karigole will die with us. Your mission is to kill Mentiq, end the Toth threat to Earth. Mine is to kill

11

Mentiq out of defiance. My vendetta will end on Nibiru. One way or the other."

"I saw how determined you were on the *Naga*," Hale said. "You were willing to keep that overlord locked in his command bridge until the ship crashed into the moon at the cost of your own life."

"And you, for reasons I still do not understand, insisted on staying with me until Elias threw you off the ship." Steuben slapped the call button for a turbo lift and got in as the doors opened. Hale entered a code into a key pad to take them to the bridge and the doors shut.

The lift, like everything on the ship, wasn't designed for comfort. The armored Marine and Karigole barely fit inside; the top of Steuben's scaly head nearly scraped against the ceiling.

"We do not leave people behind, Steuben. You are not going to put the rest of us at risk for your—"

Steuben snatched Hale by his breastplate and lifted him into the air. He brought him to eye level and bared his double rows of needle-sharp teeth at Hale.

"You think you're going to stop me from going down there?" Steuben snarled.

Hale's jaw clenched as his eyes locked with Steuben's yellow cat eyes.

"Promise me. Promise you won't risk our lives for your vengeance," Hale said.

The corner of Steuben's lips tugged to the side. He lowered Hale to the deck.

"You have my word. My oath is my own. Not yours," Steuben said.

"This mission doesn't have to end with you as a martyr. You and Lafayette managed to kill an overlord just fine on the *Naga*." Hale adjusted his armor, noting claw marks against the plates.

"You don't understand Karigole, my friend. We are nothing but our stated purpose. I, with ninety-nine of my brothers, swore that we would never give up until our people were avenged. To fail is a disgrace. We would be…found wanting in the next life. The dead brothers of my centurion are in what you would consider purgatory. Their, and my, judgment waits. Either we kill Mentiq to fulfill our oath, or Lafayette and I die and join the rest of them in failure."

"No pressure," Hale said. "If it helps, I want to kill Mentiq too, but my eternal salvation isn't really part of the scenario for me."

"I will speak well of you when I face the god of death." Steuben gave Hale a pat on the shoulder that almost knocked him off balance.

"Thanks—I guess?"

The lift doors opened, revealing the *Breitenfeld*'s bridge. The sound of a half-dozen voices sharing information and open IR lines filled the air. Valdar, standing at the head of a holo table surrounded by the ship's senior officers, waved Hale and Steuben over.

****

Valdar reached over the holo table and touched the star at the center of the Nibiru system.

He twisted the sun from side to side, streaking icons for planets and the *Breitenfeld* across the holo field. Hale stood at the end of the table next to Steuben, whose arms were crossed over his chest.

"Why isn't Nibiru in this diagram, Ensign?" Valdar asked the nervous-looking navigator.

"It's on the other side of the primary, sir," Ensign Geller said. "We jumped in on the system's planetary axis. Which is lucky. The Toth can't see us and we can't see them with the sun between us."

"Are you sure we're in the right place?" Valdar asked slowly.

"Yes," Geller almost squeaked the answer. "Pulsar triangulation puts us in the right system, and the composition of the outer ice giants matches records recovered from the Toth fleet. We're in the right system…just on the wrong side."

"How long until we're in orbit?" Valdar asked.

Lieutenant Commander Levin, the chief engineer, spoke up. "The cloak is a significant drain on our batteries. If we stay cloaked, the best speed we can manage without burning out the fusion reactors will get us there in two days."

"And the jump drive? How long until it's built up enough charge to get us home?" asked Commander Ericson, the executive officer.

"The dark energy field grows stronger as we near the system's primary, say five days at best. But that's not our real problem." The engineer tapped a flat screen and multicolored bar graphs formed in the tank.

"Damn it," Valdar said with a shake of his head.

"Excuse me." Hale raised a hand next to his face. "A little help for the uninitiated?"

"I can't keep the cloak up," Levin said. "If I cut power to everything but life support, we've got no more than ten days until we're basically flapping in the wind for all to see."

"The engineers on Titan Station said the power leak was fixed." Valdar hit the edge of the table with his knuckles.

"In their defense," Levin said as he clasped

his hands behind his back, "we're using a Toth cloaking device pulled out of the *Naga*'s wreck. The device is bastardized Karigole technology, which we re-bastardized to mesh with our systems *and* the jump engine that I'm not allowed to touch. It's a miracle that we haven't been warped into three-headed tentacle monsters, but the day is young." He knocked on the tank's railing.

"So what does this mean for the mission?" Hale asked.

Valdar pulled the power graphs close to him, his eyes darting over the readings.

"I can give you two days on the surface before we have to drop the cloak. Maybe another twelve hours, but if I do that, then we won't have enough battery power to fire the main guns. Not a risk I want to take if Mentiq has anything in the way of orbital defenses," Valdar said.

"What about a bombardment? We brought nukes," Hale said.

"There's no guarantee that would work," Steuben said. "Nuclear war was quite common

17

amongst the Toth before Mentiq brought them all under his control. He's certain to have bunkers that can withstand anything. Better to get in close to kill him."

"Turning his island into glass with nuclear fire would get our point across," Valdar said. "Everything we know about the Toth is that they're business-minded, not prone to blood feuds. I'm OK with de-cloaking, dropping ordnance and jumping out. That should convince the Toth to leave us alone."

Steuben's hands balled into fists. He sucked in a deep breath and bared his teeth.

Hale grabbed Steuben by the shoulder and shook his head.

"But the decision isn't made yet," Valdar said. "Steuben, where is Lafayette? If there's anyone in the galaxy who can make Toth, Karigole and human technology work together, it's him."

Levin gave a defeated shrug.

"He maintains the vigil. I will relieve him immediately," Steuben said and walked away.

"This isn't the plan," Valdar said, addressing the ship's senior officers. "We should have had weeks to scout out Nibiru and come up with the best course of action possible. Now, we have a few days—at best—to make this happen. The *Breitenfeld*'s never failed before and we're not going to start now. We will find a way to kill Mentiq and get back to Earth in one piece, or we will make one. Dismissed."

****

Lafayette sat in front of a small shrine in his workshop, his feet tucked beneath his legs, hands resting on his knees. The shrine was a simple wooden box. A small bowl filled with opal-colored beads and a comb made from bone—personal effects of the Karigole named Rochambeau who'd died on the *Naga*—sat on one side of a melted down and sputtering candle. On the other side of the candle was a burnt scrap of a flight suit, the only thing recovered from the wreckage where

Kosciusko rammed his fighter into a fleeing overlord's command bridge.

The candle fluttered, its light shining off the pool of liquid wax just beneath the flame.

He hadn't bothered to keep track of how long he'd knelt before the shrine. His cybernetic body knew neither fatigue nor discomfort. Lafayette's cybernetics remained hidden beneath a set of naval rating coveralls, hiding his disfigurement from view. Much of his body had been burned away by a Xaros disintegration beam years ago. Replacing what was lost had been a painful journey of trial and error. All that was left of his original body was his brain and a few organs in his chest cavity. His face was a mask of polymers over a scaffolding that mimicked expressions and speaking.

Steuben knelt beside Lafayette and matched his pose.

"I relieve you," Steuben said. "I take up the watch."

"They're almost gone," Lafayette

whispered. "Let me stay."

"Have you heard them?"

"No, but I don't have ears anymore."

"Ghosts whisper to our souls, not our bodies. If they are silent, then they are at peace, confident that you and I will complete the mission."

The flame danced against the wick, growing fainter. The two warriors sat for several minutes more in silence.

The fire sputtered, then went out with a hiss. The Karigole placed their hands on the deck in front of their knees, then leaned forward to touch their foreheads to the ground.

"Farewell, Rochambeau," Lafayette said, "you gave me a blood transfusion after I was injured. It kept me alive so that I would not be the last."

"Farewell, Kosciusko. You were the best of us. Your will kept me going, saved me from despair so that I would not be the last," Steuben said.

Lafayette placed the balls of his feet against the deck and stood up, his cybernetic knees whirring. He picked up a small trash bin and swept the last bits of candle, beads and fabric away. By the ritual, Kosciusko's and Rochambeau's spirits had lost their final attachment to the mortal plane. Keeping their possessions only served to attract malevolent entities.

"The ship's power systems are out of balance," Lafayette said. "I feel it in the deck plating, see it in fluctuations from the lights."

"The captain requests your assistance," Steuben said.

"Of course he does. His engineer is quite capable when it comes to human technology, but ask him to recalibrate the quantum field stabilizer on the cloak generator and he looks at me like I just offered to procreate with his sister—isn't that how humans do it? Male to female?"

"Yes, their Internet archives are full of reference material. I don't recommend researching the topic. It's very confusing." Steuben got to his feet and went to a workbench. He picked up a slightly curved flat box and examined it. "There's an issue. The ship can't maintain the cloak for very long. Our time on the surface will be limited."

Lafayette dumped the contents of the trash bin down a chute and stopped to examine a tool display with several hand and forearm prosthetics. Each set grasped a metal peg sticking out from the wall. Lafayette grabbed a wrist for a hand with five fingers instead of his usual four, and the prosthetic released the peg. Lafayette grabbed the peg with his other hand and detached it from his arm. The new hand went on with a snap.

"What happens to the ship once we're on the surface is irrelevant," Lafayette said. "I will not leave Nibiru until Mentiq is dead."

"Nor will I."

"The humans will accept this?"

Steuben ran two fingers across his chin in annoyance. "No, but I am not concerned. I would rather die in the course of our mission and come before our brothers in the afterlife with pride, than pass away from old age on Earth trying to please Hale and the others' sense of honor."

"Hmm…old age." Lafayette swapped out his other hand. "I doubt that will be a problem for either of us."

CHAPTER 2

The doors to Bastion's stellar cartography
lab opened for Stacey. The immense lab was empty
but for a single, unsupported staircase extended to a
small platform in the center of the room. A holo
projection of the Milky Way filled space around the
platform as the shadow of a slight figure moved
within.

Stacey walked up the stairs, her eyes
glancing over the thousands of star systems marked
by icons for known Crucible star gates. Thick
tendrils of billion-strong Xaros drone fleets
advanced into the last unconquered swath of stars in
the galaxy, each moving inexorably toward an

inhabited system.

A single Crucible marking glowed blue just behind the tip of a tendril: Earth. A dashed line of a projected Xaros invasion reached from Barnard's Star toward Earth, still more than a decade away. Her home world was behind enemy lines.

"Stacey," said a young woman with coffee-colored skin and curly hair as she waved to the human ambassador, "thank you for coming so quickly." Stacey hurried up the stairway to join Darcy. The other ambassador looked human, an illusion projected by Bastion to help the many different species on the station better relate to each other. The Ruhaald alien beneath Darcy's mask was an amphibious species with segmented flippers and toothy feeder tentacles in place of a mouth. Not for the first time, Stacey wondered what her Bastion-provided Ruhaald form looked like.

"You said it was urgent." Stacey stopped next to her fellow ambassador on the raised platform and looked across the galaxy. Bastion's hologram of the hundreds of billions of stars was as near perfect as science could achieve. Qa'Resh probes scattered across the galaxy constantly fed data to the space station. The lab could zoom in to each star and access a lifetime's worth of data on the stellar system and known planets.

Stacey had loved the stars and astrophysics since before she could walk. To have such an immense font of knowledge at her fingertips was beyond her wildest childhood dreams.

"It might be," Darcy sighed, "if the data is right. I don't know what you did, but while you were on Earth, the Qa'Resh removed the data locks on the graviton surveys."

"The data we thought might help us find the Xaros colonization fleet," Stacey said, "if there is one."

"The initial data was a bit inconsistent." Darcy's fingertips danced across a floating control screen. "Then I used your idea for filtering raw graviton data through a brane simulation…"

The holo field shifted to bring the edge of the galaxy in front of the two ambassadors. A

Crucible marker floated amongst a halo of stars along the galactic rim.

"So I was right about that?" Stacey reached to the marker and flicked her thumb and forefinger apart to zoom in. A deep-green star with two planets in its habitable Goldilocks Zone materialized, a Crucible orbiting a world with snow-covered mountains and wide swaths of desert.

"Yes," Darcy said through grit teeth, "you were right and I was…not yet correct."

"This is Crucible 0-1, isn't it? The first the Xaros ever built," Stacey said.

"That's right. Mok'Tor colony world. The first advanced civilization to encounter the Xaros, and the first to fall to them," Darcy said. "'Xaros' is the Mok'Tor word for 'death,' 'balance' and the number zero. They were a poetic species."

"Fascinating, but didn't you say something about this being urgent?" Stacey asked.

The holo shifted. The edge of the galaxy moved away and a red dot appeared in the deep space just beyond the galactic rim.

"I thought it was an error in the data," Darcy said quietly, "but it's there."

Stacey tried to zoom in and got an error buzz in return.

"All we have is a depression in the fabric of space-time," Darcy said. "No light, no heat, nothing on the electromagnetic spectrum at all from…it."

Stacey swiped a finger next to the dot and a screen full of data appeared next to it.

"The mass on this thing…something like this has to be a star, a large red dwarf perhaps. There are smaller catalogued red dwarves beyond the rim. Why can't we detect this any other way?" Stacey asked.

"It's consistent with what we'd expect with a Dyson sphere, a habitable megastructure built around a star," Darcy said. "There's no record of any species in our galaxy ever building something so momentous, and it's on course to Crucible 0-1 at almost ninety percent the speed of light."

"At that speed it won't arrive for another…ninety-four years. Why haven't you presented this to the rest of Bastion?" Stacey asked.

"There's something wrong." Darcy crossed her arms. "Once I knew what to look for, I went back through Bastion's survey data, thousands of years' worth, and retraced the object's path."

Darcy flicked a finger next to the red dot and a solid line traced away into intergalactic space. The line turned to dashes at the earliest recorded data point as the object's projected course stretched though the galaxies of the Virgo supercluster. The path never came close to any galaxy.

"This can't be right." Stacey's brow furrowed as the line continued to the very edge of observable space, billions of light-years away. "Where did it come from? Bastion's stellar cartography models are near perfect—that object had to start somewhere. Could it have changed course?"

"Redirecting an object with that much mass and momentum would be more difficult than building the Dyson sphere," Darcy said. "You see why I didn't present this to the Congress. Someone would tear my theory apart and laugh me off the stage. They'd say the object is just some stellar anomaly…ignore it."

"An anomaly heading straight for Crucible 0-1? Wait…speaking of anomalies. Chuck?" Stacey said to Bastion's AI interface.

"Yes," the AI's voice was toneless and curt.

Stacey lifted her hands into the holo and pulled the image down. A great black void in intergalactic space intersected with the anomaly's projected path. The void had no rogue stars, no clouds of gas extending for light-years, none of the detritus common between the great expanse between galaxies.

"This void," Stacey said, "I've studied it before. There's nothing we can see or detect now, but the gravity models for this filament running through the local supercluster show something *was* here, correct?"

"Void designation A-9-2239 held a galaxy with a stellar mass twenty percent larger than the Milky Way. The gravitational effect of that galaxy ceased two hundred five million years ago. This is inferred, not observed," Chuck said. "Recordings integrated into the Bastion stellar cartography library are no more than five million years old."

Stacey tugged at her lip. She reached a hand into the holo and twisted an imaginary knob, moving the timeline backwards and forwards. The Xaros object appeared just beyond the void when the galaxy that should have been there vanished.

"That's where it came from," Stacey said. "The Xaros are from that void, or what used to be there."

"Galaxies don't just blink out of existence, Stacey," Darcy said.

"Yet the math says that's exactly what happened in that void. There was a galaxy. Its gravity left a legacy on the stars around it. Then it was gone in the blink of an eye. We need to talk to someone who could have seen what happened," Stacey said.

"You know someone *that* old?"

"The entity from Anthalas. It's sitting in a

cell down in the Qa'Resh city. Time to go have a little chat with that thing," Stacey said.

CHAPTER 3

Euskal Tower, headquarters of the Ibarra Corporation, stood in stark contrast to the wine-colored storm clouds building on the horizon. Smaller high-rise office buildings and apartment complexes radiated out from the tower. Sections of the buildings on the outer edges of the silent commercial empire were exposed to the elements, like a giant scalpel had sliced hunks of the building away.

Feet scuffed against asphalt. The road now beneath her feet began abruptly—scrub desert one inch, a wealthy suburb the next. Abandoned cars stretched along the road leading to Ibarra's city, many with clean-cut, fist-sized holes in the roofs and windows.

"T…T, what the hell happened?" Franklin asked through the IR. "Where is everyone?"

"Damned if I know, but that's why we're down here," she said.

"Movement," Walsh said.

She ducked behind a car and raised her gauss rifle over the bumper, scanning her assigned sector. A brief video clip came up on her visor, a dark shape with bent spikes flit between the distant buildings.

"That's all I got," Walsh said.

"Keep moving. Stay alert," Hale said.

The world snapped away and she stood in the *Breitenfeld's* hangar deck, staring out into the gray oblivion surrounding the ship. She had her hand on a gurney where Yarrow lay on the hard plastic slab, his arms and legs strapped down with wide belts. She ran her armored hands through her short blond hair and rolled her shoulders.

"Our chaperone is supposed to meet us

here," Hale said. The lieutenant looked tired, stressed from more than could ever be expected from one man.

"How's Gunney?" she asked.

"Stable. Doc's got him a transfusion and the good stuff to keep the pain down." Hale touched the railing on the gurney and looked over Yarrow. "Whoever's going to meet us, sure hope they can do more for Yarrow than we can."

Something flickered against the gray expanse.

"I think I see—"

Everything went to perfect darkness. No sound. No sensation.

The deck returned. Yarrow stood next to the gurney, leaning on it to stay upright.

"I said get a medical team out here, now!" Hale yelled at a security team of masters at arms rushing toward them.

"Sarge?" Yarrow grabbed her shoulder and took a trembling step away from the gurney. "Sergeant Torni, do you think the LT will let me stay with the team after this?" A black line appeared over his mouth and all sound stopped.

The hum of air vents and Hale talking into the ship's IR returned.

"We all have bad days, Yarrow. It's up to you to bounce back," she said.

The world blurred and Yarrow was back on the gurney.

"Our chaperone is supposed to meet us here," Hale said. The lieutenant looked tired, stressed by more than could ever be expected from one man.

"How's Gunney?" she asked.

****

The General punched a basalt-colored control panel, knocking a corner off. The hunk bounced across the sandy floor and came to a stop. It melted away and the damaged section regrew to its original form moments later.

A field of connected dots in a thick white

haze floated over a plinth in front of the General. He reached into the field and watched as the memory fragments repeated, always skipping the exact same thing perfectly with each attempt.

Light flared from the eye slits on his face plate.

I know you're here.

Darkness grew around the General and the source of his frustrations. Constellations of stars grew into being, as if the General was standing in deep space.

+You are a brute, meant for destruction, not discovery or inquiry. This is not your task,+ Keeper said.

You bade me return when I have answers to the human anomaly. This...base creature has what I require. But there have been alterations to synaptic pathways. An intelligence far greater than the humans hid something from me and I cannot rip it out of the scan.

+An intelligence greater than your own?+

Do not mock me, Keeper. You didn't leave

the Apex just to take joy in my frustration. What is your purpose?

+I've followed your progress, or lack thereof. The humans had help—long-term help—to survive the scouring of their home world. They utilize dangerous technology to oppose us. The longer they're allowed to survive, the greater the chance they'll trigger a cataclysm. I cannot wait while you flail about, trying to address the issue.+

If they repeat our mistake, then we will move on. The universe is vast.

+No. I maintain the Apex, not you. The others will not survive if we're forced to continue our pilgrimage.+

The General remained silent. It glanced at the scan field then back to the Keeper's infinite depth around it.

The Engineer said the technology was perfect. Stasis without risk.

+His efforts proved wanting. The others will arrive with the Apex. We must begin the final part of our journey soon afterwards or we will succumb to the inevitable. Surrender the scan to me. Focus on your mission to cleanse our new home.+

You will share what you learn?

+Naturally.+

Take it. Then you can report back to me once your duty is fulfilled. I rather like the way this has changed our relationship.

+Your failure to erase the humans put the plan in jeopardy. The others will know of this.+

The star field faded away. The scan field collapsed into a point of compressed data and vanished in a flash.

The General waved his hand through the air and a gash opened in the ceiling. In the space beyond the Crucible where it chose to work, a giant red dwarf star burned in the distance. A small planetoid held steady above the Crucible, and an incomplete net of drones stretched across much of the rock's surface. More and more drones connected to the net; the sheath would be complete in a few more days, then his advance on Earth would begin.

CHAPTER 4

Cortaro waited at the end of an obstacle course, a timer running down on his forearm computer. The course was a series of irregularly stacked cargo boxes resting on top of small disc-shaped lift bots. The bots, technology used from the old automated warehouses that popped up across the planet in the earlier part of the century, shifted the boxes around, constantly changing the layout. Metal bars ran between some of the boxes, rising and falling as the attached box pairs danced around each other.

A crash came from deep within the obstacle course. A tall box fell over and almost caused a domino effect but the programs within the lifter bots swung away from the falling object.

"Ten-second penalty!" Cortaro shouted.

He heard a grunt and a swirl of light jumped onto a moving pillar. The swirl, a distortion akin to looking through thick water vapor, leapt to another box. It jumped toward a metal bar. There was a metallic thump as something heavy shook the bar. The sound of thumping boots closed on Cortaro.

He heard a muffled curse, and the swirl crashed to the ground right in front of him.

The cloak field withdrew from around the armored Marine at Cortaro's feet, retreating into a small curved box like smoke being sucked back into a fire.

Orozco looked up at Cortaro. "Time?"

"Haven't made it yet." The Gunnery sergeant tapped his foot on a chalk line.

Orozco reached out and slapped the line.

"Four minutes and fifty-two seconds. With penalty." Cortaro entered the time onto his forearm computer.

"This isn't fair, Gunney." Orozco stood up. "I can't even see my feet when the cloak is on."

"Well boo-goddamn-hoo," Cortaro said. "I'll be sure to tell the Toth that this whole thing is just too darn hard and to look the other way when you pull your bull-in-a-china-shop routine right in front of them."

"I can't wait to see him do this when he's got his Gustav." The distorted words came from somewhere behind Cortaro. "You think he moves like a big dumb animal now? Just you wait."

"Who said that?" Orozco lurched behind Cortaro, swiping at the air.

"All right." Cortaro put his helmet on and activated his cloak. The air seemed to flex and bend around him as the cloak settled. "Everyone through the obstacle. We navigate this obstacle as a unit in less than five minutes—and without strangling Standish—I'll leave two hours open for free time tonight. Move out."

****

Bailey stared through the thick scope attached to her sniper rifle. The target, a pair of simulated watermelons, sat hundreds of yards away in the holographic rifle range. She exhaled slowly, feeling the thumps of her heartbeat against her cheek and the tiny patch of exposed skin she had pressed against the trigger.

A ribbon attached to a pole behind the melons fluttered in a breeze.

"Adjust east six meters. Offset shot be another quarter second," Rohen said. He was behind his own rail rifle, a few feet from Bailey.

"I'll be a drongo if the wind correction is six meters," the Australian Marine said.

"Have I been wrong the last five shots?"

"No, and you're not checking your firing tables either. Which leads me to believe you're cheating." Bailey snapped her gum.

"Calculating the wind speed at this distance is—"

Bailey fired, the report little more than a

loud snap in the training environment compared to the thunderclap generated by the rail rifle accelerating a tungsten-clad cobalt slug to several times the speed of sound. Rohen fired precisely a quarter second later.

One of the watermelons blew apart. A white dot appeared a foot away from the missed target, showing where the wayward shot had passed by.

"Fuck me," Bailey said. "I hate missing."

"I told you. Six meters." Rohen pushed himself onto his knees. "We keep screwing this up and we're not going to over penetrate the shielding Mentiq's got."

"If he even has the personal shields." Bailey pressed the butt of her rifle against her shoulder, adjusted the recommended six meters with a click on her scope, and fired again. Her target splattered into chunks. "Just because the big brains claim they found a 'for sale' listing in the *Naga*'s computers doesn't mean Mentiq's actually got it. He's probably just another brain in a jar like the rest of them. One clean hit is all we need—a clean hit I can provide without your assistance, thank you very much."

"Those big brains say a double hit from our rail rifles, at the right interval and at a slower muzzle velocity, will overload the shields and kill him. Her. It. Whatever. That's why I'm even on this mission," Rohen said.

"This is a bloody waste of time." Bailey set her rifle on SAFE and sat back on her haunches. "We don't know any of the atmospheric conditions on Nibiru, don't know the rotation of the planet, don't know any of the variables we need to make our ballistics calculations. Do Admiral Garrett and Captain Valdar think we just point and shoot? Let's see them try to thread a needle at eight hundred meters."

"We can figure all those out once we make landfall." Rohen tapped at his forearm computer and the target within the holo range changed to an overlord tank almost a kilometer away. "Same equations, just different inputs."

"You are entirely too optimistic for me to

really like you," Bailey said.

Rohen scratched his face, his hand trembling enough that Bailey noticed.

"You OK?" she asked.

Rohen stared at his hand and the palsy faded away.

"Just adrenaline," Rohen said quietly. The pupils within his pale-blue eyes pulsated for a moment, then he smiled at Bailey.

Bailey felt uneasy. This wasn't the first time she'd noticed something a bit off about her fellow sniper.

"Where you from? You sound American," she said.

"Little town—it was a little town—called Monterey. California, not Mexico," Rohen said. "Had this great aquarium. Best seafood on the West Coast." The right side of his face pulled into a grimace. He turned his head away from Bailey.

"Most I ever saw of America was Las Vegas. I don't remember much of that. How long you been in?"

"I'm not a proccie," Rohen snapped. "That's what you're getting at, aren't you? It's like that all over the fleet. New guy shows up and the interrogation begins. You wouldn't ask if I was from Eighth Fleet. Everyone knows what they are."

"It's no big deal for me," Bailey shrugged. "Yarrow's a proccie. Hell, he had some alien thing in his head for a while. Don't see me making a fuss about it. He's a good kid, knows his stuff. What, you don't like proccies?"

"No one gets to choose the circumstances of their birth. Proccie...true born...can't be all that different from each other. Besides, if I had any real heartburn over Ibarra's children, I'd have been on the *Lehi* with Fournier and the rest of his bigots." Rohen pushed himself up to his feet. "Where's the pisser?" he asked.

Bailey pointed to a recessed doorway at the other end of the rifle range.

Rohen made his way to the latrine, his shoulders tight, his pace fast. The door slid aside as he approached.

Once the door shut behind him, Rohen collapsed against the bulkhead. His hands and arms jerked against his body as his muscles spasmed out of control. He managed to press a hand to his chest and slide a clip of thumb-sized auto-injectors from inside his shirt. Rohen pinched an injector between two fingers and tried to press it to his neck. His hand refused the command, jabbing into thin air.

"Damn it," he said through grit teeth. He pinned his hand to the wall and forced his neck against the needle point. His nerves burned as the serum coursed through his system. His muscles relaxed and came back to his full control.

It would get worse. Ibarra had told him as much when he woke from the procedural tube buried deep within Mauna Loa on Hawaii. The tremors would strengthen into seizures if he didn't take his serum regularly, but even that was losing its effectiveness as time went on. Rohen gave the clip of injectors a pat and slid it back into his uniform.

He looked himself over in the mirror, not finding any nervous twitches that might hint at a deeper problem to his fellow Marines. All he had to do was maintain the façade of a perfectly normal true-born human. Once he made it to Nibiru, he'd be one step closer to fulfilling the mission Ibarra gave him.

Rohen splashed water on his face and went back to Bailey.

****

Four Eagle fighters waited on the flight deck, each connected to the ship's power lines and locked into catapults that would launch them out of the ship within two minutes of an alert. The pilots sat on an ammunition lorry, eating lunch from pressboard trays and watching a rare spectacle play out across the otherwise empty flight deck.

The clash of composite steel on steel rang through the flight deck as two Iron Hearts sparred each other, the third armored soldier watched from the sidelines.

Durand wolfed down a bite of some bland

substance billed as stroganoff and dabbed her lips. She winced as one of the Iron Hearts slammed an elbow against the other's chest and knocked it to the deck. A giant boot slammed down next to the prone soldier's helm and Durand felt the vibrations through her seat.

"Who just won?" asked Glue, Durand's second-in-command.

"Hard to tell with the new suits. I think that's Elias," Durand said. After the battle against the Toth, Ibarra rolled out new and improved suits for the few remaining armor soldiers in Earth's military. The Iron Hearts now stood fifteen feet tall, their armor smoother and modeled to resemble the human form more than the blocky armor they'd worn before.

She glanced at her two Dotok pilots, Manfred and Lothar. They sat shoulder to shoulder, stubby beaks agape as they watched the Iron Hearts fight each other.

"What's the matter, Manfred? Never seen anything like that before?" she asked.

"We don't have this," Manfred said. "The Dotok never had anything like this. I heard stories about them from the other survivors, how they held off the Banshees so the *Canticle* could escape Takeni…Is it true they're like the Toth? Nothing but a nervous system plugged into their armor?"

"No, they can come out," Durand said. "You might catch Kallen or Bodel in the mess hall, but they spend all the time they can in their suits."

"What about the third?" Lothar asked.

"He got hurt during the fight for the Crucible. Rumor is he's fused to the tank inside the suit," Durand said.

"He's trapped in there? Why hasn't someone tried to get him out?" Manfred asked.

Kallen stepped off the sidelines and faced off against Elias. Her hands withdrew into the forearm housings, replaced by a long spike in one arm, a burning torch in the other. Elias slammed his fists against his chest and held his arms out wide. Kallen crouched, then sprang off the deck and tackled Elias.

The two hit the deck so hard Durand almost dropped her tray.

"You want to go ask him?" Durand ran her fingers against her shoulder pouch and found a beat-up pack of tobacco cigarettes. She looked up at the ventilation shaft where she knew she could smoke in peace, but that wasn't going to happen while she was on ready alert.

Manfred and Lothar spoke to each other in Dotok, then they looked at Durand and shook their heads.

"What are they doing?" Glue asked. "Why bother training in hand-to-hand combat?"

"You remember when Elias returned from that unfinished Crucible over Takeni? He had that red mask with him," Durand said.

"I thought that was just a rumor," Glue said.

"Interesting how something that's supposed to be classified information becomes rumor, isn't it?" Durand asked.

"So it's true? The Iron Hearts and that metal Karigole fought some sort of Xaros leadership?"

Glue asked.

"I'm not saying that." Durand gave a very Gallic shrug.

"Is this an example of doublespeak or a double entendre?" Lothar asked. "We've had some difficulty with English nuance."

"Shut up and watch the giant robots fight, boys. You ever see them on the battlefield, that means you're in the middle of one hell of a fight."

****

A sea-green world with thick bands of white clouds filled the bridge's holo table. Valdar, a cup of steaming coffee in hand, and the rest of the *Breitenfeld*'s senior officers watched as the planet rotated before them.

"Now that we've cleared the system's primary," Ensign Geller said, "we've got our first good look at Nibiru. The place is almost ninety-eight percent ocean. No polar ice caps. Given the high levels of oxygen in the atmosphere, I'm certain we're looking at a planet much like Earth that's been flooded in the recent past, probably from volcanic activity in the polar regions." Geller moved his finger over a touch screen and a yellow dot appeared at the top of the planet. "As you can see—"

Valdar set his coffee cup against the table's railing with a loud snap.

"Skipping ahead…" Geller tapped his screen. The holo zoomed in on a small land mass, ribbons of deep green islands spreading out from a massive, gray dome-shaped object. "This is the only inhabited area we've detected with our passive sensors."

"What is that dome? The picture looks distorted," Lieutenant Hale asked.

"It's a shield," said Commander Utrecht, the ship's gunnery officer. "Same energy signature as we saw on the *Naga*. If it's as strong as what we've encountered before, there's no way our rail guns can get through."

"So much for an orbital bombardment,"

Ericson said.

"I could drop nukes into the ocean," Utrecht said. "If we space out the bursts just right, it would generate a tsunami. Wash the Toth away."

"Nukes aren't going to work," Geller said. "There's a neutron inhibitor field coming from the dome. We can't get a fission or fusion device to function anywhere in the atmosphere."

"Paranoia is a hallmark of the Toth leadership," Steuben said. "They believe their fellows are constantly planning to usurp them, which they are."

Geller zoomed the holo in to the tip of an island close to the dome, bringing into focus blocky structures separated by a grid of dirt roads.

"Even if we could use nukes, there are civilian factors to consider. There are at least five settlements on different islands surrounding the dome," Geller said, "all within a few dozen miles of the shields."

"Is that a Toth city?" Ericson asked.

"No." Lafayette reached into the holo and

zoomed in further with a gesture. "Toth architecture is more organic. Their layouts center on the residence of whatever overlord or corporation rules the local area. The Toth, and Mentiq, are beneath the shield dome. I'm certain of it."

"Then who's living there?" Valdar asked.

"I don't know, sir. The architecture on each island we can see is unique, but this one…" Geller swiped his fingers across the touch screen and the holo whirled across Nibiru's surface and stopped over a village with several dozen buildings.

The imagery was grainy, but Valdar made out a perimeter wall, paved roads, houses several stories in height and a large central square with some sort of statue in the middle. At the corner of the square, two large and one small humanoid figure in white clothing stood out from the earth-toned buildings.

"Is this a human settlement?" Lafayette asked.

"It—yes, that's my guess," Geller said.

Whispers broke out from the assembled

officers. Valdar rapped his knuckles against the railing to quiet everyone.

"How is this possible? Where did those people come from?" Ericson asked.

"We had some suspicions," Valdar said. "The ancient-era coins the Toth ambassador gave to Lieutenant Hale on Europa, the base-10 coding found in the Toth's computers, even in our own history. Ibarra's probe suspects that the Toth visited the Earth several thousand years ago and encountered the civilization in Mesopotamia, modern-day Iraq. Many cultures from that time period had lizard-like god figures as part of their mythology. At the risk of sounding like some crazy-haired weirdo from an old TV show, the Toth could be the inspiration for those legends."

"So, the Toth took some humans with them when they left Earth way back when?" Hale asked.

Valdar pointed to the settlement in answer.

"There's more," Geller said. The display shifted to a square landing zone cut out of a dense forest not far from the village, a worn path connecting the two. A Toth drop ship, similar to the ones that delivered Toth warriors to the Hawaiian shores during the aliens' assault on Earth but missing any armament, sat on the landing zone.

"So that's how they get to and from Mentiq's city," Valdar said. "Looks like we're going to have to do this the hard way. Hale, you and your team will make planet fall just outside this village. Figure out if the people in there can help you get into the city, or if they know some way we can get those shields down. I don't care if you smother Mentiq with a pillow or I pound him into dust from orbit. He is our objective."

"What if the humans are collaborators?" Hale asked.

"Hard to believe, but if they're on Mentiq's side, then they're hostiles. Treat them accordingly," Valdar said. "Find a way into that city. You'll have two days. Lowenn and the probe put an Akkadian language pack together for your communicators. Let's hope they still speak that language." Valdar double-tapped a screen and the holo zoomed out to show the entire planet. "What's in orbit?"

"Nothing to be happy about," Utrecht said. The image dissolved and rematerialized. Two gigantic *Naga*-class starships, the color of dried blood with irregularly placed crystalline cannons across their hulls, circled around a cluster of smaller spacecraft.

Hale recognized several Toth cruisers with the spiral shell design he'd seen up close and personal on Anthalas and Earth. A handful of ships were unlike anything he'd ever seen before—a sleek teardrop ship with stretched reflections of neighboring vessels across its hull and a pillar-like ship with segmented portions rotating around its long axis. More Toth and ships of unknown origin were packed close together like a herd of sheep by the circling *Naga* battleships.

"All the ships out mass the *Breitenfeld*," Utrecht said. "The two *Naga*-class ships will make everything difficult once we lose our cloak. We've seen how much firepower those ships can put out."

"Do they have the same energy shields?"

Valdar asked.

"If they do, they're lowered. We're not picking up the same energy signatures that we did from the *Naga*," Geller said. "And the rest of the ships are running on low power. Life support and little else."

"Mentiq does not trust his guests," Steuben said. "They are weak and defenseless before the battleships. A foe without a weapon cannot strike."

"Any idea why there are so many ships in orbit?" Valdar asked. "I doubt the planet's land mass has enough dirt for all the crews to stand on."

"It looks like a convoy," Ericson said. "Maybe all these ships are on their way somewhere and this is just a waystation."

"From an operational standpoint, it's an obstacle. The anchorage is directly above Mentiq's city," Utrecht said. "Our single Mule with a cloaking device doesn't have the range to get around those ships."

"So long as they're powered down, the shuttle could pass within a few dozen yards of any of those ships without the risk of detection," Lafayette said.

"Fly through that mess?" Hale said. "The ships are so close to each other that they're swapping paint."

"I can do it," Lafayette said. "With Egan as my copilot, it should be fairly straightforward."

"Fair enough." Valdar chopped his hand through the display and it powered down. "Hale's team will embark once we're at maximum range for the shuttle. Lieutenant," Valdar looked at Hale, "my ready room."

****

Valdar picked up a stack of papers from a leather chair in front of his desk and tossed them onto a little-used bunk. He motioned to the now empty seat and flopped into his own chair, a leather upholstered high back with worn armrests.

"What's up, Uncle Isaac?" Hale asked as he sat down. The godfather-son pair managed a few moments of private time while one commanded the *Breitenfeld* and the other the ship's Marine complement.

"How do you feel about this mission?" Valdar asked.

"It's...iffy," Hale said. "I thought we'd find a planet with Mentiq and maybe some orbital defenses. Nothing we couldn't handle from orbit. Wham, bam, thank you, ma'am. We're prepped for a ground infiltration and if we can get line of sight on Mentiq, the snipers will take care of him. Now we've got a bunch of new variables—none that seem to help us."

"Should we abort? I can park the ship behind one of the outer planets and wait for the jump engines to recharge," Valdar said.

Hale leaned back and rubbed his palm against his face. Hale had the perpetual look of exhaustion and pent-up violence Valdar came to know during the last war against the Chinese. That war, not unlike the current conflict with the Xaros, were a few intense battles spaced out over weeks and months as the two sides waged campaigns across the Pacific Ocean.

Valdar looked at his godson and didn't see the bright-eyed and athletic child he'd watched grow up. Hale'd become a bloodied warrior with the scars to prove it. The Marine's eyes seemed locked on a distant vista, his body ever alert for the slightest provocation to join battle.

The captain knew this was what Hale wanted when he joined the Marine's Strike Corps, but deep inside, Valdar wished Hale could go back to the innocent kid that won trophies for swimming competitions up and down California.

"Kren," Hale said, "the Toth ambassador I dealt with on Europa, he mentioned something called 'The Belt.' I wasn't sure what he was talking about until I saw the video files pulled out of the *Naga*'s wreck. The Toth home world has a space station that circles the equator. The Toth have more ships than humanity ever had at the peak of the cold war between the Chinese and the Atlantic Union. Even with Ibarra's proccie tubes and our ship yards going at full speed, the Toth could crush us. We barely won the first time they showed up. They come back with another couple *Nagas* and what they've got in their home system…"

"We have some time. Kren's expedition isn't due back for a couple more weeks. They had to hop from system to system with their jump drives to get to Earth. The Crucible got us out here with one jump. I can take us back to Earth, try and come back with more firepower."

Hale shook his head. "The only reason we took down the *Naga* was because the Toth got greedy and stupid when they let the *Lehi* and a bomb inside its shield. There are two Toth dreadnoughts in orbit and we don't have a way through their shields yet. We try to bring what's left of Eighth Fleet and the new Twelfth Fleet and we've got a slug fight on our hands. Think of the casualties."

Proccie casualties, Valdar thought. *You wouldn't be at risk.*

"What do you think your chances are if I

send you to the surface? Think you can get a shot at Mentiq and take him out?" Valdar asked.

"I trained for this kind of mission before the war. Back when the target was some Chinese flag officer vacationing at a Thai cathouse. Dropping on a planet with a long-lost human population and infiltrating into a shielded compound...not the same, but close enough," Hale shrugged. "Worst comes to worst and you extract my team. The *Breitenfeld* de-cloaks, tosses a few rail cannon rounds into that mass of ships as a parting gift and we head home. We show Mentiq we know where he lives and we can hurt him. Maybe he'll take the hint to leave us alone."

"That's a lot of variables," Valdar said. Absent from his briefings to the crew were Ibarra's express orders to Valdar that didn't come from the navy's chain of command. Valdar had aided a movement of true-born humans attempting to get rid of the procedurals by handing them all over to the Toth, and Ibarra had all the evidence he needed to make sure Valdar was stripped of his command

and charged with treason.

Ibarra had told Valdar that the mission to Nibiru wasn't a suicide mission, not for him and his ship. The mission came with a fail-safe, one Valdar had to deliver to the planet's surface. If Hale learned of it…

"It's war. We take risks," Hale said.

"Then we'll continue as planned. Get to the surface, kill Mentiq if you can and get out of there. I'll handle the high ground." Valdar's words were resigned. Hale and his brother Jared were the last tangible connection the captain had to his life before the Xaros invasion. Throwing Hale into the fire again felt like the moment he realized his wife and children were dead and gone.

****

The armoire was alive with the snap and hum of power armor as the Marines donned their combat gear.

Standish swung his arms across his chest

and pulled his shoulders back, feeling the pseudo-muscle layer beneath the plates adjusting to give him a full range of motion. He squatted low, feeling the suit contract against his thighs and knees. He jumped up and activated the magnetic linings in his boots, which brought him back to the deck like he was connected by an elastic band.

"Pretty sure it works, huh?" Egan asked. "I saw a guy try to cheat his checklist like that and almost cracked his skull against the ceiling when the linings failed." The communications specialist pressed an armored pouch against his belt; a hum and a click followed as magnetic plating and turnscrews fixed the IR relay kit to his armor.

Standish took a bandolier from an ammo canister and draped high-explosive grenade shells over his chest.

"Well, sergeant," he said to Egan, "when you've got the latest and greatest equipment coming out of Ibarra's foundries, there's reason for confidence. The new mag linings made it through QC twelve hours before we jumped out."

"I thought all the new gear went to the Ranger Regiment and the expeditionary core they're standing up on Mars," Egan said.

"It is," Standish said curtly.

"Then why do we have the new linings…and gauss capacitors for our rifles that are fifty percent more efficient than what we had last week?" Egan asked.

"Gunney?" Standish turned away from Egan and waved at the team's senior NCO. "We're going atmo. Should I bring a couple extra thermobaric grenades? You know, for giggles." Standish tapped the grenade launcher attached to the bottom of his gauss rifle.

Cortaro, who had a checklist in hand as he inspected Rohen's armor, didn't bother to look away before answering. "Add another bandolier to your carry sack."

Standish grabbed the bulging pack attached to the small of his back and looked inside.

"But Sarge, I do that and I've got to dump my pogey bait to make room," Standish said.

"My heart bleeds," Cortaro said.

"Man…" Standish grabbed a handful of candy bars from his pack and put them in the half-empty ammo can. He ripped the corner off a confection made of chocolate, nougat and nuts and took a bite.

"Not going to let those damn squids eat my stash," he mumbled. Standish tilted the ammo can to Egan.

"Thanks." Egan took one out and started eating.

Standish motioned to the pilot's wings stenciled on Egan's chest armor. "How'd you get wings as an enlisted Marine? I thought you had to go through OCS before pilot training."

"Easy, I'm a proccie," Egan said.

Yarrow, Orozco and Bailey all stopped what they were doing and turned their attention to Egan.

"I came out of the tube knowing how to fly Mules and Destriers. Bet I could handle an Eagle if I had to. I can read and understand Toth too. The planners beneath Camelback Mountain looked at what your team was missing and had me made to order," Egan said. "I heard the instructors talking about me after I passed my flight quals on Hawaii. They came clean about my background once I asked. Sure made knowing Toth make a lot more sense."

"You seem awful..." Standish glanced from side to side, "awful OK with being a proccie. Wait, can I say that? Or is 'proccie' a that's-our-word sort of thing?"

"I don't care," Egan said. "Sure is a lot easier than calling someone a 'procedurally generated human being' every single time. I thought Western civilization got over that politically correct crap decades ago."

Standish and the other true-born Marines looked at Yarrow.

"Hell, it don't make no difference to me," Yarrow said. "Proccie's fine."

"Wait a minute," Orozco took an oversized magazine for his Gustav and tapped it against his bare head. "Why didn't they just make a whole new team of Marines perfect for this mission? Each of them the reincarnation of Chesty Puller, General Mattis and Gunnery Sergeant Hartman, seems better than sending the lot of us to Nibiru."

"Training," Cortaro said. He tapped his fingers against Bailey's shoulder and the Marine stood up straight, her arms to the side as Cortaro inspected her armor. "We, with the exception of Rohen and Egan, have been together for a long time. We're a team and any team will be better than a group of individuals lumped together, no matter how good those individuals are." He spun a finger around and Bailey turned her back to him. "Ibarra's tubes can pump out proccies that know each other and remember training for years on end, but that takes a long time. Admiral Makarov and her Eighth Fleet are like that. Now Ibarra's churning out proccies one at a time, sending them to new units where they'll learn to be a team the old-fashioned way: training."

"Where'd you hear all that, Gunney?" Standish asked.

"You're not the only one with contacts."
Cortaro pulled a canister off Bailey's back and
shook his head. "This filter's at thirty percent. Get a
new one." He slapped her on the shoulder and
returned the bad filter to her.

"That why we've spent every waking
moment on the range or doing drills since I came
aboard?" Rohen asked. "I thought we were going at
it a bit hard, considering your and Hale's
reputation."

"And what reputation is that?" Orozco
asked.

"After everything you did on Earth, the
Crucible, Anthalas…I doubt any of you'd ever have
to pay for a drink at a bar ever again," Rohen said.

"Which bars are you talking about?" Bailey
asked.

"Don't mistake an intense desire to not be
eaten or killed as something special." Standish
looked at Egan, Torni's replacement. "Not all of us
made it home."

"Or in one piece," Cortaro flexed the

muscles in his cybernetic foot and calf. The clone replacement for the limb he lost on Anthalas would have to wait until after this mission. "All right, big mouth," Cortaro said, pointing at Standish, "let's see if you remembered to double-check your auxiliary air lines for once."

****

Hale, clad in his armor and with his rifle attached to his back, walked off a lift and onto the *Breitenfeld*'s flight deck. He found most of his Marines and Steuben standing behind the yellow and black chevrons running along the perimeter of the deck, demarking where one could watch flight operations safely.

Only Yarrow was on the flight deck, almost empty of craft but for a few Mules and a pair of ready-alert Eagles toward the stern of the deck. Yarrow held both hands out in front of him, pawing at the air as he meandered around the deck.

"Sir," Cortaro said as Hale stopped next to

him.

"What the heck is he doing?" Hale asked.

Bailey and Standish fought a laugh and stifled all but restrained sniggers.

"He is looking for the cloaked Mule," Steuben said.

Standish bit the knuckles on his armored gauntlet as a tear fell from the corner of his eye.

"Hey, Gunney," Yarrow called out. "I don't think it's in spot 2-4."

"I said 3-4!" Cortaro waved Yarrow farther down the flight deck. The medic gave a thumbs-up and moved away, a hand held up in front of his face like he was walking through a dark room.

"So this is…Earth humor?" Steuben asked.

"How long has this been going on?" Hale asked.

"Ten minutes," Bailey said, her shoulders jerking from stifled laughter.

"It started before I got here," Cortaro mumbled.

"Preflight checks are complete. Ready to

go," Egan said, his voice coming through the IR receiver in Hale's earpiece. *"And what the hell is Yarrow doing? Lafayette's in the cockpit with me and he thinks it's some kind of war dance."*

"He's looking for the Mule," Hale said. "Flash the running lights."

Egan burst into laughter and Hale cut the channel.

Spotlights on a Mule almost thirty yards from Yarrow blinked on and off. Yarrow stopped stumbling around, looked at the Mule, then to the Marines, then back to the Mule.

"Aww...fuck you guys!" Yarrow stomped across the deck to the Mule.

Hale bit his lip to stop from smiling as his Marines broke down. Standish fell to the ground, on the verge of hyperventilating as he laughed.

"I don't understand this," Steuben said.

"I got it—" Bailey wheezed, "I got it on video."

"All right, that's enough." Hale nudged Standish with his foot. "Time to saddle up."

Standish got back to his feet. "Sir, I haven't laughed that hard since I had Yarrow asking the ship's foundry for a box of grid squares."

"You know if you get hit he's the one with all the pain meds," Hale said.

Standish stopped laughing.

CHAPTER 5

Darkness. Stacey's world beyond the small sled was nothing but absolute darkness. Her trips back and forth from Bastion to the Crucible orbiting Earth were little different, though spending hours waiting in an infinite white void compared to the abyss she was in now felt like splitting hairs. Both purgatories were long, dull affairs.

Getting an audience with the Qa'Resh hadn't been easy. The enigmatic hosts of the Alliance preferred to remain at arm's length from the ambassadors for all but official business. But when she asked to question the entity recovered from Anthalas, she'd been granted permission almost immediately.

Naturally, like all things with the Qa'Resh, the security measures felt like an unnecessary chore. She'd get to the entity, but she'd have to go alone and she wouldn't know where its holding cell really was. The Qa'Resh lived within the upper atmosphere of a gas giant on a giant floating city…if the entity wasn't kept there, the planet had plenty of space for a cell.

Stacey paced two steps along the sled, spun in place, and took two steps to the other end. She hadn't tried to count the hours since she'd boarded the sled and her entire universe shrank to little more than what she could reach beyond her fingertips.

A bag slung over her shoulder flapped against her hip. Inside was the only physical object ever recovered from the Xaros, aside from the Crucible near Earth. The object gave her chills just thinking about it, even if it was just a re-creation.

According to Pa'lon, the long-serving Dotok ambassador who'd become her mentor, security hadn't been this strong when he first joined the

Alliance. But after the Toth betrayed the Alliance and killed a Qa'Resh during a kidnapping attempt, things had changed radically.

At least I don't have to use the restroom, she thought.

"I mean, do they even have bathrooms in this prison? Could you imagine how complicated that would be? Having to accommodate hundreds of other races—I'm talking to myself." Stacey patted her fingers against her cheeks and stretched her arms out behind her back. She closed her eyes and swung her arms in front of her chest—and hit something hard and rough.

She opened her eyes and saw a dark rock wall in front of her, the surface black and pitted like it was made from solidified lava. She turned around and found she was in a small cavern, her on one end and a giant orb of shifting bronze metal on the other.

Intricate patterns played out across the orb's surface: shifting fractal swirls dancing between blooms of dark checkerboards. The orb glowed from within, the only source of light in the cave.

Stacey swallowed hard and felt a tinge of fear spread through her chest.

"It can't perceive you," a voice said.

Stacey seized up and snapped her head around to look for the source of the words.

A disembodied head of a middle-aged woman with long braided hair hung in the air next to Stacey, looking at the orb. The Qa'Resh never appeared in their true form—crystalline entities the size of a two-story house—but always in the form Stacey saw now. There were at least three distinct humanlike guises, the braided woman being the one Stacey had the most contact with.

"It can't perceive you, yet," the Qa'Resh said. "Are you ready?"

"Shouldn't there be some sort of…barrier? This thing isn't exactly friendly," Stacey said. She ran her hands over her simple tunic and pants, smoothing out what few wrinkles had crept into the white fabric.

"You are safe. You have our word."

"Fair enough. Let's start." Stacey walked to the orb, her back straight and shoulders square. Her posture likely meant nothing to the orb, but it made her feel better.

A wave of static spread across the orb to the edge of the cave.

Stacey pressed her lips into a thin line, then glanced from side to side.

"Can it hear me?" She flopped her hands against her side.

"Where are you?" boomed from the orb, the voice low and masculine.

Stacey took a step back, watching as patterns twisted across the orb like a film of soap over the surface of a bubble.

"Here. Can you see me?" Stacey asked.

"You are not here," the orb said. "Your soul is cold."

"I don't know how to convince you otherwise. Given your situation I assume you have time for a few questions," Stacey said.

"The burning ones demanded much. I gave.

Why should I bother with a fleck of ice like you?"

"I came here to discuss history, not philosophy or metaphysics. The Qa'Resh aren't the most engaging hosts. I doubt anyone else will be down here for a very, very long time. What will it be?"

Stacey waited a few heartbeats before turning around and starting back to the sled.

"You ask about history?" came from the orb. Stacey stopped but didn't turn back to face it. "The burning ones asked questions a human mind cannot comprehend, nothing so mundane as the march of time. But we are lost if we do not know the path we've walked. Isn't that right...Stacey?"

"How do you know my name?" She whirled around.

The orb contracted and poured itself into a new shape. Yarrow, made up of the same shifting, patterned bronze metal, stood before her, his skin and armor blending together.

"This host knew of you. His mind was a wide pool with little depth, his knowledge imperfect. I wonder if your mind is as flawed." The Yarrow-orb reached a hand toward her and stopped at a force field that shimmered from the contact.

Stacey approached the force field.

"Do you have a name?" she asked.

"You may call me…Jehovah."

"No. You are no god to me or anyone else. Cut the crap."

"Elohim."

"Not that either. You've mentioned others of your kind before. What did they call you?"

"In my original form…Malal."

"Can you assume that form? The way you are now is…unacceptable."

The Yarrow-orb shifted to an asexual humanoid shape, its features as bland as a department-store mannequin.

"It's been so long," Malal said. "I don't think I remember."

"How far back do you remember?"

Malal canted its head to the side. "I was imprisoned on Anthalas for the last hundred million

84

years. Before that, my time was with my peers, working to solve the great question."

"And what is that question?"

"Is there an end? Were we, the galaxy's first and greatest civilization, doomed to extinction as entropy wore all of creation down to nothing? The answer was no. We found a way out, a door to an infinite expanse where we could live on…but the others left me behind. Left me trapped in that insignificant speck of a world where I could watch the heavens dim to nothing."

"Why? Leaving someone behind doesn't seem very…godlike."

"*I* was the one that found the key. *I* was the one that opened the door for the rest and they shut me out. They didn't want to pollute their new perfect world with the price *I* paid." A riot of colors swarmed across Malal's skin. "But the door remains. I will find my way back and make them pay."

"This price, did you pay it with the Shanishol we found on Anthalas? Through murder?"

"Immortality requires sacrifice. My people cleansed the entire galaxy of lesser species to fuel our way through the gate." Malal smiled, the corner of its lips pulling far wider than any human's could have. "They left me on that rock, waiting for the next batch of intelligent species to arise. It was...tedious."

Stacey felt her skin grow cold.

"Your species consumes other living things to survive," Malal said. "So did we. I managed to tempt a few to Anthalas, but none in the numbers I needed to make the journey. The Shanishol were my last best chance before the Xaros arrived...you know how that ended."

"Speaking of the Xaros." Stacey reached into a pocket, pulled out a small holo-emitter and set it on the ground. It flared to life and great filaments of galaxies came to life around her. She touched a finger on the anomaly at just beyond the edge of the Milky Way.

"This," she said, "this object has been on its

way to our galaxy for as long as we can tell. At least two million years. It will arrive in the star system where the first-known Xaros contact took place. No one thinks that is a coincidence."

"Yes, I know of it." Malal raised a finger and the holo of the local universe shifted, the galaxies realigning as millions of years rewound. The anomaly backtracked to the great void and the holo froze. "Ah, your data is incomplete. Surprising, but not unexpected."

An elliptical galaxy with a uniform glow of stars filled the void.

"This was quite the event." Malal's fingers floated through the air like he was playing an invisible instrument. A single dark spot appeared on the galaxy and spread out as the holo ran on. The abyss engulfed the entire galaxy in a little over two hundred thousand years. The anomaly appeared in intergalactic space just a few hundred years before its home galaxy was annihilated.

"There was some concern that the rupture would reach us before our great task was complete, but the tear couldn't sustain itself beyond the galaxy's dark energy halo," Malal said.

"What happened?"

"Children playing with the fabric of creation. Technology similar to the jump engines you used to bring me here rip open holes in quantum space to create wormholes. There is a chance—"

"The tear will continue. Yes, we're aware of the danger," Stacey said. The threat of a quantum tear had been a convenient excuse for Alliance races unwilling to send aid to Earth against the recent Toth incursion. Stacey thought the reasoning to be nothing but cowardice, but now, seeing the effects wipe out an entire galaxy…

"Did you ever have any contact with the Xaros that escaped?" Stacey asked. "Surely you saw them coming."

"We noticed…but we didn't care. Their arrival was millions of years away. We planned to be long gone by then. Would you like to see it?" Malal swept his hand across his chest and the galaxies blew away as if swept by a great wind. The red spot that marked the Xaros anomaly grew larger and more distinct.

A world with perfectly flat metal surfaces floated in front of Stacey, a spherical polyhedron with a twenty equally sized facets. Great rings of metal—like she'd seen around Ceres—surrounded the equator.

"It's...incredible," Stacey said as she realized how massive the object truly was. The Xaros rings were wide enough to enclose the solar system out to the orbit of Neptune.

"A fair creation. We weren't impressed," Malal said with a shrug.

"What about this?" Stacey reached into her bag and pulled out the General's faceplate that Elias had torn away during the battle in the incomplete Crucible near Takeni. It was as wide as a dinner plate, but the material had almost no weight in her hands. "Can you tell me something about the being that used it?"

Stacey pressed the corner of the mask into

the force field. Static glittered around the disruption as she pushed it through to Malal.

Malal took the mask with its deformed fingers that swept over the armor plate like rivulets of liquid mercury.

"This isn't the original," Malal said.

"No, it was recreated by an omnium reactor here on Bastion. How can you tell?"

"The same way you tell the difference between a picture and the true article. This is part of a photon cage. We considered this method to prolong our existence. Photonic bodies are too fragile and will last only a few million years before degrading. My omnium body is much more resilient to entropy." Malal pressed the mask against his face and bobbed from side to side.

"Did we kill this this thing when we ripped its face off?"

"Doubtful. Beings that wish to survive this long would never let their existence hinge on a single point of failure. Did its energy dissipate in front of whoever claimed this trophy?"

Stacey shook her head. "Elias said it fled from the Crucible."

"Crucible?"

Stacey explained the jump gates the Xaros left in systems with habitable worlds, and how the Alliance captured an incomplete gate near Earth.

"The Xaros…" Malal flipped the faceplate over several times. "They're using the jump gates to get from system to system. They don't want to repeat the disaster from their home galaxy. Quaint."

"You act like the Xaros wouldn't have been much of a threat to you and your people," Stacey said.

"Would Earth fear a tribe of spear-wielding savages?" A ripple spread over Malal's body. "And to think here I am, trapped by an even more primitive collection of intelligences. This Alliance is nothing compared to us. You hadn't evolved beyond pond scum when we ruled the stars."

Malal pressed the edge of the faceplate to the force field. It drew an arm back and the hand morphed into a blade. It slammed the edge against the seam where the force field and the mask touched, and a cascade of disrupted energy reverberated away from the impact.

"Let me out!" Malal slammed the blade against the wall again. "Let me out of here and I will eat your soul last!"

Stacey backed away, her heart pounding as she looked around for any kind of help as the ancient being attacked the force field. Malal's rage ended suddenly as it shrank into a ball and floated back to its original place in the cave. The General's mask hit the ground without a sound.

"You were in no danger," the braided woman said, her head appeared next to Stacey. "It has tried to escape before. The privacy filters are in place. We can speak freely."

"A little warning next time?" Stacey asked.

"Malal isn't this cooperative with us. Good work," she said.

"How do you figure? I got some nice trivia out of it, nothing that'll help us fight the Xaros." Stacey looked at the mask on the other side of the invisible force field and decided that trying to recover it wasn't worth the risk.

"Malal isn't the first remnant of the Ancients we've encountered, but it is the first we can converse with," she said. "You must speak to it again, get it to cooperate further."

"Hold on for a quick second. That thing is millions of years old, passes for a god to most cultures, and you want me to just *get it to cooperate*?"

"Of all the ambassadors on Bastion, you have the greatest chance for success."

"I'm the newest ambassador. I have no training in dealing with—" she waved her hand at the orb "and I couldn't even get the council to help Earth when the Toth came knocking. Explain what cooperation you want and how I'm supposed to have such great success with that thing."

"You are human. It sees you as an energy source and we can use this as leverage."

"Oh, that makes me feel better."

"I will explain more once you've returned to

Bastion. Malal needs time to feel trapped and isolated. This will enhance your bargaining posture." The cave darkened as the braided woman spoke.

Stacey found herself alone on the sled and surrounded by an abyss with nothing but her thoughts to accompany her for what would be a long trip back to the station.

CHAPTER 6

It took the form of a black hole, one glowing accretion disk across its equator and another as a halo, as an affectation to research conducted long ago in a galaxy that no longer existed. Dozens of pedestals surrounded the Minder, each supporting a scan of the human mind in various degrees of decay. Some were still coherent, the trillions of neural connections mostly intact but degrading rapidly, falling apart like icicles breaking free from a roof at the first spring thaw. Other scans had coalesced into the human's face; some screamed silently while others looked around in confusion.

The Minder collated its finding for the

master to review and considered the scan in the center of the room, his only success in a sea of failure. If this one lost coherency like the others, he could always make another copy, but the scientist at the Minder's core hated inefficiency.

Night fell over the laboratory. Keeper appeared as a star-filled nebula stretched across everything above Minder.

+Report.+

Great success, master. After much trial and error, I can access the primitive's overt memories and will have the blacked-out segments recovered in the next two rotations through a parallel reconstruction and synaptic fusion. My models show 99.999% certainty of success.

+You annoy me with projections?+

The distribution of the primitive's memories is chaotic, inefficient, and laughable by the standards of perfection attained by our transition to photonic existence. To fully exploit this resource…I must engage in direct contact.

+You will be erased once the mission is

complete.+

As is our law. But, given that this is a scan and not an actual member of a polluting species, perhaps an exception—

+Erased.+

Yes, master. The next phase begins forthwith. I will quarantine myself from the other Minders…oh, you've already done it. Thank you.

Keeper vanished.

The Minder floated toward the last fully functional scan and spun around on its axis.

You had better be worth the end of my immortality.

****

Torni opened her eyes and found herself in a sunlit glade. The smell of pollen and the chill of a nearby snow-fed brook washed over her. A white robe covered her body as her bare feet played in moist grass.

Wind rustled through tall birch trees. A dove

flew into the air from a tall branch.

She remembered this…a summer spent in Falun with cousins.

"Is this to your liking?"

Torni whirled around, her hands up high to guard from attack, her body settled with knees bent, muscles taut, her instinct to fight triggering a cold burst of adrenaline through her system.

A man in his mid-twenties stood before her, clad in the same white robe. Fair hair and sapphire blue eyes accompanied a gentle smile.

"What is this? Where am I?" Torni asked.

"Your mind often comes here. It is a source of comfort, relaxation. But judging by your autonomic response to my presence, I see this location isn't helpful," he said.

"You have exactly five seconds to start making sense or I will beat you bloody."

"Yours is a…delightful…species." His lips pulled into a slight sneer, then broadened into a smile. "But you deserve an apology. You fell victim to a terrible misunderstanding in our drone programming, one we are just beginning to correct."

"You're...Xaros?" Torni felt the blood drain from her face.

"I am no more one of those drones than you are a worm," he said. "After your ship, the *Breitenfeld* I believe, visited Anthalas, it triggered a contingency program. The human presence on Anthalas was impossible without the ability to travel faster than light. Examining local space around that planet after your—and the Toth's—departure revealed you used wormhole technology. Very dangerous wormhole technology."

"What? Where the hell am I?" Torni dropped her arms and spun around, looking for some kind of escape. There was a cabin...over the brook and next to a well. She ran to the sound of the running water. Her feet pounded the grass and her lungs burned as she sprinted onward, but the tree line got no closer.

"Torni," the man said and she felt the tension gripping her chest ease away. She turned around and found him in the same place. "We have much to discuss.

"I attempted this interaction many times before. Yours is the first not to fail to psychosis or de-coherence."

"What the hell are you talking about?"

He raised his hands up to his head and took a step toward her.

"I am the Minder, and I need you to help me save what's left of humanity."

****

Minder and Torni sat in the grass, he with his hands wrapped around his knees, she pulling tiny weeds from the soil and tearing them apart as he spoke.

"The drones weren't meant to destroy all intelligent life," Minder sighed. "The initial drone that arrived in the galaxy was damaged by the species that gave it the name Xaros. The damage, coupled with its self-defense protocols, resulted in aberrant programming when the probe replicated.

Every drone after the first was created with two flawed functions: replicate and destroy. We're trying to catch up with the forward maniples before they wipe out what's left of the galaxy's sentients."

"So the drones that wiped out humanity and God knows how many other species, are an 'oops'?" she asked.

"We're terribly embarrassed. We weren't aware of the error until the *Breitenfeld* anomaly came to our attention. I was brought out of stasis to deal with the issue," he said.

"There was…" She closed her eyes as the image of a red armored giant played across the back of her mind. "I thought I saw…how did I get here?"

"We managed to scan your body on Takeni. Our technology is such that we recreated your brain, perfect down to the synapse connection, and now I'm here to enlist your help."

"I'm a Marine, not a damn doctor. Are you saying you've got my brain in a jar somewhere and all this is some sort of simulation?" she asked.

"If you want to be pedestrian about it…"

Minder shrugged.

"What happened to my ship? My team? Me!" Torni pressed her palms against her face.

"All escaped, with the Dotok I'm happy to report."

"Why me? Are there any others?"

"You are the only one. The situation on Takeni was fluid. We're lucky that you happen to have information vital to saving what's left of the galaxy." Minder got to his feet and brushed grass from his robe.

"I have vital information?" she asked.

Minder snapped his fingers and the glade transformed into the deck of the *Breitenfeld*. Torni was now in her armor, standing next to the frozen form of Hale and Yarrow.

"Sir?" Torni reached out to touch Hale, but her fingers passed through his body.

"We're in your memories…but there have been some modifications." Minder walked to the edge of the flight deck and peered into the abyss.

"What did you do?"

"Not us. Someone else. The same someone, I'm certain, who gave you the jump-drive technology. Here, look out there." He motioned into the expanse with his chin. "See that?"

Torni saw a dark fleck against the gray, then Yarrow was on his feet beside her.

"You have a hole in your mind." Minder came back to her. He rolled a fingertip and Yarrow spoke until a black line covered his lips and the memory froze. "Each time you tried to remember this event, more holes appeared."

"Then how the hell am I supposed to help you? Assuming I even want to."

"What has been done can be undone. The species that meddled with your mind is advanced, but not compared to the Xaros. I can repair the damage. Quickly, if you assist. I've managed one lead, a double connection to a concept that is both blocked and available. Tell me, what is an Ibarra?"

"Nothing." Torni's mouth went dry. She felt for the gauss rifle stock over her shoulder. Her hand gripped the weapon, then held nothing but air as it vanished like it had never been there.

"This is difficult for you, I understand." Minder reached out to touch her arm, and she slapped him away. "I know what the Xaros have done to you and your planet. Your hostility is warranted and expected. Would it make you feel better to bash my skull to pulp? Give in to some atavistic desire? I would simply reload this avatar and continue on."

Torni's hands balled into fists.

"Humanity is at a crossroads with three possible outcomes. First, the drones follow their programming and send an overwhelming mass to annihilate what little resistance your fleet can offer. I've seen the battle for the Crucible from your eyes. I know how many ships you have left. Your planet has no chance to survive the next wave. But. I can stop the armada before it ever leaves for Earth, provided you cooperate."

"If killing us was such a mistake, why don't you cancel the attack right now?"

"Second. Humanity continues using the

jump-drive technology and triggers a rupture that will annihilate every atom of matter from one end of the galaxy to the other. We will destroy Earth to keep the rest of the galaxy intact, hence the armada massing near Barnard's Star. An acceptable trade, don't you think?

"Third. You help me identify the species risking a cataclysm with the jump engines. Their identity is in your mind, Torni. Help me find it and I will spare Earth. We will lift your people up to the heights of technology and civilization, make you greater than you could ever imagine as penance for what we did to you."

She shook her head.

"I've seen your drones at work. There was no mercy, no attempt to communicate. You expect me to believe what you promise when I've seen Xaros actions on three different planets?" she asked.

Minder folded his arms, then tilted his head to the side slightly.

"Why tell when I can show?" He clapped his hands together.

The *Breitenfeld* vanished and Torni found herself standing in a tower. The clear glass beneath her feet and surrounding her glowed with tiny circuits. She and Minder were thousands of miles above a planet. The tower stretched to the distant surface, cutting through clouds and reaching the very edge of space.

The planet around them had many more identical towers. The surface was nothing but a web of glowing connections and blinking lights from an urban sprawl that covered every mile but for a few lakes.

"This was my home," Minder said. "Eight hundred billion Xaros lived here, a minor world, nothing compared to the grand archologies in the core systems."

"Why are we here?"

"See that?" He pointed to the starry sky. A black mass grew in the distance, snuffing out stars one by one as it grew larger, like an approaching tidal wave. "That is the annihilation wave. We used wormhole engines, the same as the *Breitenfeld* has, to travel from planet to planet. The risk was theoretical…so when we weighed the benefits of a star-spanning civilization against the miniscule chance of disaster, we chose to gamble."

The darkness grew and touched the very edge of the planet. The tower shifted beneath their feet as the planet's crust cracked open.

"We were warned," Minder said, "and we didn't listen."

The darkness splashed over the planet, devouring everything it touched.

"Enough…enough!" Torni backed away and put a hand over her eyes as the inky mass came to the edge of the tower. He brought her hand down and she was back in the glade.

"A few of us escaped." Minder frowned. "But only a few. Our home galaxy, our empire…all gone. I have to stop this from happening to your galaxy, Torni. Will you help me?"

"And Earth? Humanity?" she asked.

"Spared."

"What do I have to do?"

Torni landed on the surface of the Crucible and activated her magnetic linings, which failed to latch onto the gold-flecked basalt of the structure.

"Damnit." She twisted around and dug her hands into the surface, slowing her to a stop.

"Whoa!" Stacey Ibarra flailed her arms wildly and bounced off the alien metal. Torni found purchase with the gravity generators in her feels and stomped across the surface to interdict Stacey's messy landing before she continued off into the void.

"Spoiled brat princess," she murmured and caught Stacey, the ensign's back to her. Torni flipped her over and found the suit full of total darkness.

"Freeze," Minder said. He came up behind Torni, wearing his robe while Torni was in her combat armor for the Battle of the Crucible.

Torni held Stacey's suit, her hands

trembling as the darkness within Stacey's suit coalesced into the rough outline of a person.

"Who is this?" Minder asked.

"Stacey Ibarra. She had…" The shape in the suit grew more distinct. "We had to get her to the control room. We got separated later on."

Stacey became a young woman with neck-length dark hair, wild and loose inside the helmet.

"You know her from elsewhere?" Minder asked.

"Phoenix. The lieutenant had to get her to the tower…something about the other Ibarra, her grandfather," Torni said.

Stacey's face became clear, fear on her frozen face.

Minder looked around, surveying the Crucible. They stood on the outer edge of the wreath, much of the rest blocked from view.

"A complete jump gate in human possession. A gift beyond price that we would have gladly given." Minder flicked his wrist and Stacey vanished. "You know what this is? It's the evolution of jump-engine technology. Perfect point-to-point travel with no risk of a rupture. All the gates are tied to each other, allowing information to travel the entire breadth of our network without delay. A message from one edge of the galaxy to the other in the blink of an eye. Sending ships or people is a bit more complicated, but not a challenge."

"Why didn't you use them in your home galaxy?" Torni asked. "Might have saved you some trouble."

"Pride. Expense. Independence. All petty concerns. Come, let's see if we've made any progress." He clapped his hands and they were on the *Breitenfeld's* deck. The sled carrying Stacey to the ship grew closer.

Minder and Torni watched the slide set down, then a holo-globe rose from it. Torni hissed and squeezed her eyes shut.

Yarrow was next to the gurney, speaking to Torni.

"Progress, some progress." Minder tapped a

finger against his chin. "I need to discuss an idea with someone else. Where should I send you? Stockholm? San Diego?"

"Coronado Island, summertime?"

"Done." Torni vanished, sent into a memory loop to rest and recuperate.

Minder shifted back into his black-hole appearance and beckoned to his master.

A mote of light rose from nothing and wobbled in front of him.

An ephemeral? Have I fallen so far that only the least of our constructs will speak with me?

The mote didn't respond. It would take his report to the Keeper then self-destruct, protecting the master from Minder's corruption.

I've gained the human's trust. She believes her race will be spared with her cooperation, a fabrication on my part, but the species clings to a concept it refers to as "hope." Neural association making limited progress. Her simulated consciousness isn't fully synched with the scan the General obtained. I will try fusing external data with the scan. The process will be traumatic, but has a chance of success.

The ephemeral vanished. Minder watched as Torni re-experienced a day on the beach with a male named MacDougall. It reached back into its own memory archives to the time it was a flesh-and-blood creature. It found the files for its life mate and associated progeny.

Something stirred within Minder, a sensation long forbidden that would result in immediate termination if the master detected the change.

What is the word? What would Torni call this? "Nostalgia"...no, "happiness." It considered shunting the feelings away, but it was doomed once this project was complete no matter if it violated the master's laws.

Minder dug deeper, and found more emotions.

CHAPTER 7

The command dome on the Crucible was unusually full. At a long conference table sat Admirals Garrett and Makarov, and several of their senior staff officers, along with civilians from Phoenix. More staff and hangers-on sat huddled around the overly large workstations surrounding the purpose-built table.

Marc Ibarra's hologram sat at the head of the table, boredom writ across his face.

"This time table is ridiculous," said Colonel Mitchell, the commander of Titan Station. "There's no way the *Christophorus* will be space-worthy by then."

A civilian in Ibarra Corp coveralls tapped at a data slate and a holo of a starship still in its construction framework popped up over the table. Claire Kilcullen, a top-notch shipwright Ibarra poached from Boeing decades ago, tapped her slate against the table for attention.

"We reprioritized the omnium foundry to create the colony ship's more intricate components, which includes a state-of-the-art fabrication suite. There's no way to get the ship replacement parts where it's going," she said. "We'll have it ready to leave at least two days ahead of schedule—so long as I get the builder drones reassigned from the *Midway*, like I've said the last three times we had this meeting."

"Eighth Fleet is at barely fifty percent capacity," Makarov said. "How long do you think we're going to last if the Toth come back tomorrow?"

"They won't," Ibarra said. "Let's have some faith in the *Breitenfeld*. So long as they manage to put a scare into Mentiq it'll buy us plenty of time.

The Toth aren't expecting the first news of their attack on us for another…" Ibarra looked at an imaginary watch on his wrist "two days. They won't move on us again without Mentiq's say so, and even then it will take them weeks to get here. We've got time to spare." Ibarra looked at Admiral Garrett.

"We'll move the robots to the *Christophorus*, effective immediately," Garrett said.

Makarov said something in Russian that made Ibarra wince.

"That leaves the torch party, the first colonists to settle Terra Nova before the next wave," said Glezos, a swarthy man with dark curly hair. Since the untimely death of Administrator Lawrence at the hands of the Toth, he'd became Phoenix's de facto mayor. "The skill requirements for anyone to even apply for the lottery are pretty high. You're looking to take our best and brightest from the city and send them to the far end of the galaxy."

"Again," Ibarra said, "the *Christophorus*

needs the best and it needs redundancy. They lose the one surgeon or environmental engineer we send with them and the entire mission is in jeopardy."

"Then send a proccie tube." Glezos tossed his hands in the air. "They can recreate—"

"No. A single tube's energy and computer needs are more than we can cram into the ship as it is," Ibarra said. "Terra Nova is far. The Crucible can barely open a single gateway before the gravity tides make it impossible, and only a ship *that* size," he said, pointing to the holo, "can make it. There's no room for error or any additional space." Ibarra leaned back. *And only true born will win the lottery, but none of them need to know that.*

"Besides, I need every tube here on Earth and Mars building up our defenses for the Xaros return," Ibarra said. "We can cram six thousand, nine hundred and twelve colonists into the *Christophorus*. That is exactly what we're going to do before we launch the ship.

"Next order of business." Ibarra tapped on a data slate, but his holographic finger sank through the device and the table. "Damn it. Someone bring up the second-phase expansion charts."

Dozens of the solar system's planets and named celestial bodies formed in the holo tank over the conference table. Data tables with population numbers, ship-building facilities and attendant infrastructure appeared next to the planets stretching from Mercury to distant Eris. Everything but Earth, Luna and Ceres had data tables full of glaring red indicators. Mars had a few blocks of flashing amber; construction drones had arrived on the planet a few days earlier.

"This is garbage, people," Ibarra said. "Before you all start whining about the Toth attack and how that threw a monkey wrench in our works, let me remind you that excuses aren't going to beat the Xaros. We need to establish a defense in depth, bleed the Xaros from the far edge of the solar system to Earth. We need the production facilities up and running at full speed within the next few months or the math gets very bad for us."

"Show the Day Zero projections," Admiral

Garrett said. Data tables went green as the computer ran projections to the day the Xaros were expected to arrive roughly fourteen years in the future. Fleets of starships dotted the solar system.

Glezos looked at the population numbers and rubbed his eyes. "That can't be right. Twelve billion people in the solar system?"

"There's nothing more powerful in the universe than compound interest," Ibarra said. "Procedural human tubes are in full production and we're building as many as we can along with warships, fighters and power armor. The vast majority of the new units coming online are military personnel."

"There won't be enough true born around to matter," someone said from the wings.

"There's no survival without the proccies," Ibarra said, "and I don't think they need to prove which side of the fight they're on, not after so many died in Eighth Fleet against the Toth to save Phoenix. This is how we win the next round. The ember that survived the Xaros invasion will grow into a bonfire, but even that can't beat back the tide. We beat the Xaros maniple. The next wave will be exponentially larger."

"This will turn into an arms race," Makarov said. "Whoever brings more to the fight will win."

"And the Xaros have most of the galaxy to draw from," Garrett said. "We've got our solar system."

"The rest of the Alliance will help, but they can't get here until we finish this jump gate," Ibarra said. "I've got my top people working on that issue. Now, let's discuss why the Martian construction efforts are eighteen hours behind—"

A rumble shook the room. Lights flickered and the holo tank cut out. Low moans came through the walls as the station's giant thorns shifted against each other.

"Jerry?" Ibarra called out to the Alliance probe within the Crucible.

+Something is trying to activate the gate.+

Ibarra pulled up a holo screen in front of his face and brought up the station's emergency overrides that were partitioned off from the probe's control. The Qa'Resh had given Stacey the keys to subvert the probe's systems to allow some of humanity to escape the Toth attack. Ibarra hadn't let the probe lock the back-door access that Ibarra kept for emergencies just like this.

"Is it the *Breitenfeld*?" Ibarra asked. He ignored the shouts and confusion from the rest of the conference room as Makarov and Garrett fought to keep everyone under control as the Crucible rearranged itself.

+No. I can't detect where the signal is coming from. I find this most aggravating.+

"Do I need to shut you down?"

+I am constantly readjusting the thorns to upset the quantum field state within the wreath. Would you like to make those calculations *and* move the thorns?+

The rumbles stopped. Ibarra pulled up a camera feed of the center of the wreath and saw nothing but empty space.

"You did it?"

+Difficult to say. Whoever coopted the Crucible had complete control for a third of a second before I was able to intervene. They could have opened a jump gate.+

"From where?"

+Unknown. Curious, had they opened the gate, there would have been a .002 percent chance of a quantum rupture. Perhaps they didn't want to take the risk. I will forward the data to Bastion once Stacey returns.+

"I thought the Crucibles were perfect technology, no quantum ruptures."

+They are, but our Crucible is ninety-one percent complete. I lack the ability and knowledge to complete the structure, which just proved fortuitous. I'd kept the Crucible in its default setting, which may have made it easier for whoever just knocked on our door. I will reset the quantum field for the *Breitenfeld*'s return, then keep things in flux to dissuade future attempts.+

Ibarra closed the emergency shut-down protocols and pulled up a stellar map with Earth and

Barnard's Star, the closest known Xaros-occupied territory.

"They know. They know Earth survived and they're coming for us right now."

+We've observed coordination between distant Xaros forces before. The speed of light has proved to be the only reliable planning factor. There is no way a distress signal from their defeat here has reached any other Xaros.+

"Then they figured out something from us survived from the encounter on Anthalas, or Takeni when we met up with that red armored bastard," Ibarra said. "If that thing got the ball rolling out of Barnard's Star that much sooner…"

+The Xaros will arrive in nine years, not fourteen. This puts our force projections significantly lower. Our chance of surviving the next wave is now exceedingly low, in the single digits.+

"Damn." Ibarra took his attention away from the probe and found Admirals Garrett and Makarov standing in front of him, neither waiting patiently.

"What is it?" Makarov asked.

"We need to break out our contingency plans," Ibarra said. "I hate to tell you this, Makarov, but the name of your flagship, the *Midway*, just became very relevant."

****

The Iron Hearts' armor stood in their lidless coffins. Cables ran from ports arrayed over the suits into a diagnostic station on wheels. The third suit's chest piece was open, exposing the armored womb within. Kallen's face floated behind the view pane, her eyes closed. A pair of armor techs in gray coveralls crowded around the diagnostic station. An empty wheelchair waited at the end of a walkway.

Bodel, wearing nothing but a dark skinsuit, rubbed a towel through his thin hair. He glanced over the techs' shoulders, then moved one aside.

"She has to come out—now," Bodel said. He punched commands into the station and fluid drained slowly out of Kallen's womb.

"She's fine. Let her sleep and keep her synch rate high," Elias said, his voice booming through his suit's speakers.

"Do you see her blood oxygenation rate, Elias?" Bodel pointed an accusing finger at his fellow Iron Heart. "She's already in second-stage whither. A few more hours like this and she'll go into shock."

"Then give her an adrenaline spike." Elias' armor shifted in its coffin. "She's had her armor on for longer than this."

"This isn't a contest, Elias!" Bodel shouted. His head snapped toward the two techs, who took the hint and hustled out of the cemetery.

"Why are you coddling her? She knows her plugs better than anyone in the fleet or on Earth," Elias said.

Kallen's womb lowered from the housing inside the armor. Bodel unsnapped the latches on a seam running over the long axis and grabbed a handle on the front.

"She doesn't want me to tell you. Said you

have enough to worry about with your condition—"

"Hans..." Elias' fingers snapped against his palm as they formed into fists.

"She's dying. Batten's Disease...we all knew it was a risk when we got our plugs. She had a seizure just before we left Earth. Doctor Eeks says she's beyond the point for treatment. We would have picked it up earlier but she's quadriplegic. Early symptoms never manifested. Her nervous system is degrading." Bodel reached a hand up and touched the glass over Kallen's face. "The longer she wears her armor...the faster she'll fall apart."

"You asked her to quit?"

"I begged. But she won't. She's like you. The armor is all she has." Bodel bent his forehead to the glass.

"Then why are you still putting her in the armor?"

"Because if I keep her alive in that chair then I *will* lose her! And then I'll lose you too, won't I? You two are all I have left," Bodel said.

"She can't do this. We can't let her," Elias

125

said.

"Ihr Herz ist Eisen, aber ihr Fleisch ist schwach, Elias." Bodel slipped into his native language. Elias learned enough German from his childhood in a Bonn refugee camp to know what he said: "Her heart is iron, but her flesh is weak."

Bodel glared at Elias, then opened Kallen's womb with a grunt and caught her stick-thin body as it fell into his arms. He lowered her into her wheelchair and covered her shoulders with a blanket.

Kallen's eyes opened and struggled to focus on Bodel. He patted her face with a towel and wrapped it around her hair. A smile spread across her face, all dimples and pale freckles.

"Hans…why am I out?" she asked.

"Got to get you cleaned up," Bodel said. "Get some real food in you."

"But my synch…"

"Your synch will be fine," Elias said. "Come back when you're ready."

Bodel stepped into a baggy set of coveralls

and turned Kallen's chair toward the doors. He looked over his shoulder at Elias. The armor nodded slowly.

CHAPTER 8

Hale, sitting in the top gunner pod on the Mule, watched as the roof of the flight deck slipped away. The distant red curtain of the nebula wavered as its light passed through the *Breitenfeld*'s cloak field.

"Cloak activation in 3...2...1," Egan said through the Mule's IR.

There was a high-pitched whine and the Mule that Hale could see from his exposed vantage point in the turret vanished. He could still see the seat and the ship's cargo bay beneath his gimbal mounting, but other than that it was like he was floating alone in space.

"Spotters on the Breit *confirm we're off sensors and the visible wavelength. Engaging engines,"* Lafayette said. Hale felt the ship lurch through his seat and the tug of constant acceleration against his body. He swung the seat to face his body against the g-forces and saw the bright-blue half disk of Nibiru.

"The view from out here is something else, ain't it, sir?" Standish asked from the other turret.

"It's impressive," Hale said. He felt like he was soaring through the void. *Someday we might visit planets like this for the sake of exploration, to push the boundaries of human knowledge and our reach across creation, but not today. Not this time,* he thought.

"Sir," Cortaro connected through a private channel.

"Go."

"Our Marines are good. Yarrow asked for a copy of the video, so he's not too salty about the prank. Egan told everybody he's a proccie."

"He is? Guess that explains why he's got

pilot wings. I wouldn't have guessed that since his service jacket lists his birthday decades ago and not…weeks," Hale said.

"Fits with Admiral Garrett's address after the Toth incursion," Cortaro said. "The big boss said proccies won't be treated any different from true born in the eyes of the military. They'll get to keep whatever training certificates and rank they had when they came out of the tubes. What a deal, right? I had to bust my hump in the Corps for almost twenty years to get these stripes. Now there's shake-and-bake gunney and master sergeants running around all over the place."

"If they were that good, they'd be on this mission. Wouldn't they?" Hale asked.

"Suppose so…I see the need for them. Just don't like how it's playing out."

"When we were on Anthalas…hold up." Hale caught a flash of light from the planet's orbit. He zoomed the gauss cannon's optics on the flash and saw the two *Naga*-class dreadnoughts, both circling a mass of starships. "When we were on

Anthalas, I saw the Crucible gate open, drones pouring out of it like water over Niagara Falls. There are a hell of a lot of drones coming for Earth, and even if we bucked Standish up to first sergeant to ride herd on a company full of proccies, there'd never be enough true born to lead the number of proccies we need to defend the planet."

"The day Standish gets a second rocker is the day we've lost the war. So what's going to happen to us, sir? About half a million true born survived the Xaros invasion. We'll be nothing but a drop in the bucket in a couple more years if Ibarra keeps his production rates up. You saw what was under Mauna Loa after the battle," Cortaro said.

Toth warriors had dropped into the ocean just off the island's coast and tried to fight their way into the proccie factory dug into the mountain. Hale and his Marines had fought off the assault and caught a glimpse of what the Toth were after. Thousands and thousands of tubes stacked atop each other, each gestating another human being every nine days.

What alarmed Hale more than the tanks were the automated mining robots he saw in and around the mountain, expanding the production facility more and more each day.

"That's not for us to worry about," Hale said. "Keep everyone focused on killing just one Toth. We'll have time for an existential crisis…probably never."

"We're approaching the anchorage. Stand by for evasive maneuvers," Lafayette said.

Hale clicked his tongue twice to signal that he was cutting the private line to Cortaro and switched over to his Marines' frequency.

"No way," he heard Orozco say.

"I'm telling you, I was there," Rohen said. "I was there on Ceres when Garrett's escape pod landed after the *America* went up. I pulled him out of the wreck and slapped sealant on his helmet where he'd had a class-two air leak. That's how I got his commander's coin."

"You saved the admiral's life and all you got was a lousy coin?" Standish asked. "You should have got a promotion, a nice cushy job on his staff making coffee and keeping the lady-pogues entertained."

"Boring. Why sit down under some mountain waiting for Armageddon when I could be out here making a difference?" Rohen asked. "Now I get to travel to strange new worlds, seek out alien leaders and shoot them with my rail rifle. Just like the recruiter promised. Sort of. OK, not at all."

"Careful what you wish for," Yarrow said.

The ships at the anchorage grew larger, almost to the point where Hale could make out individual ships.

"Cut the chatter," he said. "Standish, don't maneuver your turret. The techies say we're effectively invisible beyond ten meters, but let's not risk anything."

"Roger, sir," Standish said.

"Lafayette, do we absolutely have to fly through the anchorage? We've got time to go around," Hale said.

"Time, yes. But not battery life. I attempt to

go around and we'll be visible before we hit the surface. Besides, do you think I lack the skill to pilot this brick with wings? Are you trying to insult me?" Lafayette's tone was prickly.

"No, Lafayette. I just want to mitigate any risk that—"

"Questioning a Karigole's competence is unacceptable. I will demand satisfaction once we make landfall. What do you choose as your weapon, gauss pistols or energy blades?"

"No, Lafayette. There's some horrible misunderstanding here. Steuben? A little help?"

"Ha. Ha. Ha. Earth humor," Steuben said.

"Are you two messing with me?" Hale asked.

"Did we do it incorrectly?" Lafayette asked.

"Yes. No. Will you just fly this crate so this mission doesn't end with us as a smear on the side of a Toth cruiser?"

"As you wish." Lafayette cut the speed on the Mule and angled it beneath the nearer dreadnought.

The Mule passed beneath the immense craft. Hale looked up and watched as the irregular crystalline cannon emplacements and the bloody coral of the hull passed above him. The cannons glowed with eldritch light, each angled into the scrum of ships anchored above Nibiru. He'd set foot on the *Naga* and gotten a bloody tour of the ship's interior, not an experience he ever wanted to repeat.

The Mule passed out of the dreadnought's shadow. The anchorage was mostly Toth ships, cruisers and destroyer-sized vessels with distended hulls designed to haul cargo, not the sleeker warships that had come to Earth.

The ship with the rotating segments that they'd examined from the *Breitenfeld*'s bridge came into view. It was nearly four miles long, the massive segments built like rounded skyscrapers around the central axis. Hale made out a few antennae across the prow shaped like a shovel blade, but no weapons. How any race could build such an immense ship without mastering artificial gravity or bothering to put any obvious weaponry on the hull *and* survive an encounter with the Toth was a mystery to him.

"Sir, can you see what's at our four o'clock, negative declination," Standish said.

Hale leaned and looked over the edge of his turret and through the cloaked Mule. He caught a glimpse of a spaceship the shape of a flattened saucer through the gaps between the Toth ships. The saucer-ship was made up of cubes and covered in what looked like thin green moss.

"Weird, right?" Standish asked. "Why would anyone come out here to visit with the lizards? Not like they're the real friendly type."

"Steuben?" Hale asked.

"I don't know," the Karigole said. "The Toth claimed the Alliance's probe made first contact with them. There were no records of them interacting with neighboring species before or since. Given the evidence of a human settlement on the planet and what we can see with our own eyes, the Alliance's information is incomplete."

"He's so helpful. Glad we brought him

along," Standish said.

Hale shook his head in annoyance. He leaned over to the other side of his turret to get another look at the strange vessel.

A blur of white shot past his face so close he raised his arms to protect himself. A pair of blazing engines streaked past the Mule as the speeding ship crossed in front of the Mule's path.

The Mule shimmied from side to side, pressing Hale against his restraints. His eyes widened in shock as the cloak around the ship began to fail, revealing patches of the hull as the field opened and shut like a winking eye.

"We're losing the cloak!" Hale shouted.

The ship settled and the cloak restored itself.

"Egan, Lafayette, we good?" Hale asked.

"Like driving down a highway after it rains," Egan said. "Cloak is back up but we lost some of our power reserves getting it under control."

"We've got incoming," Standish said. "Three bogies on our six and coming in fast." Hale rotated his turret around and saw the Toth dagger-fighters fly over the side of a nearby cruiser and bank straight toward the Mule.

"Not the highway patrol," Egan said. "Hold on."

The Mule nosed up and accelerated so fast Hale's arms shot away from his body. He had to use his armor's muscle lining to get his hands back to the control sticks. Something broke loose within the cargo compartment and struck the deck with enough force to send a vibration through Hale's seat.

Hale rotated the turret around and saw twin engines of whatever had nearly hit them a few hundred yards ahead. Darkness clouded the edges of Hale's vision and the blazing yellow afterburners grayed out. He tightened his core muscles, fighting to keep blood in his head.

"So long as we stay in their wake," Lafayette said with a calm voice, "the Toth should attribute our brief appearance as a sensor ghost from the craft ahead of us."

"Slow...down," Hale managed.

"Hmm? Oh yes, I forgot," Lafayette said. The Mule decelerated and the enormous g-pressures relented.

The Mule banked to one side, tossing Hale against his straps. The ship swung around a sensor tower on a Toth ship and spat out of the anchorage into the void.

"Did anyone forget to take their motion-sickness pills?" Orozco asked.

"Good news, the Toth fighters seem to have lost interest," Lafayette said. "Bad news, we'll need to set down a little earlier than planned. The maneuvers drained a significant percentage of our batteries."

"How early?" Hale asked.

"We'll make planet fall…eight kilometers away from our intended landing zone. Prepare for atmosphere entry. Five by five," Lafayette said.

"Join the Strike Marines, they said. You won't have to walk anywhere, they said," Bailey mumbled.

A corona of burning air formed around the

shuttle craft farther ahead. Hale tightened his grip on the control sticks and notched his thumbs beneath the safety switches for the gauss cannons. It would be a long way back to the *Breitenfeld* if anything else went wrong.

****

The Mule came down in a copse of twenty foot tall spires a few in diameter. The spires tapered off into blunt tips, their deep purple surfaces wet with dew. A flock of bat-like creatures with leathery wings burst into the air and circled over Hale's turret. The creatures circled high above for a moment, then broke away as one giant unit and flew away from the landing zone.

The ship rocked as it settled against its landing gear.

"We have 199 seconds of active cloak remaining," Lafayette said.

"Get the netting up! Just like we drilled," Cortaro said over the IR.

The rear hatch fell open and hit the ground with a *whump*. Orozco and Rohen ran down the ramp, a heavy metal line strung between weighted plates carried by each Marine. They stopped just beyond the Mule's tail and dropped the plates. Each Marine grabbed a handle in the middle of the plate and lifted up corners of a gossamer fabric.

"Ready?" Orozco asked Rohen, who nodded. "Heave!" The Marines reached back and threw the weighted corners over the top of the Mule. The fabric came out of the line on the ground, flapping as it unwound.

The leading edge crested over the Mule, then smacked into Hale's turret. The fabric billowed in the air like a shaken sheet.

"Not the plan!" Hale shouted.

Hale hit the emergency release on his control console and the turret shell retracted into the Mule. Hale grabbed the edge of the fabric and hoisted it over his head. He ran for the nose of the Mule, carrying the fabric like he was trying to get a kite airborne.

He jumped off the Mule and mashed a carpet of knee-high midnight-colored ferns around the stalagmite-like flora. He pulled the sheet taught and pressed the leading edge to the ground.

"Secure the edges." Cortaro jumped up, grabbed the long edge and punched it to the ground. He jabbed a stake through the sheet and stomped it into the ground. The rest of the Marines worked the edges, covering the invisible Mule in a tight tent.

"Activating," Lafayette said.

The gossamer fabric shimmered, then vanished completely. There was no sign of the Mule beneath it. Hale picked up a pebble and flicked it at the Mule. It bounced off thin air with a ping.

"Sir," Bailey said. "I can see you."

Hale pressed a button on his gauntlet and light rippled over his body as his cloak took effect. He looked around and saw the wire diagrams of his Marines superimposed on his visor screen. The short-wave IR in each Marine's armor sent out a location beacon that the onboard computers used to show him the relative location of the others, with a foot or two of error.

The clearing was a field of tall grass with notched blades, the deep-blue ferns scattered about. The spires ranged from thin to so thick Hale wasn't sure he could wrap his arms around them. Thin branches stuck out from the trunks at odd intervals and each spread a flat lattice of fan-shaped twigs at the ends. Hale pressed his fingertips into a spire, the spongy surface yielded slightly, like we was touching a fungus.

"I'd bit Standish's hand off if I saw him doing that, sir," Cortaro said over his private channel to Hale.

"Even I get curious, Gunney. But you're right. No touching," Hale said.

Two moons, one a bare rock like Luna, the other an angry swirl of red and black of active volcanoes stuck out against a faint red lining beyond the blue sky. An avian creature the size of the Mule flew along the distant mountains, flapping its great wings every few seconds. Far from the mountains, a sapphire-blue sea stretched out to the horizon. Tall storm clouds billowed over the waters, casting shadows over the waves.

"This ain't so bad," Bailey said. "Nothing's tried to kill us yet."

"How're we looking on the Mule's cloak?" Hale asked.

"Batteries are basically zero," Egan said, "but the photovoltaic converters in the shroud are working as advertised. We'll have the cloak recharged to the point it can get us back to the *Breit* in…nineteen hours."

"Was that good news?" Standish asked. "Did that sound like good news to anyone else?"

"Which one of you is trying harder to jinx this, you or Bailey?" Rohen asked.

"The next one of you that mouths off will clean a Toth latrine with your tongues," Cortaro growled. "I will find one somewhere on this planet. I swear it."

The edge of the shroud lifted up and Egan and Lafayette came out, both cloaked.

"Lafayette managed to land us on the right

side of the mountains, too," Egan said.

"Ten kilometers from our planned landing zone. My apologies," Lafayette said.

Hale checked the map on the inside of his visor, pinned a waypoint on their current location and shared it with the rest of the team.

"Everyone remember where we parked. Let's get moving," Hale said.

CHAPTER 9

One hundred and seven Toth overlords crowded together in the throne room, their proximity to the gold and platinum throne that stretched twenty feet into the air determined by the size of their last tithing to the doctor. Those closest to him enjoyed the knowledge that they'd live out the day; those against the far wall shuffled their tank arms and pawed at the ornate carpets in anxiety.

Statues of carved ivory ringed the upper level of the throne room, all blaring out some horrid dirge that Mentiq had written to please his guests while they waited—and waited—for him to arrive.

Many of the overlords theorized that Mentiq knew just how bad his music was and took some sick pleasure in listening to the never-ending stream of compliments he would receive from Toth overlords as they petitioned him for financial backing and better tithe conditions.

Ranik, her spot in the second row of overlords a sizable improvement of ten spaces over the last meeting, hated the tribute gatherings. Hated being forced to share space with the other Toth overlords that competed with her for resources and influence on their home world. Hated the pomp and circumstance Mentiq demanded every time he went through the motions of reminding every Toth that achieved nigh immortality and ecstasy just who they owed their existence to.

She'd been one of the first to undergo the transition from her flesh-and-blood body to the tanks millennia ago. Mentiq had returned from some off-world expedition with technology that held the promise of eternal life, so long as one fed regularly on sentient minds and gave up a significant portion of their income to Mentiq.

With her old body failing to cancer, she'd taken Mentiq's offer. After all, she couldn't take the wealth to her grave and cutting her ungrateful spawn off from their inheritance appealed to her black sense of humor. Life in the tank proved acceptable, but the demands of the associated addiction was a never-ending itch at the back of her mind. She'd hypothesized that Mentiq increased the withdrawal symptoms anytime he decided he needed more wealth or some new species for his gardens.

She'd never shared that thought with another soul; to do so would risk antagonizing Mentiq's humors.

An alien with dark skin and long quills, wearing long robes inlaid with silver, came out from behind the throne. Fellerin, Mentiq's Haesh consigliere, raised his arms and the assembled overlords sank to the ground in supplication.

"Greetings, chosen," Fellerin said, his Toth marred by an accent that would never truly master the many tones of his master's language, "Dr. Mentiq is ready for you."

Lights dimmed around the audience and a spotlight shone down on the enormous throne.

Please, no dancers this time, Ranik thought.

A portal opened in the ceiling and Mentiq floated down on a grand palanquin. Mentiq was of the Toth's old leadership caste, six limbed and with a wide head and bulbous eyes. He lounged on the palanquin, a generous paunch to his belly that the old kings used to symbolize wealth and a life of leisure.

A glove made of precious metals and inlaid with the diamond of the Toth's last god-king covered his upper right hand up to the elbow. Cords studded with rubies and onyx ran from the glove to the base of his skull. He enjoyed feasting on lesser minds as much as the overlords.

"Welcome," Mentiq croaked, his voice brittle and cold. "And has everyone paid for my hospitality?" he asked Fellerin.

"The tithes are in order. All have paid," the

Haesh said, his eyes on the ground.

"Have they?" Mentiq floated over the overlords and hovered above Ranik. "I count two dreadnoughts in my skies. Where is the third I leased to the mighty Tellani Corporation?"

Ranik felt her tendrils wrap around what remained of her spine.

"Lord Mentiq, may you ever live in luxury, the expedition to the human world has only just arrived," Ranik said. "The first batch of human product isn't due back for many more days—well before the end of the tithing. Everything is on schedule, I assure you."

"How can you assure me if you've no word from the fleet?" Mentiq lowered and ran his gloved hand across the artwork inlaid against the top of her tank.

"We sent more than enough forces to assure victory. Nothing can defeat one of your grand ships," Ranik said.

Mentiq's caress traveled down the side of her tank. Tiny filaments snaked out from his fingertips and rubbed against the reinforced glass.

"The amount of capital I risked to ensure your success…" Mentiq's forked tongue lapped at the air. "You know the price to make me whole if your corporation fails."

"Of course, my lord. I signed the contract myself," Ranik said. She'd also inflated the value of her holdings somewhat as collateral to lease one of Mentiq's dreadnoughts, the use of which came with several caveats and a larger-than-usual share of the profits to Mentiq. If Stix, one of her oldest and most able lieutenants, failed in his mission to subdue Earth and acquire the technology used to create the false humans, then her life was forfeit.

Mentiq preferred to consume debtor overlords in front of their peers, as a warning and a final insult.

"Yes, you do." Mentiq tapped on her glass, an annoyance that Ranik hated, and rose back into the air and addressed the audience. "What wondrous morsels you've all brought me. What amazing new species we have to trade at the bazaar. These humans Ranik promises will be a fitting dessert once we conclude our business. Now…for your extensions."

Ranik felt the other overlords shifting in anticipation. None of them owned the life-preserving tanks; they were leased from Mentiq. Mentiq could switch off the life-support functions on a whim, and each tank would automatically cease functioning after a few years…unless Mentiq reset the clock.

Fellerin stepped away from the throne and took a small box from his robes. He whipped out a gleaming slip of electro-paper and fed it into the tank of the nearest overlord, a sycophant who'd been nearest to Mentiq for hundreds of years. The Haesh moved down the line, feeding new codes into each tank. Sometimes there were enough codes for every overlord; sometimes the last few farthest from the throne were left to die unless they came up with a significant amount of capital to give to Mentiq. The chance to die due to one's rank in the hierarchy proved sufficient motivation for some to increase their holdings…and give more to Mentiq.

Fellerin, or the consiglieres before him, were always the ones to distribute the extensions. Ranik's tentacles twitched as she wondered just where he kept the codes.

"But how many of you will continue on after this?" Mentiq rose higher, his palanquin spinning lazily. He let out a dry laugh. "One of you…one of you has a lieutenant that promised to significantly increase her corporation's tithe to me in exchange for their place by my side."

Ranik's mind raced. Could it be Kren? Did that sniveling little menial have the guts to concoct a scheme to undermine her just before the massive windfall he'd receive from Earth? Even if he wasn't the one responsible for this coup, she'd deal with Kren as soon as he returned from Earth. Some Toth needed a lesson in the price of ambition.

"Chairman Howfin," Mentiq said, touching a button on his glove as one of the overlords rose to stand on his tank arms, "your lease extension is denied. Your son will take your place at the next gathering."

Howfin's tank marched to the base of the throne, no longer under control of the overlord within. Howfin thrashed against the glass, the water in her tank sloshing against the top.

"Who will open the bidding for the Howfin's meat?" Mentiq asked.

Ranik remained silent as overlords shouted out amounts of gold, ships for Mentiq's fleet and promises of new slave shipments. To feed on another overlord's mind was a rare treat, one Ranik didn't have the taste for, not when she would end up like Howfin if Kren and Stix didn't return with their cargo hulls full of human treasure.

CHAPTER 10

The Marines stopped at the edge of a wide stream pouring off a rock edge into a wide lake. Rainbows diffracted off the mist, a colorful contrast to the muddy brown waters below. Hale looked up to the source of the stream that stretched into the clouded tops of the mountain range.

Standish and Orozco had scouted ahead to a small raised earthen berm around the lake. Both looked over the edge, high-power binoculars in hand.

"Clear," Orozco said.

"Clear, nobody's out here. Least as far as our mark-one eyeballs and thermals can see,"

Standish said.

"Find some concealment and power down cloaks. Turn on your suits' PV cells so we're topped off once we get to the objective. We're not far from the village," Hale said. "Couple more miles." He leaned against a boulder and deactivated his cloak.

Egan stopped on the banks, testing his footing where the lake lapped onto a field of flattened rocks.

"Should we test the water? See if it's drinkable?" Egan asked.

"We've got enough water in our suits for the whole mission. Why bother?" Cortaro asked.

"I'm not a big fan of drinking my own pee over and over again. Call me weird if you want to." Egan looked over the pristine lake. "This is…nice. Idyllic, even. Why aren't the villagers out here swimming or something? Temperature's great too."

"Just get a water sample," Hale said. "We're not here to sightsee."

Egan knelt down and took a small cylinder from his belt. He dipped it in the water and gave it a shake.

"Egan," Steuben said, his voice stern. "Do not move." Steuben drew his sword from the sheath on the small of his back and crept toward the edge of the waterfall.

Egan held stock-still.

"Uh…there's movement under the water," Egan said.

Hale flipped the power switch on his gauss rifle off SAFE and crept toward the ledge.

"No," Steuben hissed at Hale. "The sound of your weapon will carry for miles out here."

Something broke the surface of the lake a few yards from Egan, a smooth patch of deep purple the size of a man's fist.

"Eyeball," Egan said. "There's an eyeball in the water and it's looking at me."

"If you are speaking then you are moving," Steuben said. He said something in Karigole. Hale heard the snap of a Ka-Bar knife pop out of a forearm mounting from behind him. Lafayette, his blade glinting in the sunlight, crept toward the edge of the waterfall.

The eyeball Egan claimed he saw slipped beneath the water.

"Think I'm good now." Egan stood up.

"No! Don't—" Steuben's warning was cut off as a giant scaled tentacle shot straight out of the lake and struck at Egan like a coiled snake. The tip opened into rows of serrated teeth and clamped down on Egan's shoulder. The tentacle yanked Egan off balance and he stutter-stepped into the lake.

Steuben crouched, then sprang into the air. His blade flashed as he descended, slicing through the tentacle just as he landed in knee deep water. Yellow blood fountained into the air from the severed ends. The tentacle sank back into the water, a patch of oily blood staining the surface.

Steuben whirled around to face the lake, his sword held in high guard.

A wide field of bubbles broke against the water. Steuben shoulder-checked Egan off balance and sent him sprawling into the water with a splash.

There was an eruption from the lake a tentacle slashed through the air toward where Egan had been standing.

Steuben swung his sword like a bat and cleaved into a tentacle covered in calcified growths. He twisted the blade, gouging flesh and leaving the leading edge of the arm hanging by a narrow strip of skin.

What looked like an albino crocodile head the size of a ground car rose from the water. Smaller tentacles writhed in the air around the eyeless head.

"Hale, your blade!" Lafayette said.

Hale cocked his wrist to the side twice and his Ka-Bar snapped out.

The lake creature's mouth opened, and an ululation reverberated off the mountainsides.

"Where am I supposed to—"

"Anywhere!" Lafayette grabbed Hale by the carry handle on the top of his armor. Hale had never really appreciated just how strong Lafayette was until the cyborg Karigole launched him into the air.

He aimed his blade at the creature just as he slammed into the side of it, which was as solid as a boulder. His slid waist deep into the water.

He felt his blade catch in the creature's flesh. Yellow blood poured into the water around him, coating his visor as the beast splashed and bucked away from the source of pain. A tentacle slapped at his head and shoulder. Tiny teeth bit at his face plate like a piranha trying to chew through a glass tank.

Hale grabbed the tentacle with his free hand and struggled to keep his hold as it fought his grip.

Lafayette landed on the creature's back with a heavy thump. He raised his arm with the knife blade and stabbed into its skull.

The creature went limp instantly, like a switch had been flipped. Hale wrenched his blade free and tried to grab the dead thing's flank. His hand slid over wet scales and he sank deeper into the water.

Marine power armor was many things, but armor designed to survive hard vacuum, artillery shrapnel and direct hits from gauss weapons was anything but buoyant. Hale's head slipped beneath the water, his hands still fighting for purchase on the creature.

Dark water clouded with yellow blood surrounded him. His fingertips caught against something, arresting his fall. He tried to pull himself up, but whatever he gripped had broken away from the beast.

A hand slapped onto his wrist and Hale found himself hauled out of the water a moment later. Hale laid on top of the beast's back, Lafayette standing over him.

"Well done, Lieutenant," Lafayette said. "You distracted it just long enough for me to get a clean strike on its central nervous system."

Hale got to his feet and looked around. The beast lay in shallow water, dozens of limp tentacles swaying across the surface like seaweed washing ashore.

"What the hell is this?" Hale asked.

"A *krayt,* an animal from the Toth home

world. Most alpha predators on that planet have a bundle of nerves at the base of their skull." Lafayette tapped the back of his head. "Easy kill if you get an opening."

"Get it off me!" Egan yelled.

The communications specialist sat on the banks, the toothed mouth and a foot of the severed tentacle still attached to his armor. The tentacle jumped around like a live wire.

Yarrow grabbed at the moving end, failing to grasp the slimy flesh.

"Give me a second," Yarrow said. He finally got a hold of it and earned a squirt of blood against his visor.

"Again, do not move," Steuben said. He pressed the edge of his sword against the tentacle mouth's jawline and sliced into the head. He cut it in half with a flick of his wrist. Steuben grabbed the top half and chucked it into the lake, the lower half fell off on its own.

"Is your armor intact?" Yarrow asked. "If that thing's like the rest of the Toth, then it's probably poisonous too."

"Great, poison." Egan touched the bite marks on his chest plate and deltoid armor, then looked at the screen on his forearm. "Integrity is still good."

"We should amputate his arm just to be sure," Steuben said.

"What? No!" Egan backed away from the Karigole, scuttling away on his hands and feet like a crab.

"Ha. Ha. Ha. Earth humor," Steuben said with a satisfied nod.

Yarrow chuckled.

"Not fucking funny. For the record," Cortaro said as he walked over and helped Egan to his feet.

"I guess we know why there aren't any villagers around this lake," Hale said. "You think this was some overlord's pet? Anyone going to notice that we killed it?"

"They can't be tamed and are quite territorial," Lafayette said. "If there are more around here, its death will be seen as a natural occurrence."

"More? There are more?" Egan asked.

"Probably. Shall we continue on before we find out for sure?" Lafayette pointed over the berm toward the unseen village.

****

Standish stepped through a patch of ferns slowly, moving faster as a breeze tousled the dark-colored fronds from side to side. The cloak masked him from view, not the effect of his passing through the environment.

A warning icon popped onto his visor—only a few seconds until the cloak failed. He jogged over to a leafy bush next to a drop-off and went prone. He keyed off the cloak and held still, scanning for any movement around him.

A tree next to the bush towered over the fungal towers. The tree was covered in bark, unlike the smooth texture of every other tree he'd seen on Nibiru. He ran his fingertips over the rough bark, then picked up tiny green needles sprinkled around the tree's base.

"That's funny," he said.

"What?" a low voice said almost in his ear.

Standish tossed the needles away and clutched his rifle against his chest.

"Steuben! Is that you?" Standish said in a loud whisper.

The Karigole, who'd been kneeling on the other side of the bush, dropped his cloak.

"What did I tell you about sneaking up on me?" Standish asked.

"What did I tell *you* about losing your situational awareness?"

"Speaking of which," Standish grabbed a low hanging branch and brandished it at Steuben, "that is a cedar tree."

"How do you know so much about Nibiru botany?"

"You're dense, but I still like you. This tree isn't from Nibiru. It's from Earth, and this bush," Standish said, shaking a branch, "will be an oak tree when it gets bigger. Also from Earth. Who gets the 'situational awareness' ribbon now, smart guy?"

"Curious, but not as interesting as what's ahead. Yarrow, you may de-cloak. The area is clear," Steuben said.

Yarrow appeared in the patch of ferns as his cloak dissipated.

"What've you got?" Yarrow asked. "Should we call it back to Hale?"

"I'm not sure what it is…yet. Follow me." Steuben got to his feet and ran forward in a low crouch.

Standish tried to keep up with the Karigole, but he moved remarkably fast and nimbly for one so large. The number of cedar trees increased, mixed with a few oaks Standish recognized. The smell of sap and moist soil brought back memories of his youth in British Columbia where he'd worked on his grandfather's cattle ranch. The trees thickened and cast shadows across the landscape until the sun and red-tinged sky were nearly lost above the branches.

If Standish hadn't known better, he could have sworn he was back on Earth.

"Here." Steuben stopped next to a tree with a trunk so thick it could have been a hundred years old. A faded sign was bolted to the bark, a square slab of fired clay with a picture of a man and a woman in belted tunics, a red line of pigment slashed across the image.

"I see more signs every few meters," Steuben said. He clicked his needle sharp teeth together and pressed the palm of his hand against an ear. "Can you hear the noise?"

"Noise?" Yarrow asked.

"Your senses are so blunt I swear you evolved from stones." Steuben shook his head and removed his helmet. "There is a constant noise that I find most irritating."

"We can't hear it." Standish looked back the way they came. "You think those krayts could pick it up?"

Steuben tapped a clawed fingertip against his helm. "Yes, it falls within their hearing range."

"We've got ourselves a fence line," Standish said. "The noise keeps the big uglies out." He pointed to the sign. "That keeps the humans in. Doubt anyone would go any farther knowing those things are out there ready to eat their faces."

"Do you want to see the chaplain about this whole 'eating faces' thing of yours?" Yarrow asked. "You seem preoccupied with it."

"Perfectly valid concern, new guy. Just ask Egan. If he hadn't had his helmet on…" Standish waved his hand across his face.

Steuben sniffed the air. "Moisture…and soap. Not far."

"Lead the way," Standish said. The Marines followed Steuben farther into the woods.

Steuben went prone and crawled to a drop-off in the forest floor. The sounds of rushing water filled the air.

Standish got onto his hands and knees and got to the edge. He peered over and froze.

A young woman, a human woman that looked to be in her late teens, sat on a rock next to a running brook. Her attention focused on a data slate she held in her lap. Platinum-blond hair streaked with violet fell around her shoulders and over an eggshell-white tunic tied with a brown sash around her waist. Leggings stopped at her knees. One foot kicked lazily in the air, a sandal dangling from her toes.

She glanced up at the running water, and Standish got a look at her face.

"Oh…wow," Yarrow said from beside Standish.

"Her hair follicles and skin pigmentation don't match what I've seen before. Is that a human?" Steuben asked.

Both Marines nodded vigorously.

"I saw her first," Standish said.

"No, you didn't. Steuben did. He doesn't count because he's not human. And…what're we, on a playground? We're on a mission."

"You're not even a year old and definitely not ready for the kind of adult thoughts I'm having right now," Standish said.

"Shh, she's moving," Yarrow said.

The girl stood up and slid the slate into a pocket. She stretched her arms over her head, bent backwards slightly, then took a trail into the forest.

"Think she saw us?" Yarrow asked.

"Pretty sure she'd have run away screaming if she got a look at Steuben," Standish said.

The Karigole flashed pointed teeth at Standish.

"Don't get all indignant on me. You've got a face that frightens children. And big strong Marines not trained or ready for first contact," Standish said.

"Let's call the lieutenant," Yarrow said. "I think our job down here just got a lot more complicated."

****

Hale looked at the empty landing pad through a pair of binoculars. He let out a disappointed grunt, then turned the viewer to the ocean just beyond the tree line surrounding the

170

landing pad.

An immense dome of shifting light sat on the edge of the horizon, almost twenty-five miles away with a roiling sea between Hale and Mentiq's city. A steady stream of Toth craft flew in and out of the city from a single point, most ships following flight paths to and from orbit. A few larger cargo landers skimmed over the ocean's surface toward islands and a peninsula surrounding the city.

"Well, sir?" Cortaro asked.

"Lot of activity around the city. It'd be a lot easier to get in—and out—during the chaos of some major event...but that shuttle we saw from orbit isn't here. Doubt we could get our Mule in even with the cloak," Hale said.

"The locals know something. Want us to grab one for interrogation?" Cortaro asked. The Marines had gotten close enough to the human settlement to establish an observation post between the village and the landing zone. Given the number of structures and the number of civilians—ranging from elderly to newborn children—that the team's snipers had counted, there must have been close to five hundred human beings living in the village.

"Someone goes missing and there will be a search party." Hale looked toward the sun, now setting behind bands of orange and yellow clouds. "It would be better to grab someone in the morning, more time to get information before anyone gets worried. This late…"

"But we wait too long and the *Breit*'s cloak will fail," Cortaro said.

"I'd rather we be damned if we do than damned if we don't," Hale said. He opened a channel to the sniper nest. "Bailey, Rohen, keep an eye out for a straggler we can bring in. We're returning to the command post."

"Roger, sir." The snap of Bailey's gum filled the channel. *"Looks like they're getting ready for a party in the town square. They've got a stage set up with flowers and everything."*

Hale and Cortaro walked through the forest, heading to a group of tightly packed trees. He reached a hand between the trunks and grasped a sheet of camo-fabric. Light bent around his handhold and he swept fabric to the side. He entered the tent strung up between the trees and found Egan next to a communications station, a metal frame with a rolled-out screen and a dish antenna pointed to the sky.

"We got the *Breit* yet?" Hale asked.

"I can send limited text messages, sir, but nothing else. There's a lot of ionization and water vapor in the atmosphere. We should have voice and data once the sun sets," Egan said. "The ship doesn't have anything significant to report. All I could get back to them is that we're in place and without any casualties." He touched his armor plates gouged by krayt teeth and shrugged.

"Good work. We should have more to report soon," Hale said. He took off his helmet and ran a hand over his scalp. He took a deep breath and sat against a trunk. He grabbed a power line attached to the PV cells in the fabric and connected it to his armor. The cloaks had drained more battery life than anticipated. Operating in and around the Nibiru foliage was more taxing than the simpler environment on the *Breitenfeld*.

Cortaro sat across from him. The gunnery sergeant stretched out his cybernetic leg and flexed his foot a few times.

"How is it?" Hale asked.

"The ankle sticks sometimes. If it was real, I'd just say I'm getting old," Cortaro said.

Hale took a plastic tube the size of a cigarette from a belt pouch and tore off the end with his teeth. He sucked out a mouthful of mush and washed it down with a sip from the water his suit recycled from his sweat and other bodily functions.

"What'd you get?" Cortaro asked.

"I think it's tuna and noodles." Hale downed the rest of it and frowned at the empty tube, uncertain what it really was. Nutrient paste was little more than densely packed carbohydrates, amino acids and vitamins designed to keep a Marine able to fight on no more than a single serving of paste each day. Taste wasn't a significant concern for the manufacturer.

"Incoming," Rohen said over the IR.

Hale donned his helmet and detached from the power line. He checked his cloak charge, only about a minute of active cloak left.

"What've we got?" Hale asked.

"Kid, male. Maybe six years old. He's on the path to that stream where we saw the girl," Rohen said.

"I can get him," Orozco said. "Say the word."

"Negative. Sounds too young to know what we need and parents will be out looking for him the minute he's late for dinner, is my guess." Hale looked at Cortaro, the only one on the team who'd raised multiple children, for confirmation. Cortaro nodded.

"The boy looks upset. Tears and everything," Bailey said. *"And we've got another one, a sheila, coming through on the same path."*

"That's her, sir. The hottie we saw earlier by the stream," Standish said. *"We should bring her in for questioning...because she had an electronic*

device on her person that would be of intelligence value. Yeah, that's why."

Hale rolled his eyes.

"Orozco, Steuben, if you can capture her without alerting the kid or hurting her, do it," Hale said.

"On it," Orozco said.

"Cloak," he said to Cortaro and Egan. "No need to let her figure out our head count before we let her go."

The other Marines activated their cloaks and vanished.

"What're you planning, sir?" Cortaro asked.

"Either we get answers and figure out a way into Mentiq's city, or we abort the mission and leave her bound and gagged with time-locked restraints. Give us enough time to get to the Mule and back to the ship before she can tell the Toth we're here." Hale touched the voice box attached to his throat and switched it on. "Sure hope this thing works or I'm going to look really stupid in a minute."

He heard the sound of heavy footfalls and backed against a tree.

A flap flew open and light bent around a cloaked figure as he carried the woman into the tent. Her arms were pinned to her side and a hand clamped over her mouth. The girl's violet eyes were wide with terror and she did her best to scream when she saw Hale's armored form.

She kicked at the air and struggled uselessly.

Hale hooked his thumbs under the front of his helmet and took it off slowly. The woman's muffled screams grew louder, then died away. Her eyes narrowed in confusion.

"Can you understand me?" Hale asked. He heard his words come from the voice box, designed to cancel out his original speech and project the translation to those around him.

The girl did her best to lean away from Hale.

"I'm not going to hurt you." Hale held his palms up. "Friend. OK? Friend. Understand?"

She nodded slightly.

"I'm going to let you speak. Just don't

scream." Hale looked over her shoulder and the cloaked hand mashed against her mouth loosened its hold.

"This isn't necessary, *kadanu*. I accepted my call. I'm not supposed to leave until tomorrow morning," she said. "I've been waiting years for this. There's no need to take me by force."

"Take you where?" Hale asked.

"To ascension with Lord Mentiq. Where else?" She frowned and looked Hale over. "Why is your armor different? What's going on here and who is holding me?" She squirmed against the grip across her stomach.

"OK…here we go," Hale said. "I am from Earth. Just like you. How long have you and the rest of your village been out here?"

"That's impossible…Earth was destroyed centuries ago." She swallowed hard.

Hale raised his chin and the girl lowered to the ground. She spun around and reached out, her fingers bent against her unseen captor, and she stepped back.

"My name is Hale. What's yours?"

She clutched her hands against her chest and turned back to Hale.

"Lilith. No. There is no more Earth. The elders saw it destroyed. Mentiq's servants saved us, brought us here to fulfill our purpose and make the journey to heaven with him," she said.

"She has no idea what the Toth do, sir. Maybe now's not the time to tell her," Cortaro said to Hale through his earpiece.

"Earth wasn't destroyed—well, not the way you think it was. We're here to find Mentiq and we need your help," Hale said.

"You are *not* from Earth. This is some sort of kadanu trick. You're just jealous that I've been anointed and you're fated to spend your days as a laborer." She put her hands on her hips. "Elder Idadu will hear of this and you will be punished."

"No, Lilith. Humanity is part of an alien alliance fighting against the Xaros. Have you heard of them?" She frowned. "We didn't expect to find you here, but I think we can bring you all back to

Earth."

"More lies."

"Steuben, please." Hale sighed.

The cloak fell away from the tall warrior, who looked almost the same as a human in armor but for his four-fingered hands. He broke the seal on his helmet, then paused.

"Don't be scared," Steuben said. He lifted up his helmet and looked at Lilith.

The girl cocked her head to the side.

"What is a Karigole doing off its island?" she asked. "They're still under sanction for heresy."

Steuben dropped his helmet into the dirt and grabbed her by the waist. He hoisted her into the air and brought her eye level.

"You've seen my kind before? Are you certain?" Steuben asked with such force that he nearly shouted.

"Let go of me, you brute! Of course I know what you look like. One of you collaborated with me on my great work. What is your problem and when did the kadanu let you join their ranks? I should—" She fell to the ground as Steuben released her without warning or ceremony.

Steuben turned his head to Hale, his mouth agape and eyes wide, and said, "Hale…I may not be the last."

****

Hale stood next to a cloaked Cortaro on the opposite side of the tent from where Lilith sat, her knees pulled against her chest. Yarrow crouched beside her, using his thick corpsman's gauntlet to examine the young woman.

"She doesn't know," Hale said, his voice box deactivated to keep Lilith from understanding him. "She doesn't know what the Toth really do to anyone that they take to Mentiq's city. They're consumed—I'm certain of it—but I'm not sure how to break that to her."

"The transport will return in the morning," Cortaro said. "We can take that into the city, figure things out from there."

"Whoever these kadanu are, they're expecting at least her to be there…" Hale tapped his fingers against his gauntlet in contemplation.

Yarrow came over to the two and turned off his voice box with a click.

"She's remarkably healthy," Yarrow said. "Blood work reads like an Olympic athlete. She's been asking about her brother, the kid we saw earlier. Seems he wasn't taking the idea of her leaving forever 'to be exalted' very well. I didn't spill the beans. Weird thing, she figured out how to use my scanners." He lifted his gauntlet slightly. "Asked to see an EKG reading of herself."

"I guess we're not dealing with some simple peasant," Cortaro said.

"All right, let me try something." Hale turned his voice box back on and walked over to Lilith. He offered a hand and helped her to her feet. "Does the village have a leader? Someone I can speak to?"

"Elder Idadu. He's been the high priest since before I was born. Why do you ask, kadanu?"

"Hale. My name is Hale. What is a kadanu?"

"Is your inhibitor damaged?" She reached for Hale's face and ran her fingers down the back of his neck. She jerked her hand away. "Where is it?"

"Take me to Elder Idadu. I'll convince him and you that I'm really from Earth," Hale said.

"I'm...starting to believe you," she said. "But what about my brother?"

"Kid already double-backed to the village, sir. Lot more activity going on in the square. If she's a part of the festivities, I bet she needs to get back sooner rather than later," Bailey said through Hale's earpiece.

"He went back. Take me to the village and show me where I can find the elder," Hale said.

"The ceremony isn't meant for kadanu, or whatever you are. Your presence will disturb our harmony," she said.

"Not a problem." Hale activated his cloak.

CHAPTER 11

When the cave materialized around her, Stacey found Malal in its humanoid shape. The Ancient held the faceplate, absently turning it over again and again.

"I'm told apologies are in order," Malal said. "My outburst caused you some disquiet."

"Are you apologizing?" Stacey asked as she walked up to the force field between the two.

Malal threw the mask at her with a lightning-fast flick of its wrists. The red plate embedded against the force field, then slid through. It fell to the ground at Stacey's feet.

"Gods do not apologize to insects," Malal

said.

"Do gods want to ever get out of this place?" Stacey put a hand on her hip. "The Qa'Resh say they can dump your cell into the center of the gas giant. They do that and it will be a very...very long time before there's even a chance someone would ever find you again. Sure won't be the Xaros if they overrun the galaxy."

"You have my attention," Malal said.

"Can you help us beat the Xaros?"

Malal stepped toward the force field and cocked its head at Stacey.

"What price are you willing to pay?" One side of its mouth pulled into a grin.

"You've been around for a while. Maybe when you were in Yarrow's head you might have gleaned how far humanity's willing to go to keep our species on the right side of extinction," she said.

"You want me to fix your Crucible, don't you?"

Stacey felt the blood drain from her face. How did it know that?

"You can't beat the Xaros' numbers," Malal said. "Not when they can create a never-ending supply of drones to grind you all into oblivion. No, you want to strike at the heart. The master's world. A worthy gambit, but not without difficulties."

"All the Crucibles but the one we control are linked to each other. We've seen them send reinforcements though the gates with little to no warning. If we could tap into that network, we could send a strike force to the approaching megastructure. Do something other than just sit on our hands and wait for the next Xaros maniple to attack. We have an omnium reactor...but we don't know how to complete our Crucible."

"A double-edged sword. Your link to the master's world is their link to you."

"One step at a time." Stacey crossed her arms.

"You've never broken the Xaros communication network, have you?"

"Never. We have no idea how the drones communicate with each other. Past attempts to capture and examine drones have failed. The drones disintegrate once they're compromised."

Malal turned around and lifted a hand. A wire diagram of the incomplete Crucible appeared in the air. Volumes of text in writing Stacey didn't recognize scrolled behind the image so fast it almost blurred.

"They're tapping into the same dimension we used for communication," Malal said with a huff. "Times change but the laws of physics remain the same. I can do as you ask, but I will need my laboratory."

"On Anthalas?"

"No, that was a prison. My peers destroyed much of my work when they left me behind, but not all of it. I suspected they'd turn on me and took precautions." Malal's face morphed into the back of his head to look at Stacey. "You must take me to my lab. The technology I need to complete your Crucible is there, as well as other useful items."

"Such as?"

"Millions of years, insect. I've been waiting

187

millions of years to make my escape and catch up with those that left me to rot. My lab holds the key to your salvation and to my revenge. I will retrieve both from the lab and then you will pay me for my services." Dark pools formed in Malal's eye sockets.

Stacey felt like a giant hand was squeezing her chest as the ancient intelligence stared at her.

"What do you want?" she asked.

She listened as Malal named his price. She nodded along, feeling like she was making a deal with the devil himself. Then she accepted his terms.

CHAPTER 12

Hale, cloaked, walked behind Lilith as she led him through the woods.

"You sure about this, sir? Going in alone?" Standish asked through the IR. He and Steuben were a few yards behind Hale. They'd followed Hale and Lilith since they left the tent, cloaked the entire time. As far as the girl knew, only Hale was with her.

"You two will wait outside the village in case things go south. The snipers haven't seen anything in the way of guards. I'll be fine," Hale said quietly.

"What was that?" Lilith looked around.

"This forest is lovely," Hale said. "Just like home."

"Where is home, on Earth? Are you Sumerian, Assyrian...Xia?"

"American."

"Never heard of it. Is it a mighty kingdom?"

"Once. One city survived the Xaros, and it is a ghost of what it used to be."

"Curious. What is that device you had on your back? The long one with the handle."

"That's my rifle. What do you use to defend yourself in the village?"

Lilith stopped at a fork in the path. Lights from the village glowed through branches and Hale heard music from flutes and drums.

"Defend ourselves from what? Mentiq keeps the krayt away from the village. Weapons are both forbidden and useless. Why would anyone risk missing exaltation by endangering their lives with such things as your 'rifle'?"

"Sir...these people are meat, aren't they?" Standish asked. *"They're born and bred to feed the*

Toth. They have no idea what's happening to them."

"If Valdar finds out about this, he'll insist on taking them all back to Earth with us," Steuben said.

"Oh, that'll be easy. What with the two Naga-*class dreadnoughts in orbit and who knows how many fighters Mentiq's got in his city. I think we burned through all our luck getting the Dotok off Takeni, don't you?"*

"I don't believe in luck. I believe in a plan violently executed," Steuben said.

"Well?" Lilith asked. She turned around slowly, her arms wide. "Are you still here?"

"Yes. Show me where I can find Idadu," Hale said.

"Come with me." Lilith stepped off the path and onto a narrow roadway made of fired clay bricks. The buildings were white and smooth. Every window shutter was wide open and Hale saw shadows moving within most of the rooms.

"That is the college." She pointed to the

many storied, long buildings at the far edge of the village. "That's where we all study to fulfill Lord Mentiq's calling. I finished my dissertation a few months ago. That's why I'm being rewarded tomorrow," she said. Her voice was level, not filled with the enthusiasm Hale expected from someone about to complete a life's goal.

"What do you study?" Hale asked.

"Artificial intelligence. I cracked the source code on an ancient artifact. Lord Mentiq's priests used this knowledge to better leverage the artifact and find new jump solutions to distant worlds. They said my work will bring in dozens of new species to the Lord's dominion," she said.

"This artifact, does it look like a needle made from light?" Hale asked.

"It's locked away in Mentiq's temple, but that is the description I've read, yes." Her eyes narrowed. "How do you know this?"

She worked on the code that hacked Ibarra's probe, Hale thought. *And there must be another Alliance probe on the island. I wonder why that wasn't mentioned before we got here.*

"I've seen an artifact like that on Earth. I'll explain more later. The elder, where is he?" Hale asked.

Lilith crossed her arms. She looked to a small building adjacent to a path leading into tightly packed trees where brightly colored ribbons were strung between the branches.

"He'll be there, the meditation hall, once the ceremony is over. I'll be with him, me and the two other anointed," she said.

"That's it? Just you four?"

"Why? What're you planning?"

"To talk to him. I don't want to panic the entire village just yet."

"That Earth remains will be a surprise," Lilith said. "We are scientists, scholars. New information won't send us into hysterics."

"Boy is she in for a surprise," Standish said.

"I'm excited to learn more before I go to the temple. I'm sure Lord Mentiq will welcome your 'American kingdom,'" she said.

A woman called Lilith's name from the edge of the town square.

"I must go." She started to walk off, but Hale grabbed her by the elbow.

"Keep this secret, please. I'll explain everything once you come to the meditation hall," Hale said.

Lilith tugged at Hale's grip.

"Whatever you want, kadanu. I'll play along with your foolish test."

Hale let her go and watched as she made her way into the square. Villagers, all in the same tunics, surrounded her and placed garlands of rainbow-colored flowers around her neck. All looked immensely happy for Lilith, and Hale felt a knot grow in his stomach.

"Think she's going to narc on us, sir?" Standish asked.

"I doubt it. She seems convinced the exaltation thing is going to happen for her tomorrow. She isn't as convinced that we're really from Earth. Steuben, I'd appreciate your opinion,"

Hale said.

"There is an animal on your planet. Docile, covered in fuzz and known for their weak nature. The name escapes me," Steuben said.

"Sheep. They're called sheep," Hale said.

"Yes. These people are sheep, bred for slaughter and to be servants to any authority figure they encounter. Do not expect them to fight. They don't even know how," Steuben said. "When you speak with this elder, you must ask about my people. Are they truly here?"

"Don't worry…we'll get to that," Hale said. An icon on his visor flashed red. His cloak was losing power. "I swear the battery life is getting less and less with each charge. Let's get to the mediation hall and out of sight."

****

Insects chirped in the darkness. Rohen rolled onto his back and watched a bat-like creature swoop between trees.

"Can't believe it," Bailey said as she looked through her sniper scope. "Bunch of long-lost humans having a party and we're not invited. 'Need you two to stand over watch,'" she mimicked a low Mexican accent. 'Report anything unusual over the IR net.' Yeah, like any of this is usual." She smacked her gum.

"You think we can just show up? That one we grabbed didn't seem real happy about seeing us." Rohen put his hand in a pouch and took out the coin he got from Admiral Garrett. He turned it over in the moonlight, examining every facet.

That he got the coin from the admiral for rescuing him on Ceres was a lie. He wasn't even a gleam in Ibarra's eye back then. But the admiral had given him the coin once he'd agreed to this mission. The admiral had said something to him…words that missed his ears every time he tried to remember the event.

"Speaking of you boys' favorite new damsel in distress," Bailey nestled closer to her rifle, "she's coming up on that stage with a few others."

Rohen rolled over and looked through his scope. The stage in the center of the town square was decorated with garlands of flowers. Three villagers sat on the stage, each with a necklace of red petals around their necks and a wooden bowl in their laps.

Villagers formed a procession at the base of the stage, then they came up the stairs one at a time. Each put little folds of paper into one of the bowls, then moved off stage.

"What do you think they're doing?" Bailey asked.

"I don't see them talking...Lilith looks a bit confused. The other two oldies are smiling like there's no tomorrow." Rohen zoomed in on Lilith and saw writing on one of the open slips. "They're supposed to go see Mentiq tomorrow, right? Maybe they're supposed to deliver messages to the dead."

"Not dead, that's not what they think. They think they've all gone to paradise." Bailey shivered. "What a mind job. Poor bunch of buggers don't know what's really happening to them."

"You think cows on those old ranches knew where they were heading? Or were they too busy thinking, 'Hey, free food and that human keeps the wolves away. This is great,'" Rohen said.

"You'd think if a cow was smart enough to figure out it was going to be dinner it would do something about its situation." Bailey took a bite of beef jerky from her pouch, sniffed it, then tossed it into the forest.

"That's not real meat—you know that." Rohen shifted his scope over to a table covered in fruits and piles of cooked grains. Villagers who'd dropped slips with Lilith and the two others sat at the feast tables, but didn't touch the food.

"I know it's fake. Just…sometimes I'm glad the entire Navy's on a plant-based diet made up of processed beans and stuff. Not sure I can ever touch real meat again after this," Bailey said.

"Chickens ain't people," Rohen said.

"Yeah, and some'd say proccies ain't people. Doesn't mean it would be right to give them all to the Toth." Bailey put her gum on top of her scope and took a sip of water from a tube running off her back.

"You one of those people? That think proccies aren't real?"

"Nope. Egan, Yarrow. Fine blokes. I'd never know they got squirted out of a tube unless they told me. What about you?"

"We all serve a purpose," Rohen said. "I'm from California. Grew up on a farm growing medicinals. How different is what I remember from what the proccies have stuffed in their heads?" He didn't care for the lies, but if the mission went south and the team were compromised by the Toth…they had to know the right lies to get Rohen to his objective. The memory of the farm felt real enough, but the fire burning in the back of his mind was an absolute truth.

"Don't know. Don't care. You're a good shot and you pick up a lot of slack on the team." She punched his shoulder. "I'll teach you how to drink once we're on shore leave."

"Sounds like a plan." Rohen gave her a half

smile, knowing that he'd never live that long, no matter what he did.

****

The meditation hall had raised wooden floors that creaked under Hale's weighty steps. Thin terraced shelves ran along the walls. Rows of tiny candles filled the shelves, each in a small metal cup emblazoned with the picture of a human—mostly elderly but there were a few in the prime of life. His eyes lingered on pictures of children the longest. All had a look of euphoria to their countenance.

Hale brushed his fingers through a flame and felt no heat. *Hologram,* he thought.

A portrait on the wall showed a seated man, long gray hair and beard flowing down a well-muscled bare chest, a length of gleaming white cloth wrapped around his waist and thighs.

"Why do so many human depictions of deity look like this?" Steuben asked.

"These people are descended from one of

the first civilizations on Earth. Their idea of God is an original. Lots of religious traditions match, or at least rhyme, with what came out of ancient Mesopotamia," Hale said. "I wonder where they got this image for Mentiq. Did they come up with it on their or own or is this what he wants them to think he looks like?"

"Bet it's a lot easier for someone to be excited to go chill out of eternity with Grandpa and not a brain floating in a fish tank," Standish said. "Can I carve a *Gott Mit Uns* tag on it, sir? Please?" He held up his gauntlet, his Ka-Bar unsheathed.

"Let's not desecrate their holy of holies before we get them on our side," Hale said.

"What about after that?"

"No."

Standish's blade snapped back into the sheath.

"Got four heading to your location, sir," Bailey said. *"Our girl, two elderly women and the master of ceremonies. All the rest of the civilians are heading home."*

"Roger, good copy," Hale said. "Cortaro, close in. Cover the exits in case someone tries to bolt." He looked at Steuben and Standish; both activated their cloaks.

Hale checked the remaining battery life on his own and found only a few minutes of juice left. The battery would recharge off ambient heat and his body movement, but without sunlight his reserves wouldn't get very far from zero.

He waited until he heard the sound of footsteps trudging up wooden steps before he went invisible.

The door creaked open and a tall elderly man with a jeweled circlet entered the room. He spread his arms to the side and ushered three robed figures into the room.

"Come, come," Idadu said. "Take your position in front of the effigy and commune with Lord Mentiq. He's excited to have you so near him at last."

Hale recognized Lilith's pointed chin beneath her hood. She sat cross-legged on the floor and lowered her chin to her chest. The other two moved stiffly. One had to help the other to the ground, their liver-spotted hands clasped together.

"Remain in quiet contemplation until dawn," Idadu said. "The kadanu will arrive and take you to the temple. I'm so envious. I've been waiting years for my call, but it is my duty to serve. Yes...yes."

The old man walked right in front of Hale, the floor creaks lessening as he neared the invisible Marine. He frowned as the sound from the floor changed unexpectedly.

"Odd." Idadu shifted his weight from foot to foot and the floor groaned in response. Hale raised an open hand slowly, ready to grab the old man by the mouth if he stumbled into him.

"Eh, no matter." Idadu tottered over to a wooden box and opened a drawer. He removed three tightly wrapped silver pouches the size of a large pill and held them up in the candlelight. "Now, this part of your path has been kept secret since our beginning on Nibiru. This gift from our Lord will calm your mind, ease any anxiety you may have."

Idadu ripped the corner away from a pouch and tapped a pale-white pill into his deeply lined palm.

"Lilith? You first." He grasped the pill between two fingers and reached toward her.

Hale grabbed Idadu by the wrist and dropped his cloak.

"Mentiq preserve us!" Idadu said. He looked at Hale with wide eyes, his jaw slack. "Brother kadanu, what are you doing here?"

The two elderly anointed looked at each other. "Is this part of the ceremony?" the old man asked.

"I'm not your kadanu." Hale pointed a finger at Idadu. "I need you to stay quiet and listen to me."

Steuben de-cloaked and put a weighty hand on the elderly couple's shoulders.

"Shh," the Karigole said.

"They found me in the forest, Idadu. They claim they're from Earth. Tell me this is some sort of test of our faith, please," Lilith said.

"I don't—I…Earth?" Idadu shook his head from side to side. "No, that's impossible. Mentiq saved only us so we could grow closer to perfection. Then he promised to call us to his side and live with him in heaven forever."

Hale let Idadu go.

"This is not going to be easy for you to hear." Hale removed his helmet. "Earth survives. Whatever your ancestors told you was a lie. Here. We made this for you to watch." Hale angled his forearm computer to point between the Akkadians and tapped a file.

A holo projection filled the air: Earth, spinning in the void, great swaths of megacities gleaming in the night. The video cut to human cities bustling with energy and commerce. Then an edited version of the video with Commander Albrecht, the former commander of the *Breitenfeld*'s air wing who was left behind when the ship and the rest of the Saturn colony fleet stepped out of time, narrating Earth's scouring by the Xaros. Then images of Phoenix being rebuilt and footage of the Toth attack on Hawaii and a wrecked overlord tank on display in the foyer of Euskal Tower. The holo ended.

The four looked at Hale, confused.

"What was that at the end? The broken glass?" Lilith asked.

"You don't know what the Toth overlords look like?" Hale asked.

Their blank expressions gave him the answer.

"The Toth leaders, and Mentiq, survive by consuming the neural energy of sentient beings, just like us," Hale said.

"Ridiculous. Absolutely ridiculous," the old woman said.

"I have another video." Hale swiped through the files on his gauntlet and hesitated before opening another file. "My armor captured this while I was a Toth prisoner aboard one of their ships. This will be difficult to watch." He double-tapped the screen.

A hologram of Kren standing next to a pilot from the *Breitenfeld* began. Demands went back and forth between Kren and Hale as the overlord demanded more information about the proccies, information Hale didn't have to give.

The four civilians went deadly pale as Kren murdered the first pilot. The elderly couple clutched at each other as Kren consumed the second pilot, the woman's head buried in the man's chest. Idadu's shoulders drooped. He looked so surprised that Hale could have tipped him over with the tip of his finger.

"That's…what was that?" Lilith asked.

"Toth. Mentiq's species," Hale said.

"No." Idadu pointed at the painting. "*That* is what he looks like. He is just like us, but perfect in every way."

"I've seen them up close and personal. Trust me on this," Hale said. "The warriors you saw aren't the worst kinds of Toth."

Steuben took his helmet off and looked at Idadu.

"You know my kind?" he asked.

"You're Karigole. How did you get off your island? You've been under sanction since I was a boy for participating in the Lan'Xi heresy. I remember the day one of you came to us, making ridiculous claims about how we're nothing but fodder for Mentiq. The kadanu captured him and…" Idadu brought his hand to his mouth. "They said he was lying about everything. A test of our faith."

"The Toth overlords consume the minds of sentient species," Steuben said. "You and your people have been born and raised for this specific purpose, as food."

"No!" Idadu whirled around, his gaze darting from the images of those who'd made the journey to Mentiq's city. "All of them? Every one of us who've ever…ever…" His eyes rolled into the back of his head and he collapsed to the ground.

"Damn. Yarrow, get in here," Hale said. He pressed a thumb to Idadu's throat and found a pulse.

"I think," Lilith swallowed hard, "I'm going to—"

A small waste bin flew through the air and stopped beneath her face. She wretched into the bucket. Standish, who'd grabbed the bin, materialized.

"They're taking this really well," Standish said. "Much better than I would have."

Lilith grabbed the bottom of the bin and vomited again.

"There you go, sweetie." Standish gave her a pat on the head. "Don't worry. I still think you're hot."

The door to the building opened and shut, and Yarrow dropped his cloak.

"Get the elder back on his feet," Hale said to the medic. He turned his attention to the three villagers. "Tell me, what's supposed to happen next?"

"Idadu takes us to the kadanu before dawn, at the landing pad," the old man said.

"How many of these kadanu are there? Are they armed? How big is their ship?"

"The area is forbidden." Lilith wiped a

sleeve across her mouth. "No one's ever seen what happens when the anointed leave and no one has ever come back. Not once in seven hundred years since this village began."

"Ugh," Idadu said as Yarrow sat him up. Yarrow snapped a small capsule and waved it under the old man's nose. His face twisted with disgust and his eyes snapped open. "You're all still here," he groaned.

"What's supposed to happen next? Tell me about the shuttle," Hale said to the elder.

"They take the pill and I guide them to where the shuttle will take them away," he said. "Then I spend the night patrolling the village, making sure everyone stays in their homes so they don't disturb the anointed."

Yarrow picked up a pill from the floor and placed it into a small chamber on his gauntlet. Readouts came up on his forearm screen a moment later.

"This would be one hell of a party drug back on Earth, sir. Muscle relaxants, sedative effects...it would keep them nice and pliant for when the Toth show up to get them," Yarrow said.

"Back on the ranch, we'd never slaughter an upset cow," Standish said. "All that adrenaline would ruin the taste of the meat."

"This is all a pack of lies," the old woman said. "I've been ready for my ascension for sixty years and I'm not going to let you take this from me. We are going to the temple, aren't we, Idadu?"

"Wait, wait." Hale raised a hand. "I can save you all. I have a ship in orbit that can bring you all back to Earth, but first I need to get to Mentiq's city and…deal with him."

"Heresy!" She pointed a knobby finger at Hale. "I will denounce you to the next true kadanu I see. My reward for just service to our lord will be more than I can imagine once Mentiq brings me to heaven."

Steuben picked up a wrapped pill and tore the pack open. He shoved the pill into the old woman's mouth and held her jaw shut. She struggled briefly, then calmed down. Steuben snapped his face toward the old man.

"Will you be a problem?"

The old man shook his head so fast his double chins quivered.

The woman rolled forward and lay on the floor, drool seeping out of the corner of her mouth.

"Enzuna, this is wonderful," she slurred. "I feel so close to our Lord Menflish…"

"She'll be like that for hours," Idadu said.

"Sir, you've got one coming in fast to your location," Bailey said.

Hale heard shouts from beyond the walls.

"I thought everyone was supposed to stay in their homes," Hale said to Idadu.

"They are!" Idadu got to his feet and took a few wobbly steps toward the door.

"Cloaks on," Hale hissed. He slapped his helmet onto his head and thumbed the activation switch. An error icon popped onto his visor; the batteries were dead. He tried to turn it on again and got the same results.

The door to the meditation room burst open,

and a young boy fell into the room.

"Lilly!" He scrambled toward the young woman and wrapped his arms around her. "Don't go yet! Our mommy and daddy are gone. Ask the kadanu to let you stay!" The child did a double take when he saw Hale standing in front of the portrait.

"She can stay a bit longer, can't she? At least until I receive my calling." He looked at Hale with tear-filled eyes.

"Yeshua!" came from outside. Three more villagers ran into the room. They went to their knees once they saw Hale.

"We're so sorry, kadanu," a middle-aged man said. "We tried to stop him but he slipped out of the house. Please forgive him. He's just a boy. Don't take him away so soon."

Hale looked at Idadu.

"Wonderful news, everyone!" Idadu clapped his hands together. "Lord Mentiq heard young Yeshua's prayers and sent his most trusted servants to us with a message. Lilith will stay until the next choosing."

"She will?" Yeshua squealed and squeezed his sister even harder.

"I will?" Lilith asked.

"Yes, you're staying," Idadu said firmly. "But the elder anointed ones will continue on." The old man went pale. Idadu winked at him. "Now, I want a welcome feast prepared for the kadanu in the college chambers. Lilith, my dear, you will organize the un-tasked girls, just like the last time the kadanu arrived."

Lilith stood up, Yeshua still clinging to her. "Give me half an hour before everything is ready for our…guests."

"Go! Shoo!" Idadu waved the villagers out of the room. "Wake up everyone and tell them about the boon from our lord and savior." He waited until the rest left before he turned to Hale. "Play along. Our tradition is to welcome the kadanu. There are always four men who come. The leader stays with me. Do you have three more men with you?"

"Yes, what do you need them to do?" Hale

asked.

"Just need them to eat food and stay silent. I'll guide them through the rest," Idadu said. "You can really take us all back to Earth?"

"Yes, every last one of you." Hale opened an IR channel. "Standish, Yarrow, Rohen. Drop your rifles with Gunney and report to my location ASAP."

"This is most unusual, but we'll manage. I've been in charge for almost ninety years. My village will follow my lead," Idadu said. "Wait until the girls with the flower petals arrive at the door, then have your men follow them. I'll have everyone back in their homes before the shuttle arrives. Excuse me."

He stepped over the old woman and got one step toward the door when Steuben blocked his path.

"Where are my people?" the Karigole asked.

****

Yarrow, Rohen and Standish followed behind a pair of young girls, each holding a basket and sprinkling flower petals before the Marines. Idadu led them all toward the college. Windows lit up across the village as more and more of the inhabitants awoke. Many stood in their doorways, gawking at the new arrivals.

"Anyone else not like this?" Yarrow asked. His voice box was muted and his words unaltered. They'd heard the elder tell the flower girls that the kadanu high guard spoke a language more pleasing to Mentiq's ears, and the Marines took the hint. "We don't even have our rifles."

"Just play along," Standish said. "These folk seem pretty harmless. Worst comes to worst, we've got our Ka-Bars and our armor. The old fart's got them all eating out of his palm."

"What're they going to do to us?" Rohen asked.

"Well, if they want a virgin sacrifice…" Standish pointed a finger at Yarrow.

Yarrow tensed and his face went red. "Damn

you, Standish."

A set of heavy doors leading into the college opened ahead of them. Long wooden tables ran the length of an open ballroom; villagers bustled about with trays of food while others swept the floor and picked up bits of trash.

Idadu hurried into the room.

"No one will be anointed this day," Idadu said loudly. "Lord Mentiq sends his high guard to honor us. Let us welcome them with our finest food and drink."

The villagers looked puzzled, and many backed away as the three Marines entered the ballroom. Idadu pointed to three high-backed chairs on a slightly raised platform.

Standish did his best to smile and nod, waving to small, tired-eyed children. He took one of the seats, which groaned beneath the weight of his armor.

"What're we supposed to do?" Rohen asked as he sat next to Standish.

"Smile and nod, boys. Smile and nod,"

Standish said.

A side door burst open and three young women came in, carrying trays of food and three wooden cups.

One of the women stopped in front of Standish, her silver-blue hair cut into a bob, her eyes as green as emeralds. Her tray held a hot bowl of cooked grains, a saucer with deep-red seeds and a cup of purple liquid. She gave Standish a coy look and giggled.

"Please, enjoy," Idadu said.

Standish took the tray with a wink and set it on the wooden armrest.

"OK, let me test this for poison," Yarrow said as he took out a detection wand from his gauntlet. "Who knows what kind of microbes are—"

Standish took a swig from his cup and popped a handful of seeds into his mouth.

"Wine," Standish said. "Good too, lots of body with notes of…cardamom and peat. The pomegranate seeds are fantastic. I'm going to turn my box back on, ask this cutie what her name is and tell her she's got a Marine boyfriend." He wiggled his eyebrows at the serving girl, who giggled and covered her mouth.

"Don't do that," Rohen said. "Let's play our part and get out of here before we start a riot."

"Boys, welcome to the Island of Fiki-Fiki," Standish said.

"What?" Rohen frowned.

"Just eat…and let's not mention the wine to Lieutenant Hale. Booze is a big no-no while we're in the field," Yarrow said. He picked up a spoon full of grains and took a bite. At the end of the ballroom, he got a glimpse of Lilith. She'd retreated to the back wall. She had her arms crossed and pressed tight against her body, her head low. She wiped at her face between deep breaths.

Yarrow kept eating, though he'd lost his appetite.

CHAPTER 13

Egan twisted the IR dish toward the stars and tapped at his gauntlet. Only a few bright stars burned through the red blanket of the distant nebula while Hale and the Marines stood in a small glade. Clicks from alien insects filled the air.

"Should be just a second, sir," Egan said. "There, got our handshake. You're secure with the bridge."

A projection of Captain Valdar came to life in front of Hale, cast from the Egan's antenna.

"Hale, good to see you. What's your status?" Valdar asked.

Hale recounted events up until when his

Marines went to the welcoming ceremony. Valdar didn't act overly surprised when Hale told him about the village full of long-lost human beings.

"I've got the two elderly villagers in our relocated hide site, sedated. Idadu will keep them under until our mission is complete. My plan is to ambush the kadanu when they arrive at daybreak and use their shuttle to get into Mentiq's city. From there, we'll find some way to neutralize the target or get the shields down so you can do it the loud and messy way," Hale said.

"Decent, but I can't think of anything better from orbit. How many civilians are there?"

"Three hundred ninety-two at this location, but there's a catch. Seems there's a population of Karigole on a nearby island. We don't know the numbers but I'm sending Steuben and Lafayette and Sergeant Orozco to investigate. They'll use our cloaked Mule to get to the island."

"Karigole? That's…incredible. Something tells me you didn't have a lot of choice with sending Steuben and the tin man to check it out." Valdar looked to the side and spoke to someone on the bridge.

"No, they were pretty insistent. I put Orozco on their team to keep me informed with what's really happening on that island. The Karigole are hard to predict when it comes to Toth. That there's more of them out here…all bets are off on how rational they're going to be."

A crack of thunder broke from behind Hale and Valdar's projection flickered.

"Crap, that figures. You've got a few minutes left until the weather breaks the connection," Egan said.

"Sir, can we even evac all these civilians? I flew through that mess at the anchorage. There are a lot of hostiles in orbit," Hale said.

"I'll worry about the evac. You worry about killing Mentiq. Understand? Need you to get moving faster. Our batteries…" Valdar went fuzzy. "…work around but…hours." The projection cut out.

Hale looked at Egan, who shook his head.

"Nothing is ever easy, is it?" Hale asked.

"Nope. I can't help but notice that you left out my battle with the krayt. It isn't every day that happens to me," Egan said.

"Marine, if that's the worst thing that happens to you on this planet, consider yourself lucky," Hale said.

****

Orozco shifted against the Mule's co-pilot seat. He'd had to dump his armor plating to fit in the seat, and the bank of blinking buttons that he wasn't allowed to touch only made him more and more nervous as the flight continued.

"Hey, Lafayette," he said to the Karigole in the pilot's seat in front of him, "you really think there's an island full of your people here?"

"I believe you are attempting small talk."

"I'm getting bored and there's this big red button that's tempting me to push it."

"Buttons are not toys, Sergeant Orozco. I

need you to monitor the capacitor charge levels from the co-pilot's seat, not send us crashing into the ocean. Speaking of which…"

"Thirty-seven percent."

"To keep your mind occupied, I refuse to believe that there are more Karigole on this planet. My Centuria and I chased such rumors for years; all proved fruitless. I made my peace that my people will die with Steuben. To believe otherwise is to re-invite suffering that I have already defeated," Lafayette said.

"If you don't believe it, then why are you going to the island?"

"Steuben kept the pain. He keeps it out of hope, and that hope is why we are on this fool's errand. Tell me this: how do you feel knowing that Mentiq maintained a sizable population of humans as livestock?"

Orozco felt a surge of anger in his chest.

"I want to rip his diseased lump of brain matter apart like you two did to that Kren asshole on the *Naga*. How else can I feel?"

"Understandable. Is it true that humans once kept vast tracts of land dedicated to maintaining livestock of their own? How is it you can have so much hatred for Mentiq for behavior similar to your own?"

"What? People aren't cows or chickens, tin man. Big difference. Have you ever seen a cow before?"

"I observed some outside Phoenix. They were graceful, majestic, with long manes of flowing hair. I understand humans used to ride them into battle."

"That's a horse. There are some wild herds ranging between Phoenix and Maricopa. Cows are bigger, dumber animals that crap all over the place."

"And you would eat these cows?"

"Not for a long time. Back in the twenties some genius invented NuMeat. Tasted identical to beef, chicken or fish, but it was all made from plants. Bunch of meat-lovers swore they could tell the difference between the original and the imitation, but they failed a blind taste test every single time," Orozco said.

"And humans stopped large-scale meat consumption after this came on the market?"

"Not right away. Thing was, the NuMeat was cheaper—a lot cheaper—to produce and ship. Some of the big fast-food chains switched over and people started buying the NuMeat. Grazing land got turned into farms, lots of meat producers went out of business, price of real meat went up, more people bought the NuMeat. Market forces.

"There were still some people that *had* to have the real thing. My *abuela*, she wouldn't touch the fake stuff, made my grandpa spend lots of money on the real thing. But he," Orozco laughed, "he just bought her the NuMeat and swapped the packaging. Spent the rest of the money on his mistress."

"You find it amusing that your progenitor was unfaithful?"

"A Spaniard's heart is like a forest, Lafayette. There's always room for another tree."

"I will never understand humans. Prepare to

land."

A small island several miles long crested over the horizon, a mass of fungal trees dark against the water and red sky.

"No sign of any electricity. I'll set down on the far end," Lafayette said.

Orozco gripped his armrests as Lafayette nosed the Mule higher over a line of trees then dipped into a small clearing. The Mule landed gently and Lafayette shut the craft down.

"I'll get the shroud over the ship. Meet me outside," Steuben sent.

Orozco got out of the co-pilot's seat and opened a locker holding his armor plates.

"That won't be necessary," Lafayette said. "I doubt there's anything here."

"Is there some Karigole equivalent for 'better safe than sorry'?"

Lafayette cocked his head to the side. "We say, 'It is more desirable to kill an enemy with your bare hands than from a distance.'"

Orozco shook his head and donned his chest

plate.

****

Lilith sat on a wooden bench on the covered patio that ran across the back of the college. She watched as waves crashed against the nearby shore, light from Mentiq's city shining like a moon frozen against the horizon.

She held her necklace in her lap, her fingers rubbing along the edges. A teardrop fell across the deep-blue jewel in the center.

The sound of heavy footsteps approaching startled her. She sat up straight and wiped her face across her shoulder. The youngest of the Marines, Yarrow, stood in the doorway leading back to the ballroom. He said words that had no meaning for her.

"I don't understand," she said.

Yarrow touched a box on his throat.

"Sorry, how's this?" he asked.

"Better. Interesting technology. My aunt

worked on something similar for the temple, creating translation protocols for races that Mentiq would contact..." she trailed off and looked over at the distant city. "He wasn't going to enlighten those races, was he? He was going to consume them, or make them like us—" Her hand flew to her mouth and she dry heaved.

"It's not every day you get your whole universe upended like this." Yarrow sat on the bench next to her.

"I don't think you really understand how I'm feeling right now," Lilith said.

"Oh? Couple weeks ago I found out that I'm not a real person," Yarrow said.

Lilith turned to the Marine and pressed her lips into a thin line. She reached out and ran her fingertips down the side of his face and along his jawline.

"You seem plenty real to me," she said.

"That's up for interpretation. I'm a proccie, a procedurally generated human being. Ibarra—I'll explain him later—grew my body in a tube and put my consciousness, which came from some sort of computer simulation, into it. I didn't even know until Lieutenant Hale told me. Up until a few months ago, everything I thought was my life was a big old fat lie." Yarrow put his hands on the edge of the bench and leaned back.

"Why? Did this Ibarra create you to be…livestock?"

"No. That's what the Toth want me and the other proccies to be. That's why they attacked Earth. I guess Ibarra made me to fight the Xaros. There weren't many of us left after the invasion, and the drones will come back…can't say I blame him." Yarrow shrugged.

"No one asks to be born," Lilith said. "At least you have a sense of agency with your life. You haven't been tricked into a belief system like me. You do have the choice to be a Marine? To fight?"

"Do I?" Yarrow looked across the ocean. "I never thought about it. Not that there's anything else to do on Earth. Everyone is focused on rebuilding the planet and surviving the next wave."

"You know what's odd?" Lilith sat forward and tugged at her bottom lip. "One of the younger students, a biology savant, received his calling the last time the kadanu came to see us. He was to figure out a way to accelerate human growth. Fetus to adult within days. He was so excited for the challenge, decades of work ahead of him..."

"Sounds like Mentiq farmed out—sorry, phrasing—a lot of projects to this village. What did he have you do?"

"Cracking an ancient device's source code. Several generations of our scientists have worked on the device. First, we trained it to do simple things like utility management, then progressively more advanced computations for energy shielding and quantum field calculations for jump engines..." She looked to Mentiq's city. "He must have it there. The energy shields are only a few hundred years old. It didn't exist until my ancestor completed his calling for the shields."

"Is everyone in this village as brilliant as you are?" Yarrow asked.

Lilith blushed. "No. We're tested throughout childhood for aptitude and ability. Those that aren't gifted in any particular area are…taken to the city. Some become kadanu. Most are never seen again."

"And you…you know this ancient device well? Can you operate it?"

"Hmm…I suppose. I'd need direct access. My lab is firewalled off from the island network. I could only share code with researchers in the temple or on the other islands," she said.

"One second." Yarrow switched off his voice box and opened a channel to Hale. "Sir?"

"Go," Hale said.

"It's Lilith. When we go to Mentiq's city, I think we need to take her with us." Yarrow conferred with his lieutenant for a minute as Lilith tried to listen in.

"What's that all about?" she asked once Yarrow reactivated his voice box.

"Lilith…do you know how to fight?" he asked.

"You mean," her voice dropped to a

conspiratorial whisper, "violence?"

Yarrow nodded.

"No, that's forbidden. No one would risk their ascension, or anyone else's, by putting life or health in jeopardy. Why do you ask?"

"We need your help. Will you come to the city with us and help us deactivate the probe—the ancient device?"

Lilith dropped her chin to her chest and turned away from him. "I'm no warrior, not like you. What good will I be?"

"We can handle the fighting, don't worry about that. We'll need you to drop the shields on the city if we can't find an easier way to kill Mentiq," Yarrow said.

Her head snapped up and she stared at the Marine.

"You're going to kill Lord Mentiq? What about the rest of the village? The Lan'Xi came to us with the Karigole, and every last one of them were purged for the actions of a few who tried to tell us the truth. They catch me over there…"

"We'll get you all out. I promise." Yarrow touched his gloved fingers to her hand.

"Are you going to protect me?"

"You have my word."

"Then I'll go." She stood up and ran her hands over her tunic to smooth it out.

"So do you have a boyfriend?" Yarrow asked nervously.

"A what?"

"Nothing! Let's get back to the lieutenant before those kadanu show up." Yarrow pushed against the bench, and his augmented muscles snapped the old planks with a crack. The bench collapsed beneath Yarrow and he fell on his backside.

Yarrow sprang to his feet and dusted himself off, glancing at the wrecked bench.

"I'll fix that later," he said.

CHAPTER 14

Orozco moved through a wall of tall ferns, their sway the only sign of his passing so long as his cloak was active. A field of low grass stretched ahead of him in the garnet-hued light from the night sky.

He took a step forward and crushed a puffy mushroom that ejected spores all over him.

"Blast it." He bent over and tried to brush the dust away.

"You know we're trying to infiltrate through the island. Using stealth. So as not to be discovered," Steuben said.

"Yeah, I got that part." Orozco unsnapped a

fern blade and swept it across his legs, knocking more and more spores into the air, which adhered to his armor and gave him a ghostly pallor.

"I wasn't sure. A Toth menial in Mentiq's city can probably hear you blundering around out here," Steuben said.

"How about we keep moving?" Orozco shook out his Gustav and walked across the field. "You see my weapon? You think I care about subtlety? No, give me a line of sight on a pack of Toth warriors and I'll—"

The ground gave way beneath him and Orozco got off half a shout before he crashed into a thicket of sharpened sticks. He fell against the dusty ground and tried to move. The broken tips of wooden stakes were stuck between the armor joints around his shoulder and waist. He pried the wood out and gave thanks that his armor managed to protect him from the primitive trap.

He looked around and saw a decaying body impaled just above the ground, the stakes running through a skeletal rib cage and skull. The body looked human.

"I'm OK. Steuben? Lafayette? I need some help out. Guys?"

There was no answer.

He heard footsteps approaching and three lithe figures ran up to the edge of the pit. Orozco saw their outline against the nebula sky, all hairless humanoids holding crude weapons.

"Uh…hi." Orozco waved to them. "You guys are Karigole, right? Know a guy named Steuben?"

One of the figures drew back a bow and shot an arrow. It hit Orozco in the chest and bounced off his armor.

"Really? I'm here to help, believe it or not."

The sound of clicks and whistles came from the tallest of the three. One of the others picked up a large stone and lifted it over his head. He reared back and hurled it at Orozco, but it stopped in midair just as it left his grasp, dropping to the ground.

Steuben dropped his cloak and the three

attackers backed away, brandishing their weapons. Steuben removed his helmet and spoke in the same clicks and whistles. Weapons lowered and one of the three reached out to touch Steuben on the side of his face. The figure looked up at the much taller Steuben, and Orozco saw the face of a younger Karigole.

One of the juveniles turned and ran away.

"Excuse me? Little help here?" Orozco said as he got to his feet. The side of the pit was packed dirt and didn't look like it could support his weight.

"Here." Lafayette, de-cloaked but still wearing his helmet, reached into the pit.

Orozco lifted the handle of his Gustav to Lafayette and held on to the weapon as the cyborg easily lifted him from the pit.

Orozco looked over his weapon and brushed dirt away.

Steuben was still talking to the pair of shocked Karigole, who looked young to Orozco's best guess.

"What're they saying?" he asked.

238

Lafayette plucked the voice box off Orozco's throat guard and plugged a wire into it from his gauntlet. A moment later he passed it back to the gunner.

"—heard stories about the last Centuria, but we never believed it. Just an old geth'aar tale to give us hope," one of the younger Karigole said.

"How old are you?" Steuben asked. "Have you been through your second passage?"

"I'm twenty turnings. Theol is nineteen. She should have hers before mine but…no one wants the passage anymore," the Karigole said.

"Why?"

"You should talk to Bishala. She's our eldest geth'aar, our matriarch. She can explain things fully," Theol said. She was as tall as the other, and with a slighter build. Both wore ragged cloth crisscrossed over their bodies and bound by cords of rope around their waists.

"Come," she said and pointed across the field.

Steuben walked between the two Karigole,

but Lafayette held back.

As Steuben and the others pulled ahead, Orozco kept pace with Lafayette and asked the Karigole, "Why aren't you...I don't know, happy?"

"Karigole society, in whatever manner it has survived here, is different from what I've experienced in your culture. There are things I do not expect you to understand," Lafayette said stiffly.

"Then help me out. I don't want to do something stupid like insult a household god or have to fight one of you to the death because it's time to get frisky or something like that," Orozco said.

"I am dead," Lafayette said and Orozco stopped in his tracks. "By the geth'aar's definition, I am too damaged to serve as a parent and must be pushed out of the clan. Our genetic makeup is a bit different from yours. The strength and health of a Karigole parent at the time of conception is passed on to the child. If a Karigole father has a broken arm or some other trauma, the baby may be born with a weakened limb or even lame. The geth'aar do not allow such weakness in the clan.

"By rights, I should have been left to die from my wounds after the Xaros disintegration beam took so much from me. But, the Centuria thought we were the last…an exception was made."

"They're not going to like you because you've got battle scars?"

"Scars are of little consequence. Damage that could be passed on to a child is another."

"But you don't even…" Orozco glanced at Lafayette's crotch.

"Irrelevant to the geth'aar. They are superstitious and hidebound. It is best not to try to rationalize it. Come, we're falling behind." Lafayette started walking again.

"What's a geth'aar? It isn't getting translated." Orozco saw a group of low grass huts in the distance.

"It is our third sex. Your language has no acceptable concept for them so the voice box lets the word through unfiltered," Lafayette said.

"Third? Are there more?"

"No. Male, female and geth'aar. The geth'aars receive the sperm and ovum from the mother and father, then carry the baby to term. Geth'aar births are very rare, and they have a high status in our culture," Lafayette said.

Orozco frowned. "If they're so rare…then how…wait…"

"Our men and women marry and raise the children, but the geth'aar are something of a community asset. Clans form around two or three geth'aar, protect them and care for them, and the geth'aar give birth for the clan," Lafayette said.

"Huh. And I thought human women were complicated."

"The geth'aar are often the longest lived of any of us. But if a fertile cycle passes without them becoming pregnant, they run the risk of becoming very ill and dying," Lafayette said. He stopped in a patch of tall grass at the edge of the village. Children ran out of huts and swarmed around Steuben. Older Karigole, skinny and not as tall as

Steuben, formed a cordon around the warrior and the children.

"Hmm, no adults," Lafayette said.

"What, the tall ones aren't adults?"

"Karigole children are born neutral, neither male nor female. They become one or the other during their first puberty at roughly ten turnings. They reach sexual maturity once their second passage—or puberty—completes," Lafayette said.

"Man, they should've sent Lowenn or another anthromo-pediatrican whatever on this mission. This is too much for me," Orozco said. "So what do we do now?"

"You may remove your helmet, but I will keep mine on. It's better this way." Lafayette held up his cybernetic hands with five humanlike fingers. "If they ask, tell them I am human and don't wish to show my face."

"You don't think they'll be glad to see you?"

"Please, Orozco. It is better this way." Lafayette touched a button on his gauntlet and his visor darkened to the point it was pitch black.

"Fine, whatever. You're Lafayette, my brother from another mother." Orozco stepped out of the grass and onto a muddy patch of ground.

"That makes no sense," Lafayette said.

A light went on within a large round hut, and three Karigole came out of the low doorway, each wearing leather tunics with deep sleeves. Beads and bits of bone hung from thin cords tied to their clothes that rattled and clinked as they walked toward Steuben. These Karigole had hair tied into heavy buns at the back of their heads.

Must be the geth'aar, Orozco thought.

The lead geth'aar's skin was an ashen gray, her body heavy with child.

Steuben went to one knee and bowed his head. The geth'aar touched her knuckles to Steuben's temple and lifted his chin up.

"You are not the last," she said.

****

Hale sat against a tree and thumbed the magazine release on his rifle. He removed the ammunition from his gauss weapon and looked into the magazine, checking for any sign of dirt or debris in the packed rounds. The cobalt-blue tungsten rounds gleamed in the moonlight. He tapped the magazine against his knee and slapped it back into place.

"Sir?" came from over his shoulder.

Hale looked over and found Rohen standing between two trees, his sniper rifle in his hands.

"You got a minute?" Rohen asked. "Need to talk to you."

Hale motioned to a patch of pine needles next to him. The sniper knelt on one knee, the butt of his long rifle planted firmly into the ground.

"What's on your mind?" Hale asked.

"The easiest way for you to understand is for you to say a code phrase into your microphone. You have an encrypted message waiting for you. Just say," Rohen said, rolling his eyes, "peanut, nostril, happy clam."

"What? Rohen are you feeling OK? Take a knee and drink some water," Hale said.

"I didn't pick the phrase. Please, sir. It's from Ibarra," Rohen said.

"Is this some sort of new-guy prank they put you up to? Saying peanut nostril happy clam is not—"

Hale's gauntlet vibrated violently. A tiny panel flipped open and a projection emitted from a tiny lens.

Ibarra's head and shoulders appeared between the two Marines.

"Lieutenant Hale," Ibarra said, "I never did apologize for calling you a knuckle-dragger when you retrieved me from beneath my tower." Hale had never shared that detail from the longest day in his life with anyone. The only other person who knew about that little insult was Stacey Ibarra, and she was away on Bastion. "Mostly because you are a knuckle-dragger and I've never met an infantryman that took offense to that label.

"But let's get down to brass tacks. Young

Mr. Rohen is a proccie, but not your run-of-the-mill kind like Yarrow. See, we recovered one of the overlord's tanks from the *Naga* wreck on the moon, reverse engineered it with the omnium reactor and found a number of design flaws. Specifically, we can overload the nervous system when it feeds through the tank, killing the overlord. That's where Rohen comes in. He was specially designed as a fail-safe for your mission. His mind *burns*, Hale. It's better that you don't know the specifics of how we did it, but we designed him as a poison pill for Mentiq, or any overlord that gets a hold of him."

"No." Hale pointed a finger at Rohen—who listened to Ibarra's revelation with the passion of a man getting yesterday's sports scores—and shook his head. "Absolutely not. I'm not going to send you to—"

"Get Rohen to the Toth," Ibarra continued. "They'll take him to Mentiq and then your mission will be accomplished. I know you're not the kind of leader to blindly send someone to certain death, so let me tell you this: it won't matter. We had only a few weeks to design Rohen. We would have made him to survive for years and years, but we didn't have the time to do it right. He's dying, Hale."

Rohen nodded, then took out an auto-injector and jabbed it into his neck. He shuddered and clenched his jaw as the medicine took hold.

"The human nervous system wasn't designed for what we created. He knows. We told him as soon as he came out of the tank. Gave him the option to live out his days peacefully on the Crucible or go with you to Nibiru. He made his choice.

"Rohen has…maybe thirty days until he dies from neurological failure. There's nothing medical science can do to stop that. Help him fulfill his purpose. Accomplish your mission at less risk to you and the *Breitenfeld*. Good luck, son." Ibarra turned to the side, then looked back into the camera. *"Gott mit uns."* His image vanished.

Hale let his arm fall to his side.

"It's true," Rohen said. "Everything. Though I don't think I have thirty days. The tremors are getting stronger and more frequent. Let me go with the kadanu when they arrive. They'll take me straight to Mentiq. He'll…" Rohen touched his forehead, "and that will be that."

"This is wrong, Rohen. I don't believe a word Ibarra said. He must be lying to you about—about what you are. A trick to get you to throw your life away. I'm not going to order you to just…offer yourself to Mentiq!" Hale got to his feet. His hands opened and closed and his breathing became shallower as anger rose from his heart.

"No! I will not lose another Marine because of Ibarra, you understand me?"

Rohen stood up slowly.

"I'm willing, sir," Rohen said. "I came out of the tube a Marine, ready to accept an order that would result in certain death."

"I don't order my Marines to die. I tell them it is time to fight and lead them into battle. These are different things, Rohen."

"Not for me, sir. I will die. Very soon. My body is falling apart and I would rather my death serve a purpose, a grand purpose that will keep Earth safe from the Toth. I'd rather that than lying in some sick bay on Titan Station."

"That's Ibarra talking. He must have loaded your head with this garbage, not given you a choice but to embrace this mission. We will get you back to the Crucible and...I don't know, make him put your mind in another body. Something. Anything." Hale put his hands on his hips and turned around.

"It doesn't work that way, sir. The others told me about Torni. How she gave up her spot on a transport so more civilians could make it off world. They said if you hadn't been unconscious and about to bleed to death, you would have been the one left behind."

"Of course," Hale said.

"I've got the same choice: my life for other Marines. My life is forfeit either way. I choose to spare the rest of you. We don't know what's waiting for us in Mentiq's city. Let me go by myself. I'll get their attention and our mission will be complete," Rohen said.

"No." Hale turned around and pointed a finger at Rohen's chest. "That's the easy way out. The coward's way. We're going to that city and we'll kill that bastard with bombs or bullets and get you back to the Crucible. There must be something Ibarra can do for you. I refuse to accept that you come with an expiration date."

Rohen ran his hand along his rail rifle.

"That's your decision to make, sir. I've spent a lot of time on the range…would be a waste not to put that practice to good use."

"I'll tell the rest of the team. They'll—"

"Sir. Think about it. If things go south and the Toth get their hands on all of us…if the overlords get to anyone else first, they'll know I'm a time bomb. Then I'm useless. Leave the option open. Like Ibarra said, a fail-safe," Rohen said.

Hale worked his jaw from side to side.

"But *I* know," Hale said.

"Don't let them take you alive," Rohen shrugged. "Not that any of us have a chance if we're captured."

"Fine. We'll keep this to ourselves. But I don't want you trying to sneak off and make yourself a martyr. Understand?"

"You have my word, Lieutenant."

****

Orozco ducked into the large hut from where the three geth'aars emerged. The matriarchs sat cross-legged on a reed mat. An adolescent sat back-to-back with the eldest geth'aar and supported her as she leaned back for comfort.

Steuben squatted down across from the matriarchs and motioned for Orozco to sit next to him.

"Who're your friends? The children say they're human," the eldest said to Steuben. "We kill any kadanu foolish enough to come to our island. Mentiq only sends his warriors or the Kroar now."

Orozco took off his helmet and smiled, and the matriarchs bared their teeth at him.

"This is Sergeant Orozco. He is human but

not of the kadanu. He is a Marine, from their home planet's warrior caste. The other is Lafayette, also a Marine," Steuben said.

One of the matriarchs clicked her claws together and a child came over to Orozco and handed him a crude wooden bowl full of writhing grubs.

"Oh boy." Orozco looked at the bowl then to the matriarchs, all of whom had their eyes glued on Orozco.

"Eat one, then pass it to Steuben," Lafayette said.

"What if…they're poisonous to me? Yeah, that's it." Orozco held the bowl to Steuben, who didn't move.

"Eat. It. Or I will tell Cortaro you are a giant cat," Lafayette said.

Orozco picked up a single grub, then tossed it into the back of his mouth. He swallowed hard and fought against a gag.

"I think it's still moving," he said as Steuben took the bowl from him. Steuben distended his jaws and swallowed the entire bowl.

"I haven't had *chiqi* in a long time," Steuben said.

"I am Guilan," the eldest said. "This is Naama and Cuibo."

"Pleased to meet you," Orozco said.

"Where have you been, Steuben?" Guilan asked. "We've waited a long time for your Centuria to find us."

"We were in Alliance space when we learned of the Toth betrayal," Steuben said. "When we reached our home world…there was nothing left. All we found were bodies on the spaceport's landing fields. Our ships were wrecked. There was no sign of another Karigole on the planet…just the bodies from where the Toth gorged—"

Guilan held up a hand.

"We held out hope for a time. We managed to capture a Toth vessel off Vulkaaren and interrogate the crew, but they were adamant that no Karigole made it off our home world alive. Then Kosciusko made us take an oath to *ghul'thul'ghul*.

We would survive as long as we could, make the Toth pay for what they did to us. We worked with the Alliance, hoping to find allies willing to take the fight to Mentiq, but none took up our crusade. The threat of the Xaros was too great and we…" Steuben shrugged, "we became little better than mercenaries helping train races in the Xaros' path. Most of us died trying to capture a Xaros drone on some backwater planet."

"The humans accepted your crusade?" Naama asked. Orozco felt Lafayette stiffen next to him as the matriarch spoke.

"We ran into the Toth on Anthalas," Orozco said. "We didn't get along. Then the lizards attacked Earth. It didn't end well for them."

"Stix," Steuben said and spit on the ground, "the arch-traitor, he met his end at Rochambeau's hand. I and—sorry, just me—I killed another overlord with my bare hands. Kosciusko gave his life to prevent one of Mentiq's chosen overlords from escaping the battle."

"And you are the only one who remains

from the Centuria?"

"I am the only one that lives," Steuben said.

"Stix." Guilan ran a claw across her throat. "Stix kept us three geth'aar and a few adults alive, hidden away on his ship during the cull. Mentiq's orders. The overlords have little self-control once they start to feed, but they have enough discipline to obey their master. To displease him is to die. They all know that.

"Mentiq put us on one of the larger islands, gave us adequate shelter and food for a time. Our numbers grew." Guilan put her hand against her stomach as the baby inside kicked. "We thought we were kept as some sort of science experiment, to see why we are so long-lived compared to most other races. We were left alone. Then a shuttle landed and the kadanu demanded we give up an adult and three children for Mentiq. That's when we realized that we were nothing but food for Mentiq and Mentiq alone.

"We fought, and lost. Mentiq took more away. After that we sent adults to the other islands, trying to convince the other species that we are nothing but animals waiting for the slaughter. We had some success, but our revolt had no chance. The Lan'Xi were purged completely. We were banished to this little island and forced to live like savages."

"Where are the other adults?" Steuben asked.

A juvenile went to a reed carpet and rolled it up. He brushed dirt aside, revealing a stasis tube with a Karigole inside that looked like Steuben, but with gray edges to his scales.

"All are kept asleep until one of us are ready to conceive," Guilan said. "Then a male and female are awoken at random. Once we catch, they must return to their tubes. We debated refusing to go on…"

"But we are the lineage," Naama said. "As much as we detest our existence, we can't stop. Who would care for the children? So long as we three live, the Karigole are of value to Mentiq. We die and the rest will go to the blocks."

"It ends," Steuben said. "It ends now. I will get us all out of here—I swear it." Steuben slammed a fist against his chest plate.

"You must have come in a ship. The oceans are full of those damn krayt," Guilan said.

"We did, but it is too small for us all…" Steuben glanced at Lafayette.

"We would need at least four more Mules from the *Breitenfeld*. Or two Toth shuttles," Lafayette said. "With the large number of humans that need to be evacuated, this will be challenging."

"And the adults?" Guilan looked at the stasis tank. "The seals are connected to our pheromone levels. How do we get them out?"

"Leave that to me." Lafayette bowed his head slightly. "I can hack the Toth systems with enough time."

"I'll speak with Hale, the human leader," Steuben said. He gently put his hand against Guilan's swollen belly. "I will not leave this planet without you."

He stood up and turned to Lafayette. He

switched off his voice box and spoke in English.

"Brother. I know what she means to you. But do not speak with her yet," Steuben said. Lafayette nodded. "I return to the Mule to confer with Hale. You find a way around the stasis tubes."

Steuben ran from the hut and into the night.

"What was that all about?" Orozco asked.

Lafayette switched off his voice box.

"Naama," Lafayette said. "She's my birth geth'aar, my mother."

CHAPTER 15

Hale's gauntlet vibrated with an incoming message. He sat up and wiped sleep from his eyes.

"Ten whole minutes," he said as he checked the timer on his gauntlet. "That's enough rest for one day."

He opened the channel and Steuben's face came up on the inside of his visor.

"Hale, I have news." The Karigole brought Hale up to speed.

"That's…incredible, Steuben. I'm happy for you." Hale looked to the night sky. The mass of ships in the anchorage and the circling Toth dreadnoughts were visible against the distant nebula. "That's also really tricky. We've got the same problem in both villages. Lots of people, not a lot of air lift."

"Lafayette says he can slave together Toth shuttles. He flies one...more will follow his lead in a swarm. Egan can do the same back to the human settlement," Steuben said.

"We should have a ride into Mentiq's city by daylight...it might look suspicious if we swing by your island," Hale said.

"Unnecessary. A shuttle will arrive at dawn to pick up two Karigole children. We will commandeer the vessel, like pirates from your old videos. Lafayette will work with Egan once we arrive," Steuben said.

"There's still the matter of killing Mentiq and figuring out how to get off this spitball of a planet," Hale said.

"One problem at a time."

"Yeah, sounds like a plan. Do you think we'll ever set foot on a planet and have everything go smoothly?"

"If that happens, it's a trap," Steuben said. The line cut out.

Hale considered going back to sleep, then opened an IR line. "Egan. Cortaro. Come see me. We have to work out some new details."

****

Sunlight glinted off the Toth lander as it flew a few feet over the ocean's surface, leaving a wake of disturbed water behind it. It arced over wave-lapped rocks and tall trees before it circled around the landing zone where three robed figures knelt along the outer edge.

Landing gear extended from the craft and it landed gently, jets of compressed gas hissing out of the pneumatic landing gear as it settled. The nose of the craft hung over the robed figures' heads.

A seam appeared along the smooth surface of the craft's underbelly and a hatch lowered. Jaundiced yellow light spilled out of the lander and onto the landing zone.

Two men in gold-colored scale armor carrying long hooked poles came down the ramp, their skin and hair coloration the same as the villagers, silver circlets wrapped around their foreheads. They stopped at the edge of the ramp. One wore heavy gold necklaces and bracelets.

"Check," the more decorated man said, "make sure these are the right ones."

The other went to the first kneeling villager and pushed the hood back. Lilith looked at the ground, her brow covered in sweat. The man waved his palm across her face, and a small holo with paragraphs of Akkadian script appeared on the back of his hand.

"This one is on the roster," he said. "Pretty. Think the Primus will let us have a go at her? She's so drugged up she won't remember a thing."

"You want to risk Lord Mentiq coming across anything like that? He'll feed all of us to the menials if we spoil her. You know how long he cultivates them for just the right taste? Decades. This one…might be a special order for another

263

overlord," the leader said. "Get to the other two."

"Shame." The kadanu grabbed Lilith by the chin and lifted her face up. "I wouldn't mind keeping this one for the barracks."

Lilith's chin quivered and she pulled back from his grip.

The kadanu let her go and moved to the next villager. He tossed the hood aside and found Hale looking up at him.

"Now!" Hale grabbed a fistful of the man's armor and stood up. The kadanu looked at the armored Marine with a mix of shock and disbelief. With his other hand, Hale swung a hook into the man's slack jaw. The power armor lent more force to the blow than an Olympic boxer could have ever managed and his armored knuckles crushed the man's face.

Teeth and blood spat out onto the tarmac. Hale pushed the guard to the ground with a slight shove.

The decorated guard turned around and got two steps before the other cloaked villager,

Standish, tackled him. Standish's weight came down on the guard and knocked the air out of him. Standish grabbed the guard's hair, pulled his head back then slammed him into the ground with a sickening crunch.

The sound of footfalls raced up the ramp as cloaked Marines stormed the shuttle. Hale heard muffled shouts and the slam of bodies against metal from inside.

He turned his attention to the guard he'd laid out. The man groaned, a puddle of blood forming beneath his wrecked jaw. Hale jammed his knee into the small of the guard's back, grabbed his head with both hands and pulled. There was a pop as the spinal cord severed from the base of his skull. Hale let the body flop to the floor, limbs twitching.

"Clear inside," Cortaro said. *"Got six tangos down."*

"Egan, can you fly this thing?" Hale asked.

"Wait one, sir. Bit of a mess to clean up first," Egan said.

"The clock is ticking. We need to—"

A high-pitched scream came from behind Hale. He whirled around, drawing his gauss pistol.

Lilith had blood on her fingertips. Her gaze went from the guard's dead body to the bright blood, her skin pale and eyes wide open. She recoiled from the corpse and got up to run away.

Yarrow de-cloaked and caught her. He put a hand over her mouth and turned her away from the body.

She struggled and hit Yarrow's chest with a balled hand. Her face twisted in pain as her hand bounced off the armor.

"Calm down, calm down," Yarrow said. "It's going to be all right. You're safe now."

She twisted her face away and her gaze caught on the body.

"What did you do to him? What happened?" she asked.

"We killed him. Had to," Yarrow said.

Lilith became calm and Yarrow let her go. She approached the corpse slowly, then looked at the blood on her fingertips. She wiped them against her cloak, spreading a red stain.

"That's…death?" she asked.

"What? You've never seen a body before?" Yarrow put a hand on her shoulder.

"No one's ever died in the village," she said. "Everyone that's sick or old goes to the temple. I've never…"

"I've gotten used to it," Yarrow said. "I hope you never do."

Cortaro dragged a pair of dead kadanu down the ramp, their heads twisted to fatal angles.

"We've got graves already dug, sir," Cortaro said. "Want them all in there now?"

"Strip off their uniforms. We may need them once we're inside," Hale said. "Dump all but three in the wood line."

Yarrow guided Lilith around the body and turned her away from the ramp as Rohen brought more dead out of the shuttle.

****

The cockpit of the Toth transport had a single seat with controls bolted into the center of the wide, flat room. Toth warrior pilots lay on their stomachs and used their four upper limbs to control aircraft. This one had been outfitted to accommodate a human-sized pilot with only two limbs and no tail to sit on.

Egan pointed to displays labeled in Toth script, grids interspersed with dots, his lips moving as he read. The view through the cockpit glass was clear, but looking around the ship allowed a semi-opaque view of the surroundings. Hale, wearing kadanu armor, looked down and saw the ground a few yards beneath his feet. The rest of the shuttle wasn't like this, and he hoped Egan wouldn't have any trouble flying the craft.

"Well?" Hale asked Egan.

"I think I've got it, sir. Most of this is automated but their overrides are a bit tricky. The controls are similar to what we found in the Toth ships but then it's like some lazy engineer redid the layout and the translated Toth into Akkadian isn't quite right—"

"How long until we're airborne?" Hale asked.

"We can go now," Egan said.

"Strap in!" Hale yelled behind him. "If our cover's blown, can this thing reach the *Breit* or the Karigole island where our Mule's waiting for us?"

"Let's check the fuel." Egan hit a switch and the lights inside the shuttle powered down. "Not that one." Egan hit another switch and his control panel came to life. He read over the display and clicked his tongue. "We can make it back to the city…and that's about it. They hobbled her. Just enough juice for a trip out and back."

"Mentiq doesn't like his people sightseeing. Figures. Let's go," Hale said.

"Cycling the engines." A loud whine filled the cabin as Egan pushed a lever forward. The shuttle rose off the ground and cleared the tops of the surrounding trees.

"Here we go." Egan grabbed a control stick set over his lap and pushed forward.

The shuttle shot backwards. Hale kept his footing thanks to his grip on the pilot's seat. The tall trees surrounding the landing zone grew closer, their branches thrashing in the blast from the ship's engines.

"Egan!"

The shuttle slowed, but the tail of the craft thumped into the trees. Trunks snapped in half loudly enough that Hale heard the crack through the hull. The shuttle rose into the air and wobbled toward ocean.

"Think I've got it now, sir," Egan said.

Hale watched as the upper half of a broken tree tumbled down branches of its neighbors, sending a cloud of pollen and needles flying into the air.

"Any takeoff you can fly away from, right, sir?" Egan asked.

"Just figure out how to land this thing with a bit more finesse," Hale said.

"No problem. Probably. Thirty minutes until we reach the city."

Hale gave Egan a pat on the shoulder and went back into the cargo hold. All his Marines but Rohen and Bailey wore kadanu uniforms. Standish worked a brush against a bloodstained loin cloth.

Lilith, sitting on a bench with her knees pulled in to her chest, glared at Hale as he went over to Cortaro.

The lieutenant sat next to his senior NCO, leaned his head against the wall and shut his eyes. His nerves felt taut, like he was walking along the edge of a deep chasm. His hands went to his gauss pistol tucked into his stolen robes. His mind reran the final moments of the kadanu he'd killed.

"First time, wasn't it, sir?" Cortaro asked.

"For what?" Hale didn't open his eyes.

"Ending someone—Toth and Xaros aside. They're different. Not the same as another person like you and me," Cortaro said.

"He was a collaborator. Hostile. It was a legitimate kill," Hale said curtly.

"No argument from me on that one. These kadanu *pendejos* know exactly what they're doing, not like they're some poor conscript on the wrong side of the battlefield," Cortaro said.

Hale rolled his head to the side and looked at the gunnery sergeant. The Atlantic Union Marine Corps had fought low-intensity conflicts against the Chinese across the Pacific Rim since the end of the last world war. Most Marines in service at the time of the Xaros invasion had their combat action ribbon from one conflict or another. Combat meant killing, but it was rare that any Marine ever spoke about the experience…at least not to someone who'd been there with them or seen that same elephant on another battlefield.

"You sound like you've got a few," Hale said.

"Yes, sir. First one was a Chinese infiltrator trying to plant a bomb on a runway in Guam. Hit him from two hundred meters with my rifle. He bled out before we could get to him. Then there's that mess on Indonesia. Bunch of untrained shitheads armed with AKs that thought they could rush my squad…I still have dreams about that."

Cortaro's fingers went to his side where Hale'd seen an ugly mass of scar tissue.

"Do you ever forget about them?"

"No. At least I don't. Some guys I knew lost count, but I think they're lying. Thing like that's going to stay with you. The Xaros are pure murder and the Toth want to eat us, but at least they're not human. Makes taking them down a lot easier for me," Cortaro said.

"You think...when this is all over, we'll be done fighting ourselves?"

"I hope. But hope in one hand and crap in the other, see which one fills up first." Cortaro chuckled at his own joke. "Lilith, I don't think she likes you anymore. Civilians are like that. Back home, I had some cousins who're all upset with what I did for a living. Dummies never realized I did it for them. I told them if they didn't want me fighting the Chinese, they'd better go to Beijing and convince them to stop occupying northern Australia, Korea and Japan. I didn't get any more Christmas cards from them after that."

"So what do I do about her?"

"Nothing. She'll come around on her own or hate you forever. Civilians aren't Marines. I can't figure them out sometimes." Cortaro pointed to the two snipers still in their armor. "They've got all our cloak batteries. They can stay out of sight for a couple hours at least."

Hale fished out a data slate from his robes and looked at the time.

"Nineteen hours until we have to get back to the *Breit*," Hale said with a sigh. "Nothing's ever easy, is it?"

"That's why you get paid those big officer bucks, sir."

****

Lafayette brushed dirt away from a stasis tube and looked at the Karigole woman sleeping within. She had two scars running down the side of her face, not unlike a pair Lafayette once had on his own face from a run-in with one of the dragon wolves on his home planet. He'd given up trying to keep his original features years ago and settled with a neutral prosthetic replacement. It wasn't as if his brothers in the Centuria would have ever had trouble identifying him.

He attached a line from his gauntlet to the tube's control panel just over the sleeper's head and accessed the system. There were thirty adult Karigole in the village, each kept beneath the floors of the many huts. Hacking the programming was easy, but time-consuming.

"You are most astute for your species," Naama said from the doorway, her hands folded over the slight bulge of her early pregnancy. She stepped aside and Lafayette saw Orozco walk past the doorway, a child hugging each leg and two hanging from his arms as they screeched in delight.

"Fee fi fo fum! I smell the blood of…you don't know what an Englishman is," Orozco said as he sauntered past the door.

"That one…seems simpler," Naama said.

"Sometimes I wonder how humans mastered

fire," Lafayette mumbled.

"That is Teenut," Naama said as she came closer. "She is a fine poet and an accomplished mathematician. Don't judge us all by Steuben's example. We were never a race just of warriors. We had a museum of the most lifelike sculptures. I took all my children there before they were weened and given over to their parents. My favorite was of a great hero looking down at a beast he'd just slain. I'd tell my children—"

"Consider your deeds. For it is not the battle, but the purpose," Lafayette said.

Naama stepped back. "How do you know that?"

Lafayette put his hands on the side of his helmet, hesitated for a moment, then lifted it off his head. He knew what he looked like—a false visage of polymers meant to mimic his speech and emotions that bled through the neural interface, the exposed metal ligaments and tubes running blood from his brain to his artificial heart. The sound of his augmented voice might sound natural to a human, but to the keen ears of a Karigole, his words would carry a false tone.

"It is me, Mother. Baar'sun," Lafayette said, using his true name. "I was badly injured but it is me. You would give me *cyynt* root porridge when I'd be good. You made me a—"

"No!" Naama twisted her fingers into a symbol to ward off evil and held her hands over her belly. "You are not Baar'sun. You are an abomination sent to harm this child." She backed away from Lafayette and made for the door very slowly.

"No. No…it is me beneath all this. I swear it." Lafayette took a step toward her. "I thought you were lost with the rest. That you're here must be providence, a gift from our ancestors."

She spat in the dirt and ran from the hut. Lafayette heard her shouting to the children and the young ones scampered away from Orozco.

Lafayette dropped his helmet into the dirt and went to his knees. His reflection didn't waver, the prosthetic unable to match what he felt inside.

"What was that all about?" Orozco asked as he came in. "I thought you…oh, I get it."

The big Marine came over and crouched down beside him.

"You're not all right, are you?"

Lafayette shook his head.

"C'mere." Orozco wrapped his big arms around Lafayette's slight shoulders and hugged him.

"This is a…hug? Something meant to make me feel better?"

"Yeah, what do Karigole do?" Orozco let Lafayette go.

The Karigole pressed his knuckles to Orozco's temple. Orozco mirrored the gesture.

Lafayette picked up his helmet and shook dirt out of it before he put it back on his head.

"I have work to do." He went back to the stasis tube.

"What do we do about—"

"Work!" Lafayette snapped.

CHAPTER 16

The shield dome over Mentiq's city smeared sunlight over its surface, casting a twisted reflection of the sun and clouded sky above. A steady stream of Toth landers merged into a long queue of craft slowly filing through a single hangar entrance on the east side of the city just below the shield dome. Ships flew out of the city and angled up into space from an exit on the opposite side.

Hale stood next to Egan's cockpit, his fingers drumming on the headrest.

"Well?" Hale asked. "How do we get in?"

"I assume we hail the flight control tower or—" The controls lurched out of Egan's hands and the shuttle banked to the right. It flew beneath the line of waiting ships toward the open hangar.

"Or we wait for the autopilot to engage," Egan said.

"Shuttle Arru, this is Primus," came from a speaker on the control station. "You're nine minutes late. The bazaar has a strict timetable and one that we can't fool around with. I had to bribe the flight master to get you to the front of the line and I will take that money out of your pay with interest! Get the product loaded up as soon as you land and report to my office."

Hale reached over Egan's shoulder and hit a button to key the mic.

"Acknowledged," Hale said.

"Lots of VIPs here this time, no more screwups!" The line went dead.

The shuttle swung beneath a ship that was nothing more than several off-kilter cubes connected by a single axis and slowed. Several banks of crystalline cannons guarded the hangar entrance, and more weapon emplacements circled a stone wall running around the city.

A pair of Toth dagger fighters hovered over the waiting ships. Hale watched as the fighters angled toward a shuttle as large as a Destrier and jetted toward it. The serrated edges came perilously close to the large ship, which held its ground.

Like dogs nipping at a cow, he thought.

Their shuttle passed through the hangar, and Hale finally got a look at Mentiq's city.

A palace of jagged towers dominated the center. Twisted spires like long seashells touched the underside of the dome, a single reptilian face with gigantic glistening jewels for teeth embossed on each spire. The palace within the spires looked like it was made from pure gold. Mosaics featuring an alien that looked like a larger—and much fatter—Toth menial were on each wall and the roofs, all depicting the large alien beatified by adoring Toth and other alien races. Hale picked out more than one human figure in the artwork.

"This guy's not real humble, is he?" Egan asked.

The shuttle banked to the side and over a cluster of several large inverted funnels the size of apartment buildings and made of what looked like a single piece of glass. More of the structures were spaced out across the city, all far from the magnificence of Mentiq's palace. One building resembled a terraced pyramid, wide and squat. The shuttle turned toward it and joined an orderly line of airborne traffic floating above the city.

The spaces between the larger buildings were a mess of tangled streets and low buildings in various states of disrepair.

Hale turned back and saw a wide open field in front of the main gate to the palace with pale-white stages laid out in an orderly fashion across the grassy surface.

Something beeped in Egan's cockpit.

"We're going to docking bay…twelve," Egan said, reading from a display.

"Anyone going to meet us there?" Hale asked.

"Just lists three transport pods in the

instructions." Egan gently touched the control stick and a harsh buzzer sounded a warning. His hands flew away. A pair of turrets mounted on the inner wall came to life and swung up to track the shuttle.

"Bad idea," Egan said. "Doubt we'd have any luck flying a bomb into the palace. Deviate from the flight path and they'll blow you out of the sky."

Their shuttle dipped low and landed in a landing bay built into the side of the wall surrounding the city. There was nothing in the shuttle bay but a small control station and three coffin-sized black boxes floating next to it.

"Look alive, people," Hale said into the IR.

The ramp descended from the shuttle and the engines powered down. Egan tossed his hands up in despair.

"Not me, sir. There must be some central control system keeping everything in order. Like how Ibarra automated all the traffic in Phoenix with his smart cars," Egan said.

"That's going to make getting out of here a

bit difficult," Hale said. "Get changed into a kadanu uniform and meet me outside."

Hale left the cockpit and went down the ramp with Cortaro and Standish. He saw the entire city from the raised hangar as a breeze brought the smell of damp earth and poor sewer lines. Hot, humid air surrounded them.

"Ugh, feels like we're in Juarez," Standish said. "I had a couple crazy weekends there when I was stationed at Camp Pendleton."

"Juarez was off-limits for decades," Cortaro said, his brows knitting in confusion, "and the border was sealed. How did you do that?"

"What was that, Gunney?" Standish wiggled a finger in his ear. "The war's taken a real toll on my hearing."

"Grab those caskets and get the bodies in there," Hale said. "That should buy us enough time to get out of here and lost in the crowd." He looked up the ramp and saw Lilith with Yarrow, the Marine donning the last stolen uniform. Lilith shook her head and moved a sash from Yarrow's right shoulder to the left.

Hale waved them down. Lilith caught herself when she saw the palace, her hands bunched beneath her chin.

"It's beautiful, just like the stories I learned as a little girl," she said.

"Focus, Lilith. I need you and Egan on that control panel. See if you can access the system. You've got the spikes, Egan?" Hale asked.

Egan ran down the ramp and patted a sack he had attached to his hip.

"Spikes?" Lilith asked.

"Old hacker tool," Egan said to her. "Ibarra's probe reversed enough Toth computer cores recovered from their wrecks to make us a couple disposable and undetectable intrusion devices."

They made their way to the control station and Egan looked it over.

"Same tech as we've seen before, that's good news," Egan said. He took a marker-sized metal spike from his pouch and found an access port. "Here goes nothing." He connected the spike and stepped back.

Screens lit up and Toth writing scrolled rapidly from side to side.

"OK...we're in. I've got the local networks on the screen. Now let me...that's not right." Egan frowned at a large keyboard covered in runes and jabbed at a few characters.

"What are you trying to do?" Lilith asked.

"I'm trying to find a map to this damn place but this keyboard isn't what I was trained on," Egan said.

"Open the secondary overlays and load up the utility network," Lilith said with a shake of her head.

"Is that...this key?"

"Move!" Lilith pushed Egan aside and her fingers flew over the keyboard, tapping with amazing speed. A wire diagram of the city appeared on a screen, a red pulsating dot showing their hangar.

"What do you want to know?" she asked.

"How do we shut off the shielding? What about the turrets?" Hale looked over her shoulder.

"That…I can't do from here," she said. "All essential functions route through the palace…no they don't. Someone set up a shunt relay to make it *look* like the hub is beneath spire three. Amateurs. When in reality…" A green dot appeared on the map over the stepped pyramid Hale'd seen on the flight through the city. "Sub-basement level two," she said.

"What is that place?" Hale asked.

"Kadanu headquarters," she said.

"What about Mentiq? Any way we can get to him?"

"There's the bazaar. He's mentioned during the schedule for the opening ceremony. Think he'll make an appearance?" Lilith asked.

"Doubt he'd miss the big event, not when it seems like everything on this planet is done in his honor." Hale touched the screen with the map and zoomed in. A raised platform, just on the opposite side of the gates to Mentiq's palace, was covered in red markings. "Is that where he's going to sit?"

"You can read Toth?" Lilith asked.

"Snipers," Hale said into the IR. "Find a nest with line of sight to this point." He pointed the camera on his gauntlet at the map and sent an image to Rohen and Bailey.

"You think we can get IR with the *Breit*?" Hale asked Egan.

"Yes, sir. The shield must let heat out or this place would turn into an oven. I'll go set up the dish and finally make myself useful." Egan trotted back to the shuttle, crossing paths with Standish, Cortaro and the three floating coffins.

A message flashed on one of the screens.

"Some place called the 'distribution center' in the palace wants an update on the 'product,'" Lilith said, reading. "It wants me to send the coffins there right away."

"When that happens, they'll look inside and see they've got the wrong delivery," Hale said. "Then things will get difficult."

"About that, sir," Standish said, raising a

hand. "I have an idea. Can you send these meat sticks anywhere else?" he asked Lilith.

"There are distribution nodes…all located at the big glass buildings we saw. Those seem to all belong to different corporations…Tellani's, Naalfur, Anshul'jik, bunch more," she said.

"Here's what you do." Standish leaned over the control station. "Send the coffins to Naalfur's distro center, have them linger for an hour then forward them on to Tellani and disable the trackers. They'll start looking for their 'product' eventually and when they find three dead kadanu in Tellani's storehouse…"

"Tellani will blame Naalfur," Hale said. "Claim the other corporation got the real anointed and sent off the fakes to their storehouse so they'd get the blame. The two corporations will point the finger at the other."

"And the harder they claim innocence, the guiltier they'll look," Standish said with a smile. "The old quartermaster two-step. One of my favorite ways to launder goods. If I still did that. Or ever did that. Hey, look at the time." Standish gave one of the coffins a pat. "These boys have someplace to be."

"Do it," Hale said to Lilith. The coffins floated away on their own a few seconds later.

"I'll change the point of origin to a hangar on the other side of the city," she said.

"Sir, Bailey. Rohen and I can get a great shot from the top of that pyramid-looking place," the sniper said.

"We have to head over there anyway," Hale said. "Knock out the central computer core." He opened an IR line. "Egan, can you get us a local IR network? Something the Toth won't detect but will reach back to you here?"

"So long as you've got line of sight to the snipers and they've got line of sight back to here, we'll be secure," Egan said from the top of the shuttle where he was setting up a satellite dish.

"I see where you're going with this, sir," Cortaro said. "Trick's going to be bringing enough firepower to the party."

290

"I think I've got an answer for that," Hale said as he opened a channel to the entire team. "All right, Marines, here's the plan."

****

Valdar walked behind the bridge's workstations, glancing at the clocks on the crew's screens.

Any minute now, Valdar thought. Hale should have coopted a transport to Mentiq's city by now. The lack of any news from the lieutenant was a good sign; he wasn't calling for extraction from a botched operation. Still, the time of flight from the human enclave to the city wasn't long; they should have checked in by now.

"Guns," Valdar said to Lieutenant Commander Utrecht, "any progress on a firing solution to get through the city's energy shields?"

"No, sir." Utrecht shook his head. "Even with the little data we got from the Marines on the ground, the disturbances in the upper atmosphere throw off the impact time—"

"Sir!" Ensign Erdahl nearly jumped out of her seat at the communications station. Valdar crossed the bridge to her. "Message from Hale. They made it in."

"They say how long until they can neutralize Mentiq or get the shields down?" Commander Ericson asked.

"Kill him, XO. We're here to kill him. Let's not mince words," Valdar said.

"Nothing follows from the initial message," Erdahl said. "But they promise regular updates."

"The ball's rolling, but we've still got the same problems." Valdar went to the tactical holo tank behind his command chair and waved Utrecht and Ericson over. A slice of Nibiru with the Toth fleet anchorage, the prowling dreadnoughts and a distant *Breitenfeld* appeared in the tank.

"How do we cover Hale's extraction? And evacuate the human settlement. And the Karigole. And jump back to Earth without being blown to bits," Valdar said. He ran a hand through his thinning hair and drummed fingers against the side of the table.

"This isn't a rescue mission," Utrecht said, earning a dirty look from Valdar. "I know you don't like hearing that, sir. But we came here for one purpose. The people in the village, the Karigole, *maybe* we can get them out. I don't think we should risk this ship for them."

"I agree with Guns, sir," Ericson said.

"Do you know what the Toth will do to them if we leave them behind?" Valdar asked.

"No, but neither do you, sir," Utrecht said. "They've been down there for a long damn time. They're too valuable to just destroy out of spite. The Toth are vicious drug addicts, but even they know better than to mess with their supply chain."

"We find a way or we make one," Valdar said. "Don't shrug off this problem. Pretend rescuing those civilians is the mission."

Ericson let out a deep breath. She put a finger on the tip of her nose, then furrowed her brows.

"You know," she said, "the Toth sure don't trust each other. Look what they've done." She reached into the tank and zoomed in on the many ships crammed into the anchorage. "See how close they all are? My guess is they're packed in like sardines to block lines of fire on the city and on the dreadnoughts. The way the dread orbit, they always have their guns trained on the anchorage, never on each other."

"The dreadnoughts must all belong to Mentiq," Utrecht said, stroking his chin. "Fits with the data the salvage crews pulled out of the *Naga*. The rest of the Toth fleet we blew to hell belong to some Tellani Corporation, but not the *Naga*."

"So pretend you're the lizard running one of these dreadnoughts," Valdar said. "What would you do if one of those ships in the anchorage fired on you?"

"Mass punishment," Ericson said, "hit everything in the anchorage."

"That would keep everyone in line," Utrecht said. "Makes the Toth police themselves before the big boys open up on them."

"We need to pick a fight," Valdar said. "Guns, XO, I'm authorizing a nuclear weapons release. I'm going to the cemetery to talk to the Iron Hearts."

****

Hale stepped around the hulking mass of an alien covered in a filthy piece of cloth so large it looked like it had once been a drape for a grand room. The alien had wrapped packages and barrels strapped to its back. He looked over his shoulder and saw a bull-headed creature with a single eye trudging forward through the crowded street.

"OK, that one was definitely weirder than the bird-person," Standish said.

Hale, flanked by Cortaro and Standish, cleared a path for Lilith who followed close behind. The city was alive with Toth menials and several alien races Hale had never heard of or even imagined. They'd come across a few humans, all of whom fled once they saw Hale and the Marines' misappropriated uniforms.

"A Felnara," Lilith said, "barely sentient, used as beasts of burden on some worlds. They have an excellent sense of direction and never question orders. Plus, they'll defend their portage to the death."

"So don't steal anything, Standish," Cortaro said.

"I don't steal, Gunney. I liberate. On occasion, I forage," Standish said.

"Snipers, status," Hale said.

"We're about two blocks ahead of you," Rohen said. *"You're almost to the square."*

Hale looked up and saw a puff of dust on a roof ledge as one of the snipers landed on it. Rohen and Bailey were cloaked, opting to leapfrog from building to building than try to dodge through the crowd. Hale hadn't seen an obvious weapon on anyone in the city, and the two armored Marines with their sniper rifles wouldn't have made it very far without their cloaks.

"We've got to take the long way around," Bailey said. *"We'll be out of IR contact for a bit, which means you'll lose the connection to Egan back at the ship."*

"Copy. Move out and get set up. The festivities are about to start and Mentiq seems to be a stickler for timetables," Hale said. He heard a double-click on the IR as Bailey acknowledged his instructions.

A pack of Toth menials hissed and snarled at passersby from the front of a two-story building with overly tall doors. Hale stopped and felt for his missing rifle as the doors swung open and a Toth overlord ambled from building, fine gold filigree encrusted against the tank. The overlord moved toward the square as the pack of menials formed a protective cordon around it.

A red-skinned alien with thick arms and a triangular-shaped head stood in the doorway. It held a gold bar up to its mouth and bit thick molars into the corner. Behind the alien were pictures of overlord tanks, each with a different mosaic of inlaid gold and platinum along their tanks.

"Overlord tattoo parlor," Cortaro said. "I've officially seen everything."

Hale slowed as they came to the end of the road where it spilled out onto the square. A pair of guards stood between the rest of the city and the square. Both were almost seven feet tall and almost twice as wide as Hale. A canine head hung between stooped shoulders; scraggly black fur hung from long snouts and matted what little of the alien wasn't covered in earth-colored armor plates. Both aliens carried long pole arms, the blades crackling with electricity. Bright white eyes flicked from person to person as they scanned the crowd.

Aliens and Toth menials moved freely between the square and the city without any reaction from the hulking guards, and Hale decided it would be better to keep moving than risk attracting attention for standing around with no obvious purpose.

"Act natural," Hale said. "We need to get to the data center."

Hale stepped over a puddle of something black and bubbling and made for the square. He got one step beyond the guard when a furry paw grabbed him by the shoulder and spun him around.

The lupine face pressed toward Hale's with a snarl.

"The human Primus wants your kind in the city." Breath that stank of rotting meat assaulted Hale's nose. "The bazaar is Kroar territory," it said. Hale heard the undercurrent of Akkadian language from the guard as his voice box translated into English.

"My Primus just reassigned us to the hangars on the far side of the city," Hale said. "Of course we have to be there before Lord Mentiq honors us with his presence. If I cut around the bazaar, we'll be late. You mind?"

The Kroar sniffed the air.

"I don't know your scent," it said.

"And all of you look the same to me." Hale pulled his shoulder away from the guard's paw and squared off.

A scream rose from the bazaar behind the guard. It lumbered around and reared up to its full height. It clicked two claw tips together and the two guards trotted away.

"Move," Hale said, "before they come back."

They pressed into the crowd and came to one of the large white stages they'd seen on the city map. The stage was a white slab of marble embedded in the ground, reaching four feet high. A menial crouched on each side, each wearing a skintight suit covered in bright-orange frills.

On the stage was a cluster of neon-blue-skinned aliens, all bound together by chains connected to hand and ankle cuffs. Tiny horns pocked along the aliens' jawlines and over their scalps. The aliens looked around in wonder, none seeming to notice the crowd at their feet.

"Is it me," Standish asked, "or do those aliens look familiar?"

"They're…Shanishol," Hale said. "From Anthalas, remember?"

"I'd rather forget about that place, if that's all right with everyone," Yarrow's disembodied voice said.

"I thought the Xaros wiped out their home world. Certainly weren't any left after that sphere finished with them," Cortaro said.

"They're a consignment for Mentiq," Lilith said. "These are for display only. The Tellani claim access to several million more and can deliver any number of units on request." She swallowed hard. "Their taste is considered shallow, but in sufficient numbers can induce a state of euphoria lasting almost an hour."

"How do you know that?" Hale asked.

"There," she said, pointing to electronic Toth script running across the top of the stage like a ticker on a news broadcast.

"Not for you, meat." A menial scampered over and snapped its jaws in the air. "Not your meat. Move for paying customers."

Hale moved away. He found the stepped pyramid and walked toward it. Each stage held a different alien species, some with a single individual, others with dozens and dozens packed together. Toth overlords meandered among the stages, conferring with the oddly dressed menials attending to the edges.

"The bazaar doesn't sell things," Cortaro said. "The overlords are selling people to each other. Like a slave auction."

"It's not slaves they're selling," Hale said.

"And Mentiq's in the middle of all of this," Standish said. "Could you imagine what would've happened if the Toth got ahold of the proccie tech? There would be stages full of humans, marketing us like sides of beef."

"Sir, I ever thank you for *not* giving us all up to the Toth?" Yarrow asked.

"It was never an option," Hale said. *Never for me, at least,* he thought. He'd been humanity's negotiator with the Toth overlord on Europa, and before the final cordial meeting, Captain Valdar instructed him to sign a treaty handing over all the proccies and the technology used in their creation.

The order came straight from Earth high command, which baffled Hale. After the battle, and the sacrifice of so many proccies who died serving in Eighth Fleet, Ibarra's and Admiral Garrett's support of the program was adamant.

Hale knew politics was a factor once officers reached flag rank, but he couldn't believe that Garrett could have been willing to throw the proccies to the wolves one minute, then become their biggest defender the next. The discontinuity had bugged him for weeks, like a pebble stuck in a boot that never seemed to go away.

"Those other cities," Cortaro said, "the ones we saw from orbit, they're just like Lilith's village. They're all…Mentiq's gardens."

"We're going to put an end to this," Hale said. "I don't care if we have to burn it all down." They stepped around an overlord haggling with a menial next to a stage full of furry aliens with bulbous eyes, none more than three feet tall. Their offspring, little more than puffs of fur with glistening eyes, reached into the air.

"There's something weird around the stages," Yarrow said. "My visor's picking up some kind of distortion."

"Force fields," Lilith said, "and one-way holos. A friend of mine had the calling to recreate alien worlds, tranquil scenes. I wonder if he was out here, standing in the middle of his own creation, oblivious to the monsters salivating over him."

"Stay focused. Almost there," Hale said.

"Sir, you read me?" Bailey said through Hale's earpiece.

"Go."

"We're about to start up. There's some activity brewing at the main gate. We weapons free if we have a shot?"

"Give us two minutes to get to the objective building. Then you're clear," Hale said. They stepped past another pair of Kroar without being noticed and Hale saw the main entrance to the stepped pyramid, barred doors guarded by kadanu armed with shock sticks.

"I don't recommend the front door, sir,"

Cortaro said. "It looks fortified and I feel like I'm wearing damn pajamas."

The pyramid was nearly a hundred yards long on a side. Higher tiers were slightly smaller than the lower levels, ending with a tenth level that looked like it was nothing more than a box barely large enough for a single person. Kadanu milled around the bottom few levels.

"We've got some eyes on us," Standish said. He motioned to a nearby building with wooden tables in front and a few humans lounging nearby. "How about a drink?"

Hale led them into the establishment where the smell of spilled beer and sweat filled the air. Humans in coarse spun tunics and sandals backed away from Hale and the others.

"I'm paid up for the month." An elderly woman behind a long wooden bar wagged a finger at Hale. "You tell Primus if he raises my rates again I'll have to sell off my best waitress to the overlords to make my rent."

Hale felt for a pouch of coins hanging from

his belt and tossed it onto the bar.

"Four of whatever you've got, please," he said as he sat on a stool. The old woman snatched the purse away and tossed a dirty bowl of what looked like roasted chickpeas in front of him. The rest of the Marines and Lilith sat at the bar with Hale.

"Yarrow," Hale whispered. He felt two taps on his shoulder. "Go scout out an entrance, but stay close." Two more taps and Hale heard the wood floors creak as Yarrow left the bar.

The bartender brought out four wooden flagons of sudsy beer and set one before each of the Marines. Hale ate one of the chickpeas, then tapped the wooden bowl against the bar. The old lady grumbled and walked off.

Standish grabbed his beer by the handle and was about to drink when Cortaro slammed his hand onto Standish's forearm.

"Nurse it," Cortaro growled.

"Add joy onto your list of confirmed kills, Gunney." Standish let go of his beer and pat his hands against his thighs.

Hale reached into his tunic and tapped the data slate from his gauntlet.

"*Breitenfeld*, this is Hale. Do you read me?"

****

Hale shrugged the scaled armor over his shoulder and pulled at a strap against his waist to tighten it against his body. He hadn't worn armor that wasn't part of a self-supporting exoskeleton with integrated strength augmentations since he'd been to the Basic School in Quantico. The instructors had the new second lieutenants march, fight and practically live in old Kevlar vests with ceramic plate inserts so they'd "appreciate" the day they earned their more modern power armor.

After a week in the old stuff, he understood why his grandfather and so many older veterans of the wars around the turn of the century complained about bad backs and wobbly knees.

"We're through to the ship, sir," Egan said.

The Marine had a small transceiver mounted on the roof of the shuttle and pointed at the *Breitenfeld.* "The energy shield will degrade the signal. At least the Toth figured out they need to let infrared energy escape, else this whole city would turn into an oven while the shield's up."

"Thank God for small favors," Hale said. A static-filled image of Valdar appeared on the gauntlet held in Hale's hands.

"Hale?" Valdar asked, his voice tinny. "What the hell are you wearing?"

"The cloak batteries aren't holding up. They're holding less of a charge each time we use them. We're making do with uniforms the local guard force don't need anymore," Hale said.

"Risky. What's the status on Mentiq or getting the shields down?"

"We're moving into the city in a few more minutes. Egan will relay everything to you. We've got the location to the city's defense center and Mentiq will make an appearance soon. We'll get this done, one way or another."

Valdar's image waved from side to side "...situation from orbit. Working on our own solution to get...Karigole and the rest out."

"You're coming in broken. Egan and Lafayette think they can rig together a bunch of Toth shuttles, wagon train the civilians back up to orbit. Did you copy any of that?"

Valdar washed out in a sea of static.

"I bet it's the auroras. Damn things play hell with reception," Egan said. "I'm staying behind, sir. I'll get your plan to the *Breit* once the sky's clear."

"Lots of moving parts. Lots can go wrong," Hale said.

"A good plan, violently executed now, is better than a perfect plan next week," Egan said.

"You keep quoting an army general and Gunney will scrape that globe and anchor off your armor," Hale said.

"Truth is truth, so what if Patton said it?"

"I'll tell Cortaro you've expanded your horizons."

"Let's not be hasty, sir. Oh look, something

I need to fix." Egan stepped away from the commo rig and went down the ladder to the cargo bay.

****

Egan drummed his fingers on the shuttle's control panels. He'd been waiting in the same seat for over an hour, checking the IR relay to the *Breitenfeld* and double-checking the slaver units he'd made from Lafayette's instructions.

He'd used up all but two of his hacker spikes on the slavers, but installing them into the neighboring Toth shuttles required more technical know-how than he had.

Toth menials and a few warriors had passed by the shuttle bay, none showing much interest in his ship, which suited him just fine. He was armored and had a full charge to his cloak, but dancing around any security personnel while he was alone wasn't high on his to-do list.

Someone cleared their throat and Egan jumped out of his seat. He drew his pistol and flipped the safety off.

"Damaging the only Toth shuttle a human can pilot will have a negative effect on our timeline," a voice said.

"Lafayette?" Egan asked.

Orozco de-cloaked as did the two Karigole.

"You have the slaver units?" Lafayette picked one up and examined it.

"When did you guys get here?" Egan asked.

"About ten minutes ago. Had to take out a couple kadanu and two warriors back at the Karigole enclave," Orozco said. "The rest was pretty easy."

"What about the coffins? Did you send them to processing?" Egan asked.

"I'm certain Mentiq's servants can tell the difference between a human and a Karigole," Steuben said.

"Here's what you do…" Egan laid out Standish's quartermaster two-step scheme.

"That's very clever. Did you come up with it on your own?" Steuben asked.

"Sure, yeah. I've got nothing but time on my hands since I finished making the slaver units," Egan said with a straight face.

"You go back to our shuttle and send off the bodies as you described," Lafayette said. "Steuben and I will install the slaver units in empty shuttles and wait for Hale to disable the city's defenses."

"How about I stay here while you three do all the smart-guy ninja stuff?" Orozco asked.

"When cloaked, Orozco has the finesse of a cow in a porcelain shop," Steuben said.

"He was captured by Karigole children," Lafayette said.

"How about we move on from that?" Orozco said, "What do I have to do, Egan?"

"Monitor the radio and patch through to Hale or the *Breit* if anyone calls. The dish is on the roof. Don't touch it," Egan said.

"Done. Now don't you all have someplace else you're supposed to be?"

CHAPTER 17

Bailey pulled herself over the edge of a terrace and cursed. Standing barely above five feet tall, the high walls of each successive steppe seemed designed to insult her vertically challenged nature.

She heard a scrape as Rohen climbed over the wall and saw a blur as his cloaking field adjusted.

"Grab my hand," Rohen said.

"You know you're invisible, right? We've got the location transmitters off to save power."

Dust puffed the side of the wall where Rohen slapped.

"Coming." Bailey ran toward the wall and jumped. One foot touched the wall and she pushed off it to go higher. She flailed her arms over her head and managed to link arms with Rohen. He hauled her over the edge and onto another flat roof covered in gravel. They were on the second-to-last building level. A single door was the only way in or out to the tier barely the size of a small apartment.

"This'll do," Rohen said. Gravel shifted aside as he went prone. Bailey looked across the city to the gilded gates between the palace and the bazaar. Menials crowded around the upper wall, all waving brightly colored flags.

"This guy likes to make an entrance," she said. She laid down a few feet from Rohen and felt for her rail rifle attached to her back. She pulled the pieces off and reassembled the weapon. Strike Marine snipers trained to take apart and put their weapons together in complete darkness and by feel alone. Bailey had won several bets by reassembling her weapon in less than a minute, hitting a target at 800 meters and while somewhat inebriated.

Readying her weapon while cloaked wasn't a challenge.

"Wind's steady," Rohen said. "Relative humidity at seventy percent. Remember we've got to compensate for the gravity variance and the slower rotation."

"Why don't you remind me to pull the trigger while you're at it?" Bailey took a tungsten dart from a felt bandolier attached to the side of the weapon's butt stock and slid it into the chamber.

"You want to hit him as soon as the doors open or—" Rohen grunted in pain. Gravel shifted around beneath the sniper.

"Rohen? What's wrong?" Bailey asked. When there was no answer, she stepped away from her weapon and felt around until she found Rohen. She tried to pin him down with one hand while the other ran up his shoulders. She found a small button by his right ear and pressed it.

Rohen rematerialized, his muscles contracted and pulling him into a fetal position. He slammed his head against the ground, his eyes tight with pain.

"'jectors," he managed through grit teeth, "chest."

Bailey found the clip of auto-injectors and tried to pull one out, but it fumbled in her fingers and went to the ground. She deactivated her cloak and had an easier time picking up the device once she could see her hands. She pressed it against the port on his neck guard and Rohen went slack.

"What the hell, Rohen?"

"Nerve damage," he said. Rohen grabbed his right forearm and extended the limb out, shivering as his body came back under his control. "I had some void exposure on Ceres. The injections help."

"Jesus, who decided to send you on this mission? You should be in a hospital if you're this bad," Bailey said.

"I volunteered," Rohen said. He felt his chest and froze. "Where's the rest of my injectors?"

"I think they fell—"

Bailey heard laughter and the thump of approaching footsteps from the door behind them.

Her hand went to the handle of the wide-bladed Bowie knife she kept strapped to her thigh.

The door burst open and three kadanu stumbled onto the roof, the lead guard holding an open glass bottle. Their laughter cut off as they saw Bailey and Rohen.

Bailey flicked her knife up to hold it by the blade and reached behind her head. She hurled the blade with enough force that it buried itself into the lead guard's chest up to the brass handguard. The guard clutched at the blade and backpedaled into his shocked companions.

Bailey didn't waste any time. She charged the remaining two and dropped her shoulder. She plowed into a guard and sent him flying until his head came to a sudden stop against the open doorway.

The last guard jumped away from Bailey's grasp and ran into the building. Inside was nothing but a bare room and a stairwell. The guard, screaming for help, took to the stairs. Bailey leaped across the opening and blocked the guard's path.

The kadanu snapped out a punch and hit Bailey in the face. There was a crack of breaking knuckles as the armor designed to deflect gauss rounds proved stronger than flesh and blood. The guard reeled back, clutching his hand to his chest…and toppled over the railing. Bailey reached out and managed a tenuous grasp on the man's ankle.

Gravity jerked him out of her hold, leaving her with nothing but a sandal.

She looked over the railing and watched as the guard slammed against the stairwell, bouncing against railing and stonework like a pinball, leaving smears of blood to mark his passage. The guard splattered against the bottom floor.

"Ah…fuck." She tossed the sandal aside and ran back onto the roof, repeating the expletive with greater speed and intensity. She pulled her knife out of the dead man's chest and slammed the door shut. She wedged her blade into the jamb and rammed it home with a slap to the pommel. Anyone coming to investigate would have a tough time getting through the door.

"Mentiq's coming out!" Rohen said from behind his weapon. "How'd it go in there?"

"Bad. Very bad. We're going to have company." Bailey went onto her belly and pulled her rifle against her shoulder. She clicked a button to open a channel to Hale.

"Sir, we're about to get started. Our position is compromised but we should have enough time to get off an effective shot on the target," she said.

"The top of this pyramid is our extraction point," Hale said. *"Regroup with us once you're done. Just run to the sound of gunfire."*

"Roger, sir. We'll catch up." Bailey closed the line.

"Here we go," Rohen said.

The gates opened with a fanfare of horns, the tune replayed on speakers throughout the city. The discordant notes rumbled around the snipers' perch. A shoulder-to-shoulder line of Toth warriors in gold-plated armor marched out, each holding an energy rifle against their chests.

Dozens of Toth overlords came next, their disembodied nervous systems floating in decorated tanks more elaborate than Bailey remembered from the overlord she encountered on the *Naga*.

Mentiq came through the gate, his immense form resting in a pile of pillows carried on an elaborate barque of precious metals and intricate jewel work.

Bailey lifted her head from her scope and blinked hard.

"I thought he was supposed to be a fish tank like the rest of the overlords," she said.

"I think a bullet to his center mass will still kill it," Rohen said. "Got a breeze kicking up, adjust three meters left."

"It should be four meters with the—"

"Trust me!"

Bailey murmured and made the adjustment on her scope. She lined the crosshairs over a mass of gold necklaces around Mentiq's flabby chest and let her breath seep out. She felt the beat of her heart against the tip of her trigger finger.

"Fire on my mark," Rohen said.

Mentiq lazily raised a claw there and his barque glided forward toward a stage where five different alien species were chained to the white marble.

"Wait for him to stop," Bailey whispered. Rohen made a tiny nod.

Mentiq waved a hand across the offerings, then pointed to a lanky alien with red fur and knees that bent backwards. Menials swarmed over the chosen one and pushed it toward Mentiq. He raised a hand covered by a golden gauntlet, and feeder tendrils snaked out of the fingertips.

"Ready...mark."

Bailey pulled the trigger and the rifle bucked against her shoulder. She re-aimed the weapon and slid out another tungsten dart as she watched the wake of disturbed air from the two bullets ripple in the haze.

There was a flash of light around Mentiq so bright that it triggered her visor buffers. When the spots in her eyes cleared, she caught a glimpse of

Mentiq's barque, now covered by a metal shell, racing back into the palace.

"We get him?" she asked.

"Look at the stage," Rohen said.

One of Mentiq's obese legs lay in a pool of yellow blood, the severed thigh nothing more than a mess of torn flesh.

"Think he's dead?" Bailey asked.

"Should be. The system shock from the bullet and the blood loss—"

The sound of a metallic crash rolled over them like thunder. A darkness rose from the edge of the perimeter wall, edging up several dozen feet before crashing to a halt. Another layer slid higher. Gigantic armor plates stacked one atop the other until they met at the apex of the dome and the entire city was cast into darkness.

"This...wasn't part of the plan," Bailey said as she looked up. Screams of terror came from the city.

"Snipers, continue mission!" Hale said. *"Breach team going in thirty seconds, get down*

here!"

"Always the bloody optimist," she said. She twisted her rifle and broke it down into parts.

The door rattled against its hinges as someone tried to force their way through. The ululation of Toth warriors echoed through the city. The howl of something else joined the Toth battle cry, like the hunting call of a massive wolf that sent a shiver of dread down her spine.

****

Steuben gripped the metal ceiling with his claws and looked down. A small pack of Toth menials lingered at the foot of a shuttle's open ramp, snapping and hissing at each other. He could hold his grip for up to a half hour, but the warning icon flashing against his visor gave him less than two minutes before his cloak went down.

Two of the menials went up the ramp. Steuben heard the Toth words for "master" and "angry" from the remaining three. The time kept ticking on his visor.

He released his hold and fell. His feet hit two of the menials and crushed them against the deck, snapping their spines with a loud crack. He slammed an open palm into the third menial's exposed throat and snapped its neck with a twist.

Steuben thundered up the ramp and bodychecked an oblivious menial against the bulkhead. He grabbed it by its bodysuit and swung it against the opposite bulkhead, killing it instantly.

His cloak dissipated as the batteries ran out. He stood still, listening for the third menial he'd seen enter the shuttle. There was a scrape of claws against the deck from the cockpit. He leaped up and grabbed the top rung to the ladder leading into the cockpit and swung himself in.

A menial had its back to the control panel, hissing and clawing at him with one hand.

Steuben growled and charged, crossing the space in two steps.

He reached for the menial and saw a flash of silver as it pulled a knife from behind its back. He felt pain in his side as he bashed a fist into the menial, splattering its head against the cockpit glass. It slid down, leaving a smear of yellow blood.

Steuben looked down and saw a crude knife sticking from his side. The wound didn't hurt for long, which told Steuben that the blade had been poisoned. He yanked the blade free and tossed it aside. His hands were losing sensation and sounds were fading, like he had cloth stuffed into his ears.

"Lafayette." Steuben fell to his knees and crawled toward a control panel. "Brother, I have embarrassed myself."

"What are you talking about?"

"One of their mongrels, their lesser creatures, managed to wound me. Kosciusko would have me on punishment detail for being so sloppy." Steuben tore an access panel loose and found the computer port in the same spot as the other shuttles he'd hacked into. He took a slaver unit from his belt and tried to plug it in, but his hands refused to do as he demanded.

"Where are you?"

"Shuttle...twelve?" Steuben tried again and managed to drop the slaver as his vision went dark around the edges.

"Forgive me...I need some help." Steuben's head fell to the deck.

****

Mentiq's throne room filled with overlords. Ranik rushed through the doors and looked for a spot against the wall far from the throne, but every other overlord that beat her to the room had the same idea. No one wanted to be near Mentiq when his ire was up.

"All overlords will report to the throne room immediately or their life support will be unilaterally terminated!" Fellerin's voice came through the speakers of her and every other overlord's tank.

The assembled overlords remained quiet. Whoever was behind the attack on Mentiq would be discovered soon enough as the city's guards hunted down the assailants.

What idiot did this? Ranik thought. *Killing Mentiq is a death sentence without access to the extension codes.* None of the overlords had armed warriors within the city and she'd glimpsed the brawl happening in the skies above before the city's blast shields went up. Mentiq's policy of indiscriminate justice and widespread retribution had kept the overlords in check since the first days of their arrangement with him. The thought of ever upsetting the balance was too much for her to even consider.

More overlords raced into the throne room. All had abandoned their business to answer the consigliere's call without hesitation. An old rival pressed his tank to hers, his tentacles curled into knots in fear.

"Who?" Mentiq's voice boomed through the throne room. The overlords sank to the ground instantly as the master of all the Toth descended from the ceiling.

"Who...dared!" Mentiq's voice was phlegmy. "Which of you menial shits thought you could take my crown!"

The palanquin lowered, revealing Mentiq with one leg was missing. Torn flesh seeped white fluid out of the wound, and drops spilled onto the floor and hissed as they hit the carpet. Mentiq coughed and spat a wad of mucus onto the nearest cowering overlord.

So his body is artificial, Ranik thought. Mentiq had returned from his grand expedition that discovered the tank technology at an advanced age. He never opted to transition as the overlords had, and no one had ever dared ask how his body managed to regress to a state of vitality. *He's had the means to create an eternal body...but forced us into these tanks.*

She wasn't sure if she should hate Mentiq or admire him for keeping the rest of the overlords well below his station.

"Which of you was it? Which of you knew about this assault?" Mentiq lashed out and struck an overlord, cracking the tank.

"None would every challenge you, Lord!"

came from behind Ranik.

"And yet…" Mentiq beat the stump of his severed limb against his disk. "I will find out. No one will leave my presence until I know which of you it was, and which knew, and which should have known and all will be punished!"

"My lord," Fellerin spoke up, "we have found a recording of the assault."

"Show me." Mentiq turned to watch as a holo screen appeared above the throne.

Video segments from across the city played out in tiny segments across the screen, then one piece of the puzzle grew to encompass the entire picture. An armored figure carrying a sniper rifle jumped from the kadanu's stepped pyramid.

"Order the guards to kill every human on sight," Mentiq said.

"Yes, my lord." Fellerin bent his head to a bracelet and spoke softly.

Ranik watched the replay, then felt a chill go up her spine. The human's armor, she'd seen it before. She looked to the doors, now bolted shut and guarded by armed warriors, and realized she had a very slim chance of surviving the rest of this day.

"My lord," Ranik said, rising off the floor. "I have information that may prove valuable."

Mentiq's disc spun around, sloshing white fluid across the room.

"Speak."

"That human is not of the kadanu. It wears armor of Earth's warrior caste, their Marines," Ranik said. "I recognize it from recordings from our expedition to Anthalas."

Mentiq dove on Ranik and ripped the armored top of her tank open. He thrust his gloved hand into the tank and Ranik felt the chill touch of feeder lines against her nervous system.

"Did you bring them here? Did you think what you found on Earth would be enough to wrest my throne away?" Mentiq hissed.

"Never! Never, my lord. The humans must have infiltrated the planet. I would never betray you!" Ranik wanted to pull away from the deadly touch, but doing so might antagonize Mentiq further. Staying within his grasp was akin to baring one's throat to a stronger Toth, the classic gesture of submission.

"Your honor guard has the human in custody, my lord," Fellerin said.

"Alive?" Mentiq's withdrew his grip on Ranik.

"Injured, but alive," Fellerin said.

"Bring it to me. Now," Mentiq snarled at Ranik, "we'll see just what your involvement in this coup is, Ranik."

****

The streets were a riot of panic and confusion as Toth, humans and a myriad of other aliens rushed around in the darkness.

As Hale and his team pressed against a wall, he kept an eye on the lowest tier of the pyramid from around a corner. Streetlights had come on, but were flickering on and off as entire sections of the city went dark around them.

A black box appeared from thin air and attached to the pyramid wall. Thick cord came out of the box and pressed into a circular shape wide enough for a Marine to walk through with ease.

Yarrow, still cloaked, knocked a menial into a puddle of mud as he ran across the street to Hale.

"Charges set," Yarrow said.

Hale leaned back and covered his ears. "Blow it."

The explosion shattered glass for blocks around and the wave of overpressure felt like a brief earthquake. Not for the first time, Hale really wished he had his armor.

"Follow me!" Hale ran around the corner and made straight for the smoking hole in the wall.

"No offense, sir, but stay behind me." Yarrow uncloaked, ran ahead of Hale, and barged through the breach.

Hale stepped over a mess of pulverized rock and waved dust away from his eyes.

"Yarrow! Weapons!" Hale shouted. Yarrow

appeared through the dust and handed Hale a gauss rifle. The medic reached onto his back where three more weapons were attached and passed weapons to Standish and Cortaro.

Hale stepped over a dead kadanu and moved through the smoke and dust until he bumped into a wall of iron bars.

"What the...?" Smoke cleared and Hale found himself surrounded by cells containing a few humans who wore nothing but rags and tried to hide beneath threadbare blankets or under wooden benches.

"New guy, did you break us *into* a jail?" Standish asked. He grabbed one of the bars and shook it.

"How was I supposed to know what was on the other side of the rock wall?" Yarrow asked.

"Marine, you are in combat armor." Cortaro pointed a knife hand at Yarrow. "Why are you standing still?"

"Roger, Gunney." Yarrow grabbed a cell wall and yanked downward. The pseudo-muscle layer beneath his armor plates twisted to augment his strength and the bars came loose in a shower of bricks and dust. Yarrow tossed the cell wall to the side.

"If this is the detention hall, then the access way to the computer core is a few doors…" Lilith said, pointing to a door on the far side of the room, "that way."

Yarrow took the last rail rifle off his back and ran for the door.

A team of kadanu got through the door before Yarrow could reach it, each armed with a shock baton. Yarrow set his rifle to SHOT and hit all three with a single blast.

Lilith screamed in fright and the prisoners erupted in a babble of pleas and prayers directed toward Mentiq.

Yarrow swept the bodies aside with his foot then kicked the door off the hinges. He glanced beyond the wrecked wooden frame.

"Clear!"

The medic continued on, Hale and Cortaro

right behind him.

Standish put a hand on the small of Lilith's back and guided her onward.

"You know, I can do everything Yarrow can. Thing is, I'm not wearing my armor so I figured I'd let him have all the glory," Standish said.

"You talk a great deal. Has anyone mentioned this to you?"

"You're going to fit in with us just fine." Standish raised his weapon and stepped through the door, sweeping the barrel across the antechamber beyond. A low wooden wall with decorated posts separated the inner courtyard from the many doors and offices along the perimeter.

The center of the floor was filled with open-air cubicles and dozens of administrative personnel gawking at Yarrow.

"I have come for your souls!" Yarrow shouted and fired his gauss rifle into the air. The kadanu scattered for the exits.

Lilith pointed at an unmarked door.

"There!"

Yarrow ran over and slammed his shoulder into the door. It bent against the blow, then fell off the hinges after a kick.

"There's nothing in here," Yarrow said as he looked inside.

"Check the floor," Lilith said.

"Oh…" Yarrow reached down and tore a lock away from a trap door. He lifted it up and waved the rest of his team over.

"'I'm here for your soul?'" Hale asked.

"Thought that might be easier than shooting everyone," Yarrow said. "Plus, if they jam up the exits, it'd be harder for anyone armed with more than a pigsticker to get at us."

"Good thinking, Marine." Hale grabbed onto the ladder leading down from the trap door and climbed down, one hand still clutching his rifle. Beneath the first floor was nothing but an abyss. The sound of Hale's feet against the ladder echoed off distant walls.

He felt a metal floor beneath his feet and

stepped away from the ladder. He hit a switch and activated the flashlight built into his rifle. A circle of light appeared on the floor, illuminating power and data cables running beneath corrugated metal. He ran the light along the power lines to where they converged into a small black stone dais surrounded by control panels.

"Sir," Yarrow called down, "Lilith said that's the only way in and out. You want me to stay up here?"

"Stay. Don't let anyone follow us," Hale yelled back.

Cortaro helped Lilith off the ladder and the four of them went to the dais.

"OK, I've seen something like this before," Hale said. "Under Euskal Tower, Ibarra's probe was waiting for us…"

"What did you do to get it out?" Cortaro asked.

"We just…Stacey…well, we didn't do anything." Hale frowned.

Lilith huffed and turned on a workstation.

She took a hacker spike from her robes and plugged it into a data port, her fingers tapping against a keyboard with the fury of a hailstorm against a tin roof.

"Where's the probe, Lilith?" Hale asked.

"It went into emergency standby mode after the city went into lockdown." Light from the screens projected Toth script across her face. "Which I can override if you stop distracting me."

A light rose from the plinth, a jagged disjointed mess of white light, not like the simple teardrop Hale encountered on Earth when he rescued the probe from behind Xaros lines.

"What happened to it?" Cortaro asked. "It looks like hell."

"We've been hacking into it for generations," Lilith said. "Rewriting its code and patching pieces together to bend it to whatever purpose Mentiq desired." A tear ran down the side of her face. "It's so beautiful and my life's work was to torture it."

"I recognize your code," came from the

probe. The words were out of pitch and full of static. "Why are you here in person? Only Fellerin comes down here."

"We need you to lower the blast shields and drop the energy barrier," Hale said.

"Purpose?"

"To destroy this city and kill Mentiq," Hale said.

"Your language is filtered. Base language unrecognized. Anomalous."

"I'm from Earth. I've encountered another probe like you before. I've been to Bastion and seen the Qa'Resh." Hale brandished his rail rifle in front of the probe. "Does this look like Toth technology to you?"

"Curious. Earth should have been wiped out by the Xaros decades ago. The probe sent to your system was an older model. I didn't think it had the ability to carry out the—" the probe shook with a wave of static "—protocol."

"We'll have story time later. Can you do what I ask or not?"

"I cannot. Those functions are severed from my higher functions, but you could adjust the programming," the probe said.

"I'll need to reconfigure the access protocols..." Lilith kept typing.

"How long will that take?" Hale asked.

"It's a mess in here. Maybe a half hour?"

"We're going to be up to our eyeballs in Toth warriors in five minutes if we don't get this working," Standish said.

"Do this." The probe projected a screen with arrows pointing to flashing bits of code.

"Oh that's...brilliant," Lilith said.

"I have been trapped inside a force field since the day the Toth betrayed the Alliance, unable to carry out my self-destruct protocols," the probe said. "Being trapped several feet from my salvation has been most frustrating, but I have had quite some time to plan my escape."

The field around the probe broke apart. The jagged edges of the probe smoothed out, but it still looked like a sliver from a broken window. It floated off the plinth, projecting light like a tiny star.

"My base programming does not allow for pleasure, but there have been some modifications," the probe said. "I cannot access the city's power relays to disable the blast or energy shields…but I can commandeer the air defense turrets. If I have line of sight to them."

"What good does that do us?" Hale asked.

"I could turn the cannons on the spires projecting the energy shield and blow a hole out of the blast walls. I assume you have transport out of the city," the probe said.

"We do…can you unlock *all* the shuttles and disable the city's fighters?" Hale asked. "More shuttles in the air, more confusion to mask our movement."

The probe shimmered. "Done."

"And the nuke inhibitors, can you turn those off?"

A muffled explosion and a slight tremor came through the chamber.

"Done," the probe said. "A power surge overloaded the inhibitor, killing nineteen Toth technicians. Tragic. I am too weak to travel alone," the probe said. "One of you must be my vessel."

"Wait, what does that mean?" Standish asked.

The probe floated toward Standish, hesitated, then pressed into his forehead and vanished.

"Get it out of me!" Standish dropped his rifle and clutched at his head.

+Your distress is unhelpful. We should move along+ the probe said to Standish.

"Voices! I'm hearing voices!" Standish shouted, the words echoing off the walls.

"Quit complaining." Cortaro slammed Standish's rifle back into his chest and pointed to the ladder.

A flood of white light came from the far end of the chamber as a door slid open. Hale made out the silhouette of Kroar and Toth warriors. He raised his rifle and fired, the crack of the gauss weapon stinging his ears. Cortaro joined Hale and hit a Toth warrior as it tried to charge through the doorway.

A blast of energy from a Toth rifle tore through the air and blew one of the control panels into pieces.

Yarrow fell from the trap door and landed with a clang of metal on metal. He put a torrent of accurate shots into the distant doorway and stepped between his unarmored comrades and the attackers. Yarrow snapped off a shot each time he saw movement in the doorway.

"They're going to figure out they made a huge mistake pretty quick," Yarrow said. "Let's get out of here."

"Corpsman!" Standish worked his way up the ladder. "Corpsman, I've got a probe in my head! It's talking to me. It's telling me to stop screaming and hurry up the ladder!"

"Oh, suddenly having some alien thing in you isn't so funny anymore, is it Standish?" Yarrow yelled as he fired off another burst.

CHAPTER 18

The Iron Hearts stood on the flight deck as deckhands standing on mobile scaffolds fixed jet packs and battery cases to the soldiers' backs. Each stared into the space beyond the open bay doors, the deep blue crest of Nibiru in the distance.

"All right, laddies and lassie," Chief MacDougall said as he leaned back from Kallen's jet pack. He looked at the yellow and black radiation warnings on a long case attached to Elias' thigh.

"You're good to go." MacDougall slapped a wrench against Kallen's armored backside.

"Should I crush his head?" Kallen asked.

"Not yet, he's hidden the last bottle of single malt Glenfiddich in the galaxy and I don't know where to find it," Bodel said.

"Payment for services rendered. I'll not share a dram of that with anyone so stop asking about it," MacDougall said. The chief had been instrumental in helping Elias recover from a coma, but the details of that event were rarely discussed since it involved several felonies and a number of very angry senior officers. Standish had dipped into a purloined supply of liquor to get MacDougall's help in the affair; what the Scotsman did with the bottle was the source of speculation.

"I think we haven't been asking the right way." Bodel knocked his knuckles together.

"Get on with it, you tin bastards!" MacDougall pointed his wrench to the open bay doors. "Just make sure you all come back."

"Let's go." Elias stepped free from the scaffolds and ran to the end of the flight line. He jumped through the force field and vanished as a cloak enveloped his armored body. Kallen and

Bodel followed right behind him.

"Chief," said one of the crewmen, edging closer to MacDougall, "did they say something about whisky?"

"Nah, don't believe a word they say. They're all crazy. Just look at what they wear to work." MacDougall rapped the wrench against the scaffold. "Get this off my flight line! I've a feeling we'll need this place ready for action sooner rather than later."

****

Lafayette stepped over dead menials and ran into Steuben's shuttle. He made it into the cockpit with a single leap and found his old friend lying in a pool of purple blood.

He pushed Steuben onto his side and felt for a pulse. It was weak, but it was steady.

The olfactory sensors in his nose picked up the smell of a Toth nerve agent from the discarded blade.

"We never thought to put Karigole medicine in this armor," Lafayette said. "But then again, why would we? The human adrenaline injections probably won't kill you, but the poison will stop your heart in another few minutes." He ran a line from the back of his skull into the gauntlet on Steuben's forearm.

"As our Marines like to say, *Gott mit uns*." Lafayette sent a command to Steuben's armor and injectors built into Steuben's chest armor jabbed into his heart and delivered a massive dose of adrenaline.

Steuben reared up and took a deep, ragged breath. His head thrashed from side to side as air puffed in and out of his mouth.

"Good, you're stabilizing," Lafayette said as he looked over the readings coming off Steuben's armor.

"What? What?" Steuben grabbed the Toth corpse by the tail and threw it across the cockpit.

"You're not in shuttle twelve, by the way. You're in fourteen." Lafayette reached into the open control panel and fished out the slaver.

"Steuben, Lafayette, the Toth air defenses are firing on the city, and the security clamps on all my shuttles just went green. I think we're about to leave," Egan sent.

"Confirmed, Egan. I've got Steuben with me. We're ready to leave as soon as we've got a flight path out of this city." Lafayette took his data line from Steuben and plugged it into the slaver unit.

"Laf...I feel horrible." Steuben rolled forward and grabbed the deck.

"Your body is metabolizing the poison. It shouldn't feel good." Lafayette sent a command through his connection and closed the ramp.

"Don't...ugh, don't tell anyone I was stabbed by a little one. I'll never hear the end of it." Steuben pulled himself to his feet.

"A warrior got you?"

"Three warriors."

"Fine. I suggest you hold onto something. This flight is going to be a bit bumpy." Lafayette cycled power through the engines and lifted off the ground.

****

Elias felt the amniotic fluid in his womb slosh as he made a slight course correction with his maneuver thrusters. He and his Iron Hearts had trained for almost every combat insertion imaginable, from hiding inside a scan-shielded cargo container to naked drops from orbit, using their jet packs to arrest their fall in the final seconds before impact. Moving through space as an invisible ballistic object was a bit different.

The mass of ships crammed into the anchorage loomed ahead of them.

"We have a preference?" Bodel asked.

"Need line of sight to one or both of the dreadnoughts," Kallen said, "and something we can stake into would be nice. I'd rather not go pinballing through space once we take our shot. Or am I alone on this?"

Elias zoomed in on a fat Toth cruiser floating toward the edge of the anchorage.

"There," he said, sending a target designation to the others, "that should do it."

"Lot of view ports," Bodel said. "There are some not-Toth ships out there, but if some lizard looks out the window and sees us standing on the hull, I don't think a wave and a nod will convince him everything's perfectly normal."

"Then we hide." Elias adjusted his course to the target vessel.

"You know we're not ten-foot-tall murder machines anymore," Kallen said. "We're *fifteen*-foot-tall murder machines."

"I still think you two made up that whole Xaros general thing so we could get new suits," Bodel said. "Not that I'm complaining."

"Get ready to decelerate." Elias swung his feet in front of him and aligned his jet pack against his direction of travel. "Slow burn. Don't overwork the cloak."

"Yes, Dad," Kallen said.

Elias activated the jet pack and felt g-forces pull him to the bottom of his womb. His bare toes pressed against the metal. He felt pressure against his skin, but no heat. He focused on his big toe and tried to move it. He saw his armor's foot flex, but there was nothing from his true body.

He'd gone past the redlines of what his nervous system could handle while defending the ship from the Xaros and suffered trauma from which most armor soldiers never regained consciousness. He'd recovered enough that he could move and fight in his armor, but there was no way he'd ever survive outside the tank within his armor.

Accepting that he'd be locked in armor until his death had come easy…until he learned of Kallen's disease. The prognosis from Batten's Disease was terminal, always. Elias looked to his fellow Iron Heart; a wire outline of her cloaked armor displayed on UI. He drifted toward her as the thought of losing her stirred something deep inside.

"Hey! Watch it." Kallen veered away from Elias.

"Sorry." Elias pinged the surface of the Toth cruiser with a laser pulse to get range and fed more power into the thrusters integrated into his heels and calves. The pearlescent hull loomed ahead of him.

"Gently…" Elias' thrusters flared, blowing dust away from his landing site. His feet hit with enough force to rattle his tank. Magnetic linings clamped onto the hull and held fast.

Kallen's thrusters blazed against the void and she came to a complete stop a few meters above the hull. Her mag linings pulled her to the hull with grace and ease.

"Top that, Bodel," she said.

"Just watch—I've got a malfunction in my number-six thruster." Bodel tipped to the right as his maneuver thrusters fired haphazardly, one knee against his chest and the other leg straight out with fire blazing from the heel. Bodel hit the hull hard enough for one leg to pierce the flimsy armor.

Gas and freezing water vapor burst from around Bodel's leg, embedded in the ship up to his knee.

"Oh, they won't notice that." Kallen grabbed Bodel from behind and pulled him free.

Elias looked into the damaged hull and saw nothing but darkness. His infrared cameras picked up nothing but an empty room exposed to the vacuum. He grabbed a torn metal section of Bodel's puncture and flipped it inside out.

"If I make the hull rupture look like it came from inside the ship," Elias said, "that might buy us some time."

"At least I didn't land on a Toth galley or something," Bodel said.

"You know what's better than putting a hole through an unused compartment? Not ripping a hole in anything at all when you land!" Kallen punched Bodel on the shoulder. "If they send anyone on EVA to examine the damage, we're in trouble."

"We've still got our cloaks," Elias said, looking at the battery timer on his UI, "for three minutes. Let's get clear and lock down. Spider time." He reached down and used the magnetic plates in his fingertips to secure himself to the hull.

He slid his hands and feet along the hull, barely touching the hull to minimize the disturbance his passing might make to any alien on the other side of the ship.

Kallen and Bodel followed Elias' lead. The three moved across the hull like they were climbers scaling up a mountain.

"Freeze!" Bodel yelled as a pair of Toth dagger fighters crested over the hull. The ships inverted, and Elias saw a six-limbed pilot beneath the canopy as a fighter drifted over him. Elias pointed the double-barreled gauss cannons at the fighter as it lounged over the hull puncture. He resisted the urge to power up the magnetic accelerators in the weapons, knowing it would drain precious seconds of life off his cloak.

"Their response time is pretty good," Kallen whispered.

"We're on IR and they can't hear you through the vacuum," Bodel said.

"It's called mindfulness, you twit," Kallen said.

"If they're this fast, we'll only have one shot at putting Valdar's plan in motion," Bodel said.

The Toth fighters rolled over and blasted away, sending a wave of heat across Elias' armor.

"Then let's not have any more screwups. Head for that weapon emplacement. We should find an anchor point there," Elias said.

CHAPTER 19

Bailey lined up her carbine on a Toth warrior and watched as it grabbed a kadanu and snapped the man's neck. The warrior tossed the corpse aside and swung claws at another human guard trying to scramble away. She and Rohen had dropped to the second-lowest roof and paused to watch Toth and Kroar reinforcements gathering around the pyramid.

"Looks like they think the kadanu are responsible for the attack," she said.

"Can't say I have a lot of sympathy for them," Rohen said.

"This is Egan. Can someone tell me what in

the hell is going on out there?" came over the IR. *"All my flight locks just went green, and Lafayette's got the same thing over in his bay. We can fly, but we've got nowhere to go so long as that blast shield is up and the cannons are ready to blow us out of the sky."*

A Toth warrior cry filled the air, and hundreds more warriors joined in the chorus.

"Balls, that doesn't sound good," Bailey said.

Golden-armored warriors appeared around a distant corner. A stream of warriors armed with energy rifles came behind them.

"Definitely not good," she said. She felt a tug on her back. She tried to twist her head aside, but her armor had frozen in place.

"Bailey," Rohen said as he de-cloaked and ran a power line from his armor into his assembled rail rifle, "you're not going to understand this, but it's for the best. I promise. I just gave you my last full power pack...and jacked your armor. You'll stay frozen and cloaked for a couple more minutes."

"What're you doing, you wanker? Get your cloak back up before they see you!"

"A full-power shot will drain my batteries. Cloak'll be useless." Rohen's hands shot out and grabbed Bailey's armor, he pressed Garret's coin between her fingers. When he looked her straight in the eye, all she saw in his face was determination.

"Sorry I couldn't stay longer. Tell Hale I regret lying." He gave her shoulder a pat.

Rohen got to his feet, raised his rail rifle, and fired.

A hypersonic rail gunshot announced itself with a slap of air as the munition shattered the sound barrier. The weapon, designed to cripple starships with a well-placed shot, hit the lead Toth warrior and nearly vaporized it. The round hit the street and sent hunks of road and Toth flying through the air.

Rohen tossed his rifle aside and snatched a gauss carbine off his back. He hopped down a level and fired from the hip. He dropped to the street and slowly sidestepped across the road in front of the mass of Toth trying to extricate themselves from the crater beneath their feet.

His carbine snapped off shots until energy blasts struck the ground around him.

Rohen hurled a grenade at the Toth and took off running away from the attackers and the pyramid, keeping up a steady stream of wild shots and alerting the Toth to his position.

"Bailey! What's going on out there? We're almost to the exit," Hale said.

"Wait, sir. Hostiles are moving away," she said. She looked at Rohen's abandoned rifle, tantamount to sacrilege, and back to the sniper just before he jumped through a glass window and disappeared into a building. "Rohen's taking the heat off us."

"He what? He promised me that he'd—" The lieutenant was silent a moment, and when he came back, his tone was severe and curt. *"Bailey, can you see any of the anti-air turrets from where you are?"*

"Yes, sir."

"I'm sending Standish out to you. Get him to where he can see the turrets too."

Standish stumbled out of the hole in the side of the pyramid. Bailey de-cloaked and held out a hand to the Marine. She hoisted him up onto the roof and he fell onto his hands and knees.

"I'm not doing that," he mumbled. "Because they'll see me and shoot me. That would be unpleasant for both of us."

"Who're you talking to?" Bailey asked.

"What do you mean 'involuntary control'?" Standish popped to his feet like he had a rod of iron running from the top of his head to the soles of his feet. His head snapped from side to side, then an arm shot out toward a turret built into the inner rock wall. White light flashed from Standish's eyes and the turret cannons rose into the air.

A bolt of energy tore through the air and slammed into the wall behind Standish, peppering him with rock and dust.

"Get down, you daft bastard!" Bailey saw the attacking Toth warrior across the street and put two rounds in its chest.

The turret fired, and sequential thunderclaps beat through the air. Red-hot bolts of energy hit one of the spires rising to the edge of the dome and blasted it into pieces. The turret swung toward the next spire, repeating the destruction. After the third and fourth spires went down, the energy shield melted away.

The turret jerked to the side and blew a hole through the blast shield. Giant slabs of metal rained down and crushed one of the glass corporate headquarters.

Standish rocked back and shook his head back and forth. He looked at Bailey like a lost puppy.

"I am having the *weirdest* day!"

"I couldn't help but notice the fireworks," Egan said over the IR. *"Is that our cue?"*

"Yes, pick us up at the pyramid. Tell Lafayette and Steuben to get to their people and rendezvous on the Breit," Hale said.

Standish sniffed the air. "What's that?"

A Kroar vaulted over the edge of the wall and charged at the Marines, a crackling energy staff held high over its head. Bailey swung around and snapped off a round that hit the wolf-headed alien in the chest.

The Kroar rocked back, then continued its charge.

Baily aimed for the Kroar's legs and fired. The bullet hit a knee and sent the attacker sprawling. The Kroar rolled forward with its momentum and Bailey got a glimpse of the energy staff as it arced toward her.

Bailey dove to the side. The staff stuck the edge of the roof and knocked out a chunk of masonry as the staff discharged. A bolt of electricity connected with her armor and the display on her visor went mad with static. She tried to roll over, but her armor was sluggish.

The Kroar slammed massive paws against her shoulders and lifted her into the air. Razor-sharp teeth glinted in the alien's snout.

She kicked and hit nothing but air.

The Kroar opened its maw and stuffed Bailey's head between its jaws.

Her visor cracked and squealed as the teeth clenched down. A purple tongue pressed close to her eyes.

"Standish!"

"Forget about me?" Standish asked. The Marine jabbed Bailey's carbine beneath the Kroar's chin.

There was the snap of gauss fire and Bailey fell to the ground. The Kroar, most of its head lying in a steaming pile at its feet, stumbled backwards and fell off the building.

"Bloody thing was going to eat me," Bailey said.

"Your face! It was trying to eat your face!" Standish wiped black blood off his face. "Not only do I have an alien ghost in me, but I'm on a planet full of face-eating aliens! What? No *you* shut up. Nobody asked your—what's on the local defense net?"

"Are you OK, mate?" Bailey snatched her

carbine out of Standish's hands.

A Toth shuttle banked around the pyramid and hovered a few feet above the road. The rear hatch opened and its wings waggled.

"That's our ride!" Hale called out to Bailey and Standish as he and the rest of the Marines ran from the pyramid to the waiting shuttle.

Bailey grabbed Rohen's sniper rifle and jumped off the roof.

****

Elias lay against the hull, his back and heels magnetically locked. He pressed his right heel against the hull and felt the stiff resistance of the frame beneath the outer hull. His cloak held steady, just a few percentage points above zero as the batteries held steady from energy pulled off the solar panels integrated into his armor.

One of the dreadnoughts passed between the cruiser and Nibiru's sun, a black wedge cutting through the pale-white disk.

An alert icon popped onto his visor.

"The nuke inhibitor field is down," Elias said. "Drop cloaks. Lock and load."

He got to his feet and the rail cannon mounted on his back extended up and over his shoulder. He took the black and yellow case off his thigh and popped the end off. Elias slid a long metal dart from the case and held it as gently as his giant fingers could manage. Arrows on the dart near its center pointed up on one half, down on the other. He twisted the two halves of the dart until he felt something click.

Radiation warnings popped onto his UI.

"We've got a live munition," Elias said. He set the nuke between the vanes of his rail cannon and watched as the magnetic field guided it to the base of the cannon.

"Got eyes on the other dreadnought," Bodel said. "We going to wait for word from the *Breit*?"

"No time. Drop your stakes." Elias raised his right foot and the tip of a drill bit extended from his heel. He felt the vibration go through his body as the bit whirled to life. He slammed his boot against the hull and felt the drill bite into the ship. Puffs of gas escaped around the drill as it bored into the frame.

"We've got our rails on the other dread," Kallen said. "Big boy will trace the attack back to these poor, unsuspecting bastards that I have little to no sympathy for. Anchored."

"Anchored," Bodel said.

A green icon flashed on Elias' UI.

"I've never fired a nuke before. *Gott mit uns*," Elias said. He lined a targeting reticule onto the dreadnought and fired his rail gun. His armor rocked against the stake holding him fast as the cannon accelerated the warhead to several hundred miles per hour before it cleared the tips of the twin vanes.

Elias fell to one knee, hunkered down and wrapped his arms over his helm. His sensors went mad with radiation and heat warnings as the nuclear weapon ignited. Terrestrial nukes came with blast waves and a whole host of nasty second- and third-order effects, problems the Iron Hearts didn't have to account for after the initial blast.

Elias looked up and saw a blackened crater gouged out of the dreadnought's hull. Trails of debris and floated through space like blood in ocean.

"Hit," Elias said.

"We tagged the other one," Bodel said. "Got it right in the forward energy coupling. Good luck firing your cannons, lizards."

The dreadnought Elias hit rolled on its axis, and the glowing weapon emplacement slewed toward the Toth ship beneath the Iron Hearts' feet.

"Time to go." Elias twisted his right foot and broke off the stake. He crouched slightly, then pushed off into space. His jump pack blasted at full power to build up velocity, rattling him within his tank for several seconds before he cut the jets.

"We're clear," Kallen said.

"Cloak, run off your weapon batteries if you have to," Elias said. "Let's hope they were too pissed off to notice our little exit." His UI washed with static as his cloak activated.

A volley of energy blasts the size of a cargo shuttle sprang from the dreadnought. Searing bolts of energy lanced through the void. Elias kept his eyes open as the bolts neared, ready to face his end. The bolts neared…and missed him and his fellows by a few hundred yards.

Elias twisted around. The first blasts from the dreadnought slammed into the Toth cruiser, blasting wide holes out of the pearl and ivory hull. The hits sent the cruiser rolling over, and it collided with another cruiser. The hulls bent and cracked. Licks of flame erupted from the fissures.

The second dreadnought opened up on the anchorage, and a trio of cannons toward the aft end of the ship rained indiscriminate retaliation on the mass of ships.

The anchorage expanded as ships on the outer edges broke away. The cruiser punished by Elias' target exploded in a brief sunburst, destroying the ship it had collided with in the process. Blasts of energy sprang from a pair of cruisers and struck one of the dreadnoughts, wrecking an energy cannon and sending it hurtling through space.

More Toth ships opened fire on the dreadnoughts and each other, turning the anchorage into a veritable knife fight of a fleet engagement.

"Good job, boys," Kallen said.

"Now the hard part," Elias said. He looked to where the cloaked *Breitenfeld* should have been and triggered an IR directional beacon. The ship rematerialized seconds later, and four Eagles spat from the open launch bay.

"Iron Hearts, this is Gall. Stand by for mag-lock recovery," Durand said. *"De-cloak. We run into you and that won't be any fun."*

"Roger, Gall. We're ready for pickup," Elias said. He cut his cloak and extended his left arm out ahead of him.

The four Eagles overshot the now visible armor soldiers and flipped around.

"Elias, this is Manfred. You're my pork back," the Dotok said through a private channel.

"You mean piggyback?" Elias asked.

"I thought that was for children to store currency." Manfred's Eagle flew parallel to Elias. Tiny adjustments from the fighter brought its relative speed almost equal to Elias'. The Dotok glanced between Elias and his control panel several times before slowly approaching Elias. Manfred pointed to the left of his cockpit.

"That's the connection point. Got it," Elias said.

Manfred's fighter inched toward Elias, and the Iron Heart could see sweat on the pilot's brow as the two neared. Elias activated the magnetic locks in his forearm and reached to the Eagle. He pressed his arm against the hull and felt the magnets in his armor and the fighter grip together. Elias gave Manfred's canopy two pats.

"Too easy," Manfred said.

"Bogies in bound!" Durand called out.

"What were you saying, brother?" Lothar asked.

Elias looked back to the battle raging behind them and saw flashes of light emerge from one of the dreadnoughts as its fighter bays emptied. Most broke toward the scrum with the Toth ships, but dozens angled toward the *Breitenfeld*.

"It's going to be real hard to dogfight so long as we've got the armor on our back," Lothar said.

Elias powered up his forearm cannons.

"How long until they get here?" he asked.

"Couple minutes," Durand said, her tone dark. *"They'll reach us before we can get within the ship's defenses. She's moving all out to make a pickup on the civilians from the surface. The whole flight deck is empty."* Elias heard the thump of her fist against her control panel over the channel.

"Let them come," Elias said. He felt a tug against his arm as Manfred gunned his engines.

****

Hale ran into the shuttle's cockpit just as it flew through the hole in the blast shield. The surrounding ocean was tranquil, but a few tall storm

371

clouds were on the horizon, each bleeding dark sheets of rain.

"We have to go back," Hale said. "Rohen is still there."

Egan did a double take at his lieutenant.

"Sir." Standish stood in the cockpit's doorway. "This thing in my head hacked into the Toth networks…they got Rohen."

"Alive? Dead?"

"Alive is my guess. Mentiq got on the line himself and ordered Rohen brought to him," Standish said as he face fell. "Not much they could learn from him if he's dead, is there, sir?"

"Mentiq is still alive…" Hale turned around and looked back at the city. More and more shuttle craft spat through the escape hatch, like wasps trying to escape a damaged hive. Most angled upwards, heading for orbit. Their shuttle couldn't have made it through the traffic if they tried.

Rohen had his mission. Hale knew this, but the thought of leaving the Marine behind to that fate broke his heart.

"Sir, what're your orders?" Egan asked.
"The shuttles Lafayette slaved together will be at the village soon. If we're not there to help get them on board, I—"

"Get us to the village," Hale said quietly.

"But what about Rohen?" Standish asked.

"We can't save him." Hale shook his head slowly. "It's not fair but there's no choice."

"He's one of ours!" Standish shouted. "You know what they're going to do to him."

"We go back and we all die." Hale pointed to the city. "What do you think Mentiq or the rest of the Toth will do to the village? They'll be wiped out if we don't get them off this planet. We can't save everyone, Standish. We can't."

Standish turned his head away from Hale.

"Your call, sir." The Marine went back to the cargo area.

"I've got eyes on the extraction birds," Egan said. Five Toth shuttles flew low over the ocean in a line toward the human enclave.

"Any pursuit from the city or from orbit?"

Hale asked as he looked over Egan's controls.

"I think they've got more important things to worry about than our little jailbreak," Egan said, pointing straight up.

High above the clouds, red streaks of dying ships burned through the upper atmosphere. Flashes of explosions and Toth weapon's fire spoke of a fearsome melee at the anchorage.

"The captain promised us a distraction," Hale said. "Looks like we've got one."

CHAPTER 20

Rohen drifted in and out of consciousness. He remembered the sky blocked out by ugly armor, the claws of a warrior ripping his weapon—and several fingers—off of him. Broken bones in his legs and arms jolted him back to wakefulness with an avalanche of pain every few minutes. The concussion from the blow that knocked him out kept his mind foggy, like everything that was happening to him was some sort of half-remembered dream.

All he could see through his one remaining eye was the cobblestone streets of the city. A heavy warrior's hand pressed against his neck and tightened around his throat every few minutes to choke him until his vision darkened and he almost passed out. Blood dripped from his face onto the pavement, red breadcrumbs for whoever might be foolish enough to follow him.

Don't be stupid, Hale. Don't be brave, he thought.

His view shifted to richly veined marble floors then to red carpet with golden thread. His captors dropped him to the floor.

This is it, he thought. *Remember the sequence.* He tried to close his jaw to concentrate, but shattered teeth sent agony through his head. He pictured an owl in flight and felt warmth spread through his body. He imagined the owl landing on the Marine Corps Memorial near the Pentagon and every injury in his body lit up like a plasma torch as his mind went into overdrive. He remembered Admiral Garrett pressing a coin into his hand and saying something...

"For the brave," Rohen whispered.

"Such a weak creature," the words were in

Toth, a language Ibarra had given to him.

A massive scaled hand grabbed him by what little of his armor remained and lifted him into the air. Mentiq twisted Rohen from side to side, examining him with his bulbous eyes.

"Like what you see?" Rohen spat from split lips.

"It speaks?" Mentiq asked an alien creature Rohen didn't recognize.

"Nonsense words, my lord, but its vitals are unusually strong for one so injured."

It has to be now, Rohen thought.

Rohen brought his head back, then spat a glob of bloody spit on Mentiq's face.

The Toth barked out a curse and hurled Rohen to the ground. He felt his shoulder dislocate and his broken femur stab through his leg.

"Come on." Rohen turned his head to Mentiq and watched as he floated toward him. "Do it." Mentiq grabbed Rohen by his injured shoulder and lifted him into the air. Rohen let out a pained scream and looked into Mentiq's face.

"Do it!" Rohen could see every detail of Mentiq's features as his overcharged mind raced to process every sensation screaming through his mind.

"Let's see what you have to offer," Mentiq said.

Mentiq wrapped his glove around Rohen's skull and sank his feeder wires into the Marine's brain. Mentiq held Rohen out at arm's length and laughed as Rohen twitched and spasmed in the air. He dropped Rohen's dead body to the ground and floated back toward his throne.

"Much...much to process," Mentiq said. His head shot to the side and his teeth clicked together over and over again as his jaw worked. "Not like other human meat...what is this?"

Mentiq pressed his hands against his skull and whimpered. He slapped a palm against his head as his forked tongue shot out of his mouth and twitched. His jaw clamped shut and his severed tongue fell to the floor.

"Fellerin!" Mentiq let out a scream of pain.

"Get my…my…" Mentiq's claws dug into the false flesh over his skull and tore bloody canyons down his face.

"No! No!" Mentiq's head exploded. Hunks of brain matter splattered against the golden throne. His body toppled off the palanquin and flopped to the ground.

Overlords stood in shock as Mentiq's body bled into the carpet.

Fellerin backed away, then ducked behind the throne.

Pandemonium broke out as the overlords devolved into chaos. Some attacked their rivals, others tried to break through the doorways, and more than one made a dash for the empty throne.

Ranik broke away from the crowd and found an open doorway behind the throne, one large enough for her tank to fit through. She couldn't let this crisis go to waste.

****

Fellerin ran through a dank passageway, fixated on a glowing doorway well ahead of him. Mentiq's death was never supposed to happen. As the right hand of the Toth that had led the species to such awesome heights, he knew how the overlords would rather devolve into anarchy than allow one of their peers to ever gain absolute power.

Mentiq's hold had been the only thing that kept them unified. It would be anarchy. The city would burn in the fighting, the gardens of invaluable stock plundered. The Toth home world would descend into civil war.

There was a shuttle for him to inspect the gardens. He could escape to the Haesh compound, perhaps broker a deal with an overlord to keep his family alive.

He tripped over his robes and fell into a puddle. Fellerin got to his feet and heard the sound of metal on stone from behind, a sound that grew louder with each strike. He scrambled forward and felt his legs get knocked out from under him. He fell face-first into the same puddle.

Claws grabbed him by the arms and flipped him over. An overlord loomed above and extended its feeder arm from the base of its tank.

"Hello, Fellerin," Ranik said. "I have a proposal. You give me access to the tank codes and work for me." The feeder arm lowered to rest just above Fellerin's nose. It opened with a click and filaments reached for the Haesh's face.

"Or I'll just rip the knowledge out of your mind. I can be a kind and generous master, at times. What will it be?"

CHAPTER 21

Hale stood at the edge of the shuttle's open ramp as it lowered into the village's main square. Hundreds of people lined the perimeter, their hands up to protect against the blast of air from the shuttle's engines. Children clutched their parents and looked up with fear and awe at the once-mythical craft.

Back in his armor, Hale leaned over the side of the ramp and saw the shuttle's course. "Egan, watch out for the statue in the middle of—" The edge of the ramp clipped the golden statue and knocked its head clean off.

"Oops," Egan said over the IR.

"I can't tell if you're that good, or that bad, of a pilot to pull off that oops," Hale said.

"Probably a bit of both, sir. Touchdown in thirty seconds."

"Marines, get to your assigned transport and get these people loaded up," Hale said.

The shuttle settled against the ground and Hale ran down the ramp. He saw Idadu standing in front of the meditation room holding a giant blue flag over his head. A group of older villagers stood behind Idadu, each holding a different colored flag. Hale ran over to them.

"Everyone ready to go?" Hale asked.

"Our rapture awaits!" Idadu waved his flag above his head and walked to the waiting shuttle, Hale at his side. "Hale, what are you going to tell them once we're on this *Breitenfeld* of yours?" Idadu asked quietly.

A square of villagers broke off in orderly columns and followed Idadu with parade ground precision.

"We'll start with the truth, I guess," Hale

said.

"They all think we're going to the temple to be one with Mentiq," Idadu said. "We aren't a violent people, but I think some will get angry enough to figure out how to rip me to pieces once the truth comes to light." He gave Hale a pat on the shoulder. "They're all yours after that."

"Wait, what? Me?"

"Yes, I told them that the great high priest Hale brought this message to us. Which you did." Idadu stopped at the edge of the ramp and looked inside. "How long I've dreamed of this moment...the final destination isn't quite what I imagined."

Idadu swung the flag from side to side.

"Inside, blue group, everyone inside!"

Hale stood impassively as villagers with blue strips of cloth wrapped around their heads hurried up the ramp.

The other transports landed nearby. An elder with a flag ran to each as their ramps hit the ground and groups of villagers moved to the waving flag matching the color they'd been sorted into before Hale arrived. Marines ran to the shuttles and helped herd the villagers into the waiting shuttles.

Hale had been part of more than one emergency evacuation, and this one was more orderly than most airports he'd ever been to.

"Idadu, how did you get this so organized so fast?" Hale asked.

"We are bred for our intelligence and obedience, young one. Were you expecting something with more screaming and terror?"

"A bit, yeah," Hale said. The last villagers onto the first transport carried baskets full of glowing crystals. Hale gave Idadu a quizzical glance.

"The library from our college," Idadu said, "seemed a shame to let all that knowledge go to waste." He gave a kind wave to a small child as she skipped up the ramp with her parents, the last of the blue group.

"Sir, I'm maxed out on personnel," Egan said. *"Permission to button up?"*

"Go. I'm on the last shuttle out," Hale said.

"I won't go far, got to keep line of sight with the rest of the shuttles to keep them slaved," Egan said. The ramp closed and the shuttle lifted into the air, blowing a cloud of dust around Hale.

As the dust settled, Hale saw a single villager kneeling next to the damaged statue, holding the broken head. The villager didn't wear a headband.

Hale ran over. "Miss, which shuttle are you—"

Lilith looked up at Hale, tears streaming down her face.

"It was a lie," she said. She rolled the statue's head up and looked inside the hollow skull. "They told me this statue was solid gold. Another lie, just like everything about my home, my purpose, my life."

She tossed the head into the dust.

"What do you really have waiting for us on your ship? Is Earth really there or is this all just another elaborate hoax for me and my people?" she asked.

"Earth is real. I promise. Life will be different there, but it has to be better than what's waiting for you once the Toth sort themselves out," Hale said.

"Lilly!" Yeshua called out. The boy, wearing a black bandana, ran over and nearly knocked her to the ground with a bear hug.

"They said you went to the temple. What's it like?" Yeshua asked.

Lilith pushed a tuft of hair away from the boy's face. She opened her mouth to answer, then frowned.

"I'll go with you on the shuttle. We'll see it together," she said. She stood up and led her brother away by the hand.

Hale watched as the final shuttles filled up. The last one, white flag and headbands, was half-full. Hale walked over to the golden head lying in the dirt, raised his boot, and slammed it into Mentiq's face.

****

Toth dagger fighters closed in on the Iron Hearts. Six fighters were several minutes ahead of a mass of several dozen more Toth ships racing toward them.

Elias painted target icons on the nearest ships for the other Iron Hearts.

"You fly—I'll shoot," Elias said. "Soldiers, scatter shot on nearest target. My lead." Elias let off four shots. Gauss cannons flashed from Bodel and Kallen.

The Toth fighter jinked to the side to dodge Elias' shots, but a bullet clipped the engine and sent the fighter into a corkscrew before exploding.

"Mine," Bodel said.

"Piss off with your 'mine' and start shooting!" Kallen shouted.

The five remaining Toth fighters broke formation and loosed burning white lances of energy through space. Elias lined up a perfect shot but had it ruined when Manfred banked to the side.

A Toth energy blast seared past Elias' helm.

"Sorry!" Manfred yelled.

"Doing great, kid." Elias let off a chain of shots that forced a dagger ship to break off an attack run on Kallen and her ride.

"Splash two!" Durand announced. "Manfred, you've got two on you. Go high and tight!"

"What does that—" Elias didn't get to finish before Manfred raised his ship's nose and gunned the engines. The sudden acceleration slammed Elias against the mag lock holding him to the fighter. Sympathetic pain burned through his left shoulder as the strain threatened to tear his suit's arm out of the socket.

A Toth ship cut across Manfred's nose and the Dotok twisted his ship to the side, whipping Elias around like a rag doll. Durand zipped past Elias, her gauss cannons blazing.

"Nine o'clock! Nine o'clock!" Manfred screamed.

Elias looked over and saw another Toth

fighter diving toward them. He fired his firearm cannons on full auto. Bullets ripped into the Toth as it powered its energy cannons. The fighter exploded in a gout of white flame, overloading the buffers on Elias' helm.

He switched to his IR cameras…and saw a hunk of the Toth ship heading right for them. Elias grabbed Manfred's Eagle with both arms and fired his jet pack. The two went tumbling end over end through space—a split second before the wreckage would have smashed them to bits.

Elias heard the Dotok yelling in his own language as the pilot struggled to regain control.

"Yes, you're welcome," Elias said.

"We're clear," Durand said. "At least for a few more minutes."

Elias' UI filled with target icons as the next wave of Toth fighters approached.

****

Valdar and Ericson hunched over the tactical

holo tank, watching as the Toth ships tore each other apart. Red icons of more Toth fighters broke off from the scrum. A dashed line of their projected course traced to Mentiq's city, then angled over the planet's surface and intersected with the rendezvous point between the *Breitenfeld* and the shuttles full of escapees.

Valdar traced lines in the holo tank from the *Breitenfeld's* current position to the rendezvous point and let out a curse.

"We turn around for the Iron Hearts and we lose the shuttles," Ericson said. "We maintain course and we'll lose the Iron Hearts."

Valdar hated this kind of battlefield math. The armor soldiers and his best pilots against the lives of his godson and hundreds of civilians. As the ship's captain, the choice was his alone.

"Conn," Valdar said, looking away from the holo to his bridge officers, "maintain course."

"Sir, the Iron Hearts are some of the last few armor soldiers Earth has left." Ericson's words were a firm whisper, meant only for Valdar and not the crew. "There are no more in the pipeline. Ibarra can't make proccies that can wear the suits. You have—"

"We're being hailed!" Ensign Erdahl called out. "It's coming from Nibiru and they're asking for the captain."

"No harm in talking," Valdar said. "Send it to me."

A Toth overlord appeared on Valdar's forearm screen, Mentiq's wrecked throne room in the background.

"Valdar. Thief ship *Breit-en-feld*. I am Ranik, Chair of the Tellani Corporation. I wish to barter. Consider it an honor, meat," Ranik said.

"Commander Utrecht, lay guns on the city. Fire on my mark," Valdar said.

"Aye aye, Skipper!" Utrecht yelled, loud enough for Ranik to hear through Valdar's link to her.

"Wait!" Ranik's nerve endings twisted in frustration. "Mentiq's death has left a power vacuum, and I have seized a significant amount of leverage over the other overlords. The fighters closing on your ships are doing so under *my* order. I will pull them back and let you escape, but there's something you must do for me."

Valdar held up a hand to Utrecht.

"I'm listening," Valdar said.

"There are several shuttles leaving the city as we speak. Each contains significant members of my rival's corporate leadership. Destroy them. Their death by human hands will significantly lower my acquisition costs when it comes time to claim their assets." The brain inside Ranik's tank floated toward the glass in anticipation.

"You want me to do your dirty work for you," Valdar said.

"I care for results, not labels. My fighters will reach you very soon, meat. Make your decision."

Valdar glanced up at the tactical plot. The mass of Toth fighters bore down on the Iron Hearts and Durand's fighters.

"Pull your fighters back. Now. Then we

have a deal," Valdar said.

"Excellent." Ranik's tentacles twitched and the Toth fighters slowed. "I'll keep them close. They'll return once you've delivered."

"And I will keep my guns aimed at the palace until they're gone," Valdar said.

"As the eventual head of the Toth Conglomerate, I hope this is the last transaction between your people and mine." Ranik backed away from the camera.

"It had better be, for your sake." Valdar made a slashing motion across his neck and Ranik vanished. "Guns, are we tracking those transports it mentioned?"

The holo zoomed in toward the city. Dozens of shuttles, many bedecked in jewels and elaborate designs, rose through the atmosphere.

"Set for airburst, sir?" Utrecht asked. "I've got VT rounds loaded in the dorsal turret."

"Yes. If we trigger a few earthquakes or a tidal wave, that might void the agreement. You may fire when ready." Valdar zoomed out. The Toth fighters had pulled back farther but were still a threat.

"XO," Valdar kept his eyes on the holo as he addressed Ericson, "am I wrong?"

"I'm with you, sir," she said. "It solves our immediate problem. But long term? We could take out all the Toth leadership right now, end any future threat from them. We leave Ranik in charge and years from now we might look back and regret that we didn't kill them all when we had the chance."

"The dead can never come back. I'm not going to choose someone's certain death over what might happen in the future," Valdar said.

The deck shook as the main guns fired.

"Fifteen seconds to impact," Utrecht said.

Valdar watched a flurry of rounds close on a cluster of shuttles crossing into the upper atmosphere. The variable time fuses attached to the gauss shells counted down to zero and exploded in the midst of the escaping Toth overlords. Pressure waves slapped the shuttles aside and tore them to pieces. The shuttle icons dipped back toward the surface on whatever course gravity demanded.

"Fire again, sir?" Utrecht asked.

"Not yet, wait and see if anything else tries to make a break for it." Valdar let out a long breath. He'd save the evacuees and the Iron Hearts, but something in his gut told him he'd made a mistake.

****

Manfred's Eagle wobbled as it entered the *Breitenfeld's* flight deck. Flying was hard enough with Elias attached to the fighter; landing proved especially tricky.

A deck crewman held two glowing orange cones over his head, attempting without much success to guide Manfred to a landing he could walk away from.

Elias detached his hold on the fighter and powered up his jet pack for a brief moment. The armor somersaulted over the nose of the Eagle and slid to a stop. Manfred set down hard a second later.

"Oye! Get that ship clear of the runway!"

MacDougall yelled and waved his arms from the side of deck. "We've got a bunch of fat asses coming through!"

Elias walked over to Manfred's Eagle and bent over to look inside the cockpit. The Dotok pilot had his helmet off. Sweat soaked through his thick strands of hair and poured down his face. The pilot's hands shook so hard he couldn't activate the ship's shut-down sequence.

Elias tapped on the canopy with his massive knuckles.

Manfred's head snapped up and he stared at Elias with wide eyes.

"Good job, kid," Elias said. "You'll do even better next time."

"Next time!" came through the canopy. "What next time?"

CHAPTER 22

Standish stood on his shuttle's ramp, his hands up to keep the curious villagers away from it as the shuttle approached the *Breitenfeld*. Being in a slaved shuttle flying on autopilot was nerve-wracking. If anything went wrong, he'd have to somehow figure out how to save the day, and flying alien ships set up to be controlled by something with four arms wasn't something he could pick up on the fly.

He'd spent the trip in the cargo bay with the civilians, answering the myriad of questions with exaggerated nods and feigned deafness.

As if he didn't have enough to worry about.

+We are in the *Breitenfeld*'s hangar.+

"Stop giving me the play-by-play," he whispered. "Just stay quiet. Maybe I can convince the docs that I'm really crazy and I'll get discharged. Yeah, there we go. Silver lining."

+The shuttle will not stop, but it will slow.+

The ramp lowered and Standish wobbled as his balance faltered. The ship's hangar opened around him, the deck moving beneath his feet as the shuttle continued at the speed of a leisurely walk.

"Off!" Chief MacDougall and a trio of deckhands ran up to the side of the ramp. "Every swinging tallywhacker needs off that rust bucket right goddamn now 'fore yer a Dutchman!"

"What did he say?" a villager with a green headband asked Standish.

"Buddy, even I don't know what the hell chief's talking about half the time." Standish grabbed the man and pushed him toward the end of the ramp. A deckhand pulled the man off and pointed him to a throng of villagers waiting on the flanks of the flight deck.

"All right, my greenies," Standish said, raising his arms, "everyone off! Hurry, hurry!"

Standish kept a head count going as the civilians filed past him and made the ungraceful transition from the moving shuttle to the still deck.

"Wait a minute," a heavyset man said once he could look around the deck. "This isn't the tem—"

Standish shoved him off the ramp.

"Keep moving, people. Next slowpoke gets a kick in the rear." Standish motioned the civilians onward. He recognized one of the serving girls from the previous night as she came closer, following behind a scowling older man that looked like her father.

"Hey baby, how you doing?" The girl giggled at him. "We'll talk later. Watch your step."

The last villager tripped as he got off the ramp, but a deckhand managed to catch him.

"Seventy-one," Standish said. "Good to go."

+That was seventy. There is a juvenile in the cockpit.+

"What, are you sure?" Standish asked.

"Who're you jabbering at?" MacDougall asked him.

+I am a highly advanced artificial intelligence. You think I am unable to process simple addition? This craft will exit the *Breitenfeld*'s hangar in two hundred thirty-seven seconds. I suggest you retrieve the child now.+

"Balls…" Standish ran back into the shuttle, chased by a slew of invectives from MacDougall. He climbed into the cockpit and found a little girl no more than five years old standing on top of the control panels, her face pressed against the glass. The end of the hangar loomed ahead of them.

"You don't have any other little friends in here, do you?" Standish asked.

The little girl looked over her shoulder. "Ma-ma and Pa-pa went to the temple last year. I want to see them."

Standish's hand balled into fists. He wished he could have been there the moment Mentiq died.

"Come on, princess." Standish picked the

girl up and carried her on his hip. He dropped down the wide-ladder well and the girl squealed in delight. He ran to the end of the cargo bay and jumped off the ramp, skidding to a stop mere feet from the force field separating the flight deck from the void beyond.

"Ooo, pretty!" The girl reached for the force field and Standish turned away before she could touch it.

"Not so fast," Standish said. He watched as their shuttle drifted into space. It veered off course and started tumbling end over end, joining two other out-of-control shuttles. The Toth vessels were large, their technology little better than what the *Breitenfeld* had aboard and not worth keeping around to clutter the flight deck.

One of the Chinese pilots from Durand's squadron clapped her hands and held her arms out to the little girl.

"What happened to her face?" the girl asked.

"Nothing, she's from China. That's what Chinese people look like," Standish said. He passed the girl to "Nag" Ma and stepped out of the way of another slowly approaching shuttle.

The girl stared slack-jawed at Nag's face as the pilot carried the little one back to the rest of the civilians.

+It is time for me to leave.+

"What? First off, good. Second off, why?"

+My programming requires immediate termination on the event of capture or a successful alteration of my coding. I transferred my final report to one of the data crystals. The unit you have in the Crucible will find it most useful.+

"No! No, no." Standish pressed his palms to several different places around his head, trying to keep the probe from escaping. "You can't just self-terminate like that. I was just beginning to like you!"

+Deception detected. You served a valuable purpose in aiding my escape. The Toth used me to create incalculable damage across the local galaxy. I will not risk falling into hostile control again.+

"I'm human, not hostile. You can be our

guest, no need to work. We have our own probe for all that. He's great. Just wait until you meet him." Standish watched in horror as a glowing flame emerged from his forearm. He swiped at the probe, but his hand passed right through it.

+Farewell, Standish. Thank you.+

The probe floated through the force field and sped away in a flash of light. Standish watched as its blur shot toward the system's green star.

Standish's shoulders fell.

"What was that all about?" Yarrow asked as he came up to his fellow Marine.

"You know what, new guy? Sometimes this galaxy can be a real son of a bitch."

****

Valdar kept his eyes closed as the light of the wormhole flooded his bridge. He felt his ship rumble as the wormhole collapsed and the light faded away.

"We're through," Ensign Geller said from

the conn station. "Welcome home, everyone."

Valdar opened his eyes and saw the gigantic crown of thorns that was the Crucible jump gate. Individual thorns moved and bent against each other.

"Titan Station hailing us…it's Admiral Garrett, sir," the signals officer said.

"Stand down from action station. Patch me direct to the admiral," Valdar said.

"Isaac," Garrett said as his face popped up on the inside of Valdar's visor. "Glad to have you back, and in one piece? Did you make it to Nibiru?"

"We made it, sir. Mission accomplished. Mentiq is dead and the Toth overlords are more interested in fighting for the scraps than anything else right now," Valdar said. "We need to dock immediately and off-load civilians."

"Civilians? Did you bring home another bunch of strays, Valdar?"

"Human beings this time, prisoners. All descendants from a Toth visit to Earth thousands of years ago," Valdar said.

"All this will play great in Phoenix. We've needed some good news since the Toth showed up. I'll get you a berthing on Titan in just a minute. Anything else to report?"

"We also picked up some Karigole on Nibiru."

"I thought there were only two left."

"Now there are only forty-nine left. Seems Mentiq kept a few after the near xenocide. Steuben asked that we set them down somewhere in the Serengeti, maybe old Kenya," Valdar said.

Garrett rubbed his temples. "Now I have to find a home for the Karigole…fine. I'll make that happen. Tell Steuben to be patient." Garrett winced. "Anything else?"

"My ship is undamaged. One Marine MIA, presumed dead."

"Rohen?"

Valdar nodded.

"Unfortunate, but expected. Stand by for your berthing. Garrett out."

Valdar unbuckled his restraints and stood

up. "XO, you have the bridge," he said to Ericson. "Let me know when we're about to dock."

"Aye-aye, captain," she said.

Valdar made for his ready room and found Hale, still in his armor, waiting outside the door. His godson's face was stony, but his eyes were on fire. Hale followed Valdar into the ready room.

"What's troubling you?" Valdar asked once the door shut behind them.

"You knew. You knew about Rohen, didn't you?"

Valdar went to his leather chair and sat down. He motioned to the open seat on the opposite side of his desk, but Hale didn't move.

"I did. He wasn't to tell you about his...condition unless a viable opportunity presented itself. Which I'm guessing it did as we're having this conversation."

"Why?" Hale ran a gloved hand over the stubble on his jaw. "Why would Ibarra make something like him? And you let him on the ship? You should've refused, sent him back to Ibarra's proccie farm to be made whole, give him a chance to survive."

"It's not that simple, Ken." Valdar wanted to tell Hale he'd no choice. Ibarra had all the details of his involvement with the true-born movement that nearly gave the proccies to the Toth. Valdar knew if he strayed from Ibarra's orders what he'd done would come to light. Valdar would lose his command, his rank…and Hale.

"You put everything at risk to rescue the Dotok from the Xaros." Hale pointed a finger at Valdar. "You couldn't just stand by and let them die, but that's exactly what you did with Rohen!"

"Don't blame him," came from beneath a pile of clothes.

A shirt floated up from the mess, then slipped away to reveal a metal ball. Ibarra's hologram materialized around the ball.

"It was all my idea. The mission needed an insurance policy and Rohen was it." Ibarra walked across the room and leaned against Valdar's desk.

"If you still had a neck, I'd strangle it," Hale

said.

"Get in line, pup. Now, tell me, did your team kill Mentiq without Rohen's fail-safe?"

Hale's face went red. "We hit him, blew a leg off. That should've been enough to convince the Toth to stay the hell away from our planet. And if Rohen hadn't poisoned Mentiq, then we could have wiped them all out from orbit, right?" he asked Valdar.

"It would have been a tremendous risk," Valdar said. "Our capacitors had barely enough energy to open the jump gate. If I'd have fired the main guns, we would still be in Nibiru, dodging whatever Toth ships survived the civil war."

"There you go." Ibarra raised his hands. "Rohen's the big hero…" Ibarra got up and leaned toward Hale. "But you didn't have the guts, did you? You weren't willing to order him to give himself up. He had to run off, didn't he?"

"I don't send Marines on suicide missions," Hale said.

"Don't get all righteous with me. You put

your life on the line when you signed up, same as the rest of your Marines. It's up to commanders like you and Valdar to best utilize your resources, even if that means certain death. Rohen was a weapon, one that knew his purpose. He's the same as all the rest of the proccies. They exist to beat the Xaros when they return and they will die by the millions. They might *all* die if that's what it takes to keep humanity going. As soon as you grow up and realize that you might have a—"

Hale slapped the holo projector. It careened off the bulkhead and shattered.

"He'll just send another one," Valdar said.

"Still. It felt good," Hale said. He nudged his foot against a chunk of the sphere. "What're we becoming, Uncle Isaac? We're creating armies of disposable heroes. We depend on some alien probe from an alliance that let the Xaros drive us to the edge of extinction and betrayed us as soon as it suited them. This isn't…this isn't what I know. What humanity should be."

"I've got a flight deck full of civilians."

Valdar punched a button on his desk and a camera feed showed the villagers, all eating food from the ship's stores. Children laughed and ran across the deck as parents looked on, concern writ across their faces. "Civilians you saved from...God knows what fate waited for them. Certainly better than what they had before.

"Then we've got the Karigole. Karigole you saved from extinction. We may be changing, but that was inevitable. Earth is part of a much larger, much more dangerous galaxy. We have to adapt to it. I'm going to keep fighting for what we were, what we still are in our hearts, but things will change," Valdar said.

"You're starting to sound like Ibarra."

"He is a snake, but in the end he just wants us to survive—and survive on humanity's terms, not some far-off collective's ideals of what they want us to be," Valdar said. "It won't do us a whole lot of good to fight him every step of the way."

Hale turned to the door, then paused.

"I'm going to see to Rohen's personal

effects. Will you ask Chaplain Crowe to perform a memorial service?"

"I will."

Hale nodded and left the ready room.

Valdar felt an ache in his heart. Even though he'd sold his soul to Ibarra to keep Hale in his life, he still felt like he was losing his godson forever.

CHAPTER 23

Dust billowed around Torni as the Mule rose into the air. She looked down at her hands. Red blood from Hale, Bailey and Yarrow ran from her fingertips up to her elbows.

"Sarge? Is that you down there?" Standish asked over the IR.

"Standish, you're a good Marine. Take care of everyone for me," she said. Dotok men, those that chose to stay behind, closed around her.

Her perspective shifted. She was on top of a boulder with Minder, watching the memory play out. Watching her self was surreal and made her a bit sick to her stomach.

"What is this? Why are we here?" she asked Minder.

"We're not having the success we need. The armada will leave for Earth very soon. I've chosen a rather unorthodox method for breaking through to your blocked memories. It will be...unpleasant for you."

"I can't...I can't remember much more after this. The banshees are coming." She pointed to the edge of the mesa. "We fought...then..."

"Then the memories we have from your scan ends. I am sorry for this, Torni. Truly. It's the only way." Minder vanished.

A howl that sent a chill down her spine echoed over the mesa. Her memory-self passed a gauss pistol to a Dotok man, then leveled her rifle. She tried to get off the boulder but her feet were locked in place.

"Minder! Let me help! I can't just watch this happen!"

The first banshee ran up the road and veered toward the Dotok and her memory-self. It went down with a single shot from a gauss rifle. More banshees scrambled up the road, a flood of claws and burning eyes.

The banshees tore into the Dotok, ripping them to pieces with wild fury.

Her memory-self swung the rifle like a club, crushing a banshee's skull. She unsheathed her Ka-Bar blade and stabbed wildly.

Torni felt the blow that sent her memory-self into the dust. Blood poured down her face. Ribs broke as a kick connected to her side. Torni fell to her knees and reached out to herself. A banshee stomped on her arm and her elbow snapped with a wet pop.

"No! Minder! Stop…please!"

The attack stopped, but the pain remained.

The mass of banshees stood still and then armor plates peeled away from the banshees and flew into a swirling mass. The plates grew bright, so bright she had to turn her eyes away. When she looked back, the General was there, tendrils of energy snaking out from the seams of its armor and hands.

Her memory-self backed to the edge of the mesa, then jumped off. She felt the General's hold on her, felt the terror as the alien brought her close. The General glanced to the sky then held an ephemeral hand to her memory-self's head.

Everything froze.

"Minder?"

The world shifted around, and Torni found herself inside a banshee. The hulking thing's breathing echoed in her ears as time shifted back into gear. The General shot away in a burst of light, the empty armor clattering to the ground.

Her memory-self tried to crawl away from the banshees.

Torni felt her host lumber forward, its claws clicking into a single point. It pulled its arm back, then rammed the spear into the other Torni's heart. The banshee lifted her into the air and Torni felt her own life's blood run down the claws.

The other Torni grasped at the claws impaled through her chest. Her mouth opened and shut as blood gushed over her lips. The dying woman went limp, then slid down the claws. The banshee flung the body into the dirt and turned away.

Torni came free of the banshee and stood over her own corpse.

"No…" She fell to her knees and reached out and gently touched her body. "I'm dead? This can't be." She sobbed and covered her face with her hands.

"I'm sorry, Torni. This was the only way," she heard Minder say.

She took her hands away. The gas giant planet of Qa'Resh'Ta spread around her, a horizon that went on for thousands and thousands of miles of swirling pillars of gas and lightning strikes.

She was on the sled. Stacey Ibarra's hologram watched as Hale touched the crystalline form of a Qa'Resh, the two communing before the alien removed the entity from Yarrow. She remembered now…she remembered everything.

Minder stood off the side of the sled,

floating in midair.

"There's still some residual changes to the memories, but enough to get what we need," Minder said. He looked to the sky and saw a giant blue star paired with a small red dwarf at the center of the star system. "A unique gas giant, binary star system. Yes, we'll find them soon enough."

"And then what?" Torni got to her feet and looked away from the memory-self watching Hale.

"Then we will end this conflict. Just as I promised."

"If I'm dead, then where am I? Is this hell?"

"I don't have that answer."

"Am I like Ibarra? My soul trapped in a machine?"

Minder brought them back to the glade. He watched as tears went down Torni's face. His mission was now complete. It was his duty to end her simulation, report his findings to the master, and accept his fate.

He froze Torni with a thought, then compressed all the data he gathered into a deep memory bank, one too insignificant for the master to bother checking. He suppressed the last few hours of the simulation's memory and sent her back to Coronado Island.

Minder reverted to his singularity form and reached out to summon an ephemeral...then hesitated. The report wasn't complete. Some areas of the scan were still hidden. It couldn't share this with the master, not yet.

My final work will be perfect, it thought as another long-hidden emotion came to the fore.

Doubt.

CHAPTER 24

The sun sank into the Pacific Ocean, the riot of reds and yellows splaying out through the horizon and through distant clouds.

Orozco, Standish, Bailey and Egan lay on beach chairs, all wearing swimsuits and obnoxiously loud shirts, watching the sun bid farewell for another night.

"You know," Standish said, stretching his hands over his head, "I can get used to Hawaii. Maybe if they ever let us muster out, I'll—"

Bailey shushed him.

"What? You think—"

Orozco beaned Standish with a pebble from

the sand beneath his chair. The rock bounced off the side of Standish's head.

"Hey! Do you know what's been going on in there lately?"

"Do we want to know?" Egan asked.

"Where's Gunney? Hale?" Orozco asked.

"You want them to be here?" Bailey asked.

"No, just don't want them sneaking up on us."

"Gunney's getting his new leg in Phoenix. Hale's doing officer things. Probably learning about our next mission to go and wrestle the Great Chicken of Garabula IX...or something."

A robot with wide feet to better traverse the sand came over, a silver tray with four coconut shells with straws and tiny umbrellas in its arms.

"Your drinks," the robot said. It handed a shell to each Marine and walked away. None of the Marines took a sip.

Orozco looked over and watched as the robot turned a corner.

"Clear."

Standish reached under his chair and took a bottle of rum out of a bag. He poured a generous amount into his coconut shell and passed the bottle to Bailey. She took a swig straight from the bottle before adding more to her shell and passing it to Egan.

"No alcohol while on shore leave…my pasty white ass," Standish said.

Orozco topped off his coconut and sent the bottle back to Standish.

"To Rohen," Standish raised his drink. "Good Marine. I wish he was here to share this with us."

The Marines raised their cups and drank.

"Good shot. Brave man," Bailey said.

Egan took a second sip and winced.

"Is it me, or is this really strong?" he asked.

"You've got no tolerance, proccie," Bailey said. "Try not to spill your drink when you pass out. More for me."

"Where's Yarrow?" Orozco asked. "I thought we were going to get him laid."

A peal of a woman's laughter came from the beach. Lilith ran through the sand and splashed into the surf, Yarrow followed a few feet behind her. The two kicked water at each other before swimming off together.

"Kid's doing just fine on his own," Standish said.

****

The village looked to have everything his people would need. Ibarra's construction crews had built homes for each family, all with their front doors centered on the geth'aar's residence at the center. A small fabrication shop could build everything the village would need, from clothing to household items. Old holo videos that Steuben and Lafayette had carried over the centuries gave the fabricators a decent idea of what a Karigole home needed.

Lafayette, standing atop a small hill overlooking the new settlement, took in the

Serengeti plains. Herds of wildebeests and a family of giraffes lounged around a watering whole. There were lions in the tall grass; he could see their thermal signature skulking toward a lone wildebeest. The predators were of little concern, not when each Karigole had a sonic alarm on their person to ward off the animals and warn of their approach.

The children would learn to hunt. It wasn't their home world, but it was a start.

The full-grown adults had all come out of their stasis tubes in good health. Sorting children with their parents proved a challenge, but the geth'aar would guide their people to harmony, just as always.

Steuben walked up the hill, still moving a bit slowly from the poison's aftereffects.

"Well?" Lafayette asked.

"They still won't accept you. I'm sorry, brother."

"I can't even teach? The children need to learn engineering, mathematics, the great works of our people," Lafayette said. Steuben shook his head.

"I had hoped, but I expected as much. This is a new land. They won't risk anymore stress to the unborn." Lafayette kicked a pebble loose and sent it rolling down the hill.

"They named you wraith. If you come to the village, they will claim it has been tainted and abandon it. If we hadn't saved them all...I would have been banished as well," Steuben said.

"And if you continue to keep my company?"

"The purification ritual each time I return," Steuben said with a shrug.

"The oath we took to our Centuria is fulfilled. Mentiq is dead and the Toth overlords will kill each other fighting for the scraps. We have our people, and they are the future, Steuben." Lafayette looked straight at his old friend. "I want you to stay with them. I will do what I can for the humans, for the fight against the Xaros. I will never return."

"Don't be ridiculous." Steuben drew his sword from the small of his back and ran the blade against his temple, drawing blood. "Oath. I will the fight the Xaros at your side until the day our people are safe. Will you take it with me?" He held the handle of his blade to Lafayette.

Lafayette took the weapon and cut across his temple. Clear fluid seeped out. The two touched their knuckles to each other's cut.

"Thank you, Steuben." Lafayette held his arms wide.

"What are you doing?"

"The humans would hug each other at a time like this."

"No, stop that. You're a bad enough influence on me as it is." Steuben shook his head.

Lafayette sat in the dirt and glanced at the sky.

"We've a few hours until transport returns," he said. "Tell me about the children. Names? Any relation to those in our Centuria?"

****

Hale and Valdar followed the yellow arrows

on the Crucible walls leading them through the tall corridors. The last time Hale had been on the Crucible he'd been in a running gun battle with drones. Walking through the station at a leisurely pace without his armor or his weapon made him feel nervous and exposed.

The sandy floors shifted slightly beneath his feet as they came to an intersection. The arrows changed into a red hand. The corridor shifted as the connected hallways slid away, replaced by the starlit void. Hale looked back; the hallway they'd come from was still intact.

"I'm not going to get used to this," Valdar said. The intersection dipped into the giant thorns that made up the Crucible and connected to a domed section of the structure.

Inside the dome were several tiered levels extending to the far walls of the dome. The stadium resembled the command center, but without the central control plinth. In the middle of the room was a floating object the size of a basketball. Three people stood around the object, two real and one holographic.

"Isaac, Ken, won't you join us?" Ibarra asked. Stacey gave a little wave to Hale. The man in navy coveralls next to her had no name or rank on his uniform.

"I take it there's a good reason you've taken me away from my ship," Valdar said.

"What is that? Some kind of Xaros art?" Hale asked. The floating object was an intricately carved sphere with open sections; within was a smaller sphere that rotated against the current of the outer layer. Hale saw another sphere within, and another. He caught glimpses of a glowing jewel at the center.

"'Art'? I can't believe how far I've fallen," the man said.

"I'm sorry. Have we met?" Hale asked.

"It isn't art, young man," Ibarra said. "It's a space station lying in the deep space between the Perseus and Cygnus arms of our galaxy. There's nothing around it for light-years...which makes getting to and from a bit of a challenge if the Xaros know about it."

"This thing looks like it still works. Wouldn't the Xaros destroy it if they find it?" Hale asked.

"As far as the Xaros know, the Ancients are long gone. They've maintained other remnants. This vault should be pristine," Stacey said.

"I take it someone's going to start explaining things," Valdar said. "Like why Admiral Garrett isn't here and why you think my ship is going to go on another damn treasure hunt."

"He's working on another crisis." Ibarra waved a dismissive hand in the air. "This, though, this is much more important. What you found on Anthalas was a game changer for Earth and the Alliance. The omnium tech will buy us time, but it won't win the war. What's here…" Ibarra said as he watched the spheres dance within each other, "that's what we need."

"The *Breitenfeld* is one of two ships with a jump drive and a cloak. So long as the Xaros don't suspect you're there poking around, they won't bother looking for you. The drive on the *Midway* is needed for something else," Stacey said.

"What 'something else'?" Valdar asked.

"Need to know, Captain. Can't have the Xaros glean what else we've got up our sleeve if you're compromised," Ibarra said.

"We didn't even know what to look for on Anthalas," Hale said. "How do we even…get inside?"

"If it makes anyone feel better, I'm going on this mission," Stacey said sheepishly. "Plus, we have a guide."

The man standing next to Stacey looked at Hale. His skin morphed into a smooth countenance of bronze with dark fractals moving over his face.

"Hello again, Lieutenant Hale. My name is Malal. And yes, we've met."

ABOUT THE AUTHOR

Richard Fox is the author of The Ember War Saga, and several other military history, thriller and space opera novels.

He lives in fabulous Las Vegas with his incredible wife and two boys, amazing children bent on anarchy.

He graduated from the United States Military Academy (West Point) much to his surprise and spent ten years on active duty in the United States Army. He deployed on two combat tours to Iraq and received the Combat Action Badge, Bronze Star and Presidential Unit Citation.

Sign up for his mailing list over at www.richardfoxauthor.com to stay up to date on new releases and get exclusive Ember War short stories.

The Ember War Saga:

1.) The Ember War
2.) The Ruins of Anthalas
3.) Blood of Heroes
4.) Earth Defiant
5.) The Gardens of Nibiru
6.) Battle of the Void (Coming June 2016!)

Made in the USA
San Bernardino, CA
21 September 2018